All the best!

Dream Chaser

Angie Stanton

~ ~ ~

For Tip.

Your humor, kindness, and generous spirit
will stay with me forever.

~ ~ ~

Also by Angie Stanton

Love 'em or Leave 'em

The Jamieson Collection:
    Rock and a Hard Place
    Snapshot
    Under the Spotlight

Snowed Over (Novella)

Royally Lost

Waking in Time

http://angiestanton.com/

Chapter 1

"Give me everything you got!" I urged.

"Alright, Fearless Wonder. Whatever you want." Kyle grinned, eager to launch me skyward before Coach came back.

"Willow, are you sure you want to try this? It's like the most illegal stunt on the planet! You'd never be allowed to do a toss with four twists in competition," said Jilly, my best friend.

"Positive. Come on guys, let's go." The rest of the cheerleading squad watched as the guys set their arms in load position. I placed one hand on Rick's shoulder and the other on Kyle's.

"Oh my god, are you sure?" Jilly said, from her spotting position.

"No guts, no glory! Ready when you are," I said to the guys and stepped on their hands, and balanced in a crouched position.

I loved flying more than pretty much anything. The rush of adrenaline and the fast flips and turns were my addiction. I especially loved the sensation of the free fall and the whoosh as my bases would cradle catch me in their arms.

"One, two," Kyle called, and they dipped with each

count. On three, with their combined power, they launched me skyward.

I pushed off with my legs to get the ultimate height. Like a bullet I shot up, kicked and then twisted my body as fast as possible, once, twice. Gravity took over and I twisted two more rotations as I free fell back toward the cradled arms of my bases.

And then something went wrong.

Turns out it that it's true—when you think you're about to die, everything moves in slow motion. Like that commercial where a kid spills a glass of grape juice and the housewife moves in slow motion across the room to stop the mess before it splatters on her pristine beige carpet. But the juice splatters on the carpet anyhow, just like I hit the mat.

I heard a loud pop as my body slammed into the mat. My world went dark.

*　*　*

I lay staring at the bright overhead lights of the emergency room as reality set in. A bulky brace was wrapped around my neck. I couldn't even tilt my head to look down at my feet. The doctors and nurses at St. Mary's Hospital must have thought I was in trouble too. They'd stuck wires on me for a heart test the second I arrived, and then, when satisfied my heart wouldn't quit, whisked me away for x-rays.

I focused on the ceiling tile and tried to remember what happened.

One moment I was flying high above the team, the next my catchers made a botched attempt to save my landing. My body slammed at an awkward angle to the safety mat.

I squinted as the lights shone down and made me the star of the wrong show. The piercing pain in my shoulder and the constant blip of machines reminded me I lived. Every few minutes the blood pressure cuff threatened to squeeze off my arm as it tightened to take a reading. Another torture device pinched at my finger.

"How are you doing, Willow? Okay?" A nurse wearing a lavender smock asked as she entered data into a computer attached to the wall. She caught my eye and smiled. "You have some very worried friends who'd like to see you. Would you like me to bring them in?"

"Oh, I guess." My head felt foggy and my ears seemed to hear echoes as if I'd taken strong meds. "Did you put something in my I.V.?"

"Nope, no meds. Not until the doctor knows what's going on and gives the okay."

I tried to look to the side, but pain and the brace stopped me. "Are my mom or dad here yet?" I shivered in the flimsy hospital gown. Normally, I didn't need my parents around, but this was different. I felt off and couldn't put my finger on why.

"Cold? Let me get you a warm blanket. Your dad is on his way. I'm not sure about your mom." She pulled a blanket out of a warming cabinet and spread it over me. "I'll send your friends in." She pulled the curtain closed and left.

I shifted under the covers to reach the bed controller. Pain shot through my shoulder and upper back, and sent me flat again.

"Oh my god, Willow, are you okay?" Jilly rushed to

my side. She peered down, her eyes swollen from a recent cry. Her thick red hair framed her worried face as she took my hand.

"Yeah, I think so," I said, but I really didn't know. It was so good to have her by my side, but weird to be in a hospital bed.

"We were so worried." Rick gripped the bedrail and wrinkled his forehead in concern.

"Don't be. It wasn't your fault. I pushed you guys to let me try it." I knew better than to experiment with such hard tricks, but I had been so sure I could nail a quad. I thought I actually had. Until I hit the mat.

"You scared us to death!" Jilly said. "You were just lying on the floor kind of twisted up. Everyone was totally freaking out!" She bit her lip. "They're all in the waiting room. The nurse said only two at a time."

The idea of the team waiting to hear how I was doing was kind of embarrassing but not a surprise. What affected one of us affected all of us. That's what our coach, Ms. Klahn, always drilled into us. Our squad had plenty of close calls before, but never one that included an ambulance ride.

My shoulder throbbed more than ever. It better be okay; we had a huge competition coming up and I couldn't miss it.

At that moment, the curtain pulled back, and my dad appeared with my little sister, Breezy.

"Willow, honey, how ya doing?" His worried expression touched my heart.

"Dad." My voice broke a little. I hadn't realized how much I needed to see him; a weight lifted from my injured shoulder.

He approached the bed and patted my leg. That small contact brought my anxiety down a couple notches. He fixed me with one of his meditative Buddha gazes. Dad believes he can solve just about anything with a calming look, a deep breath and a cup of tea. This time I welcomed it.

"Where's Mom?"

"Her flight arrives at eight, and she's coming straight here," he said.

"My, we've got a full house in here." A towering older man in a white coat walked in. "Hello, I'm Doctor Tyler. You must be Willow."

"Yes." I straightened in the bed. "This is my dad." I gestured to my ponytailed father.

"Hi. Ralph Thomas." Dad stepped forward and shook the doctor's hand.

"And these must be friends." The doctor nodded toward Jilly and Rick.

"Yes, they were there when I fell. And this is my sister Breezy." Her round eyes stared mesmerized at the jagging lines on the heart monitor.

The doctor took his stethoscope from around his neck and placed it in his ears. "Mind if I take a little listen?"

I nodded and he listened to my heart and lungs through the thin gown.

"Are you able to sit up so I can listen from the back?"

"I think so." I tried to sit up. A sharp pain shot through my shoulder, and I let out an embarrassing yelp. A sheen of perspiration dampened my forehead as I fell back to the bed.

"Well that's not good. Tell me what happened to bring you in today."

I wiped my uninjured arm across my face to hide the welling tears. Reality and pain were sinking in. "I'm not exactly sure. We were practicing a stunt."

"What kind of stunt?" Doctor Tyler asked.

"Oh, sorry, cheerleading. We're getting ready for Regionals and were playing around."

Screwing around was more like it, but I didn't want to admit that.

"We've won State the last three years," Jilly added. "And Nationals last year!"

"Anyway, we were lined up, and everything seemed normal during the toss. It wasn't until the catch that I realized something was off, but by then it was too late." I shuddered, which sent pain down my arm as I remembered that instant.

Rick spoke up. "One second everything was fine, and the next she was coming at us head first." He cast me a pained look. "We tried to catch her, but it was too late. She landed kind of shoulder and head first and at an angle. Kyle tried to throw his knee out to slow her fall."

"So you're one of those girls they flip in the air?" Doctor Tyler asked, ignoring the horrific accident description. He leaned against the wall.

"I'm a flyer. That's what they call us, the ones who, you know, fly in the air."

"How high up do you go?" he asked, as if he were an excited fan and not my doctor.

"It depends, but usually about fifteen feet and on big stunts even more."

"And you like that?" he asked in disbelief.

"Yeah," I said. "At least I used to. Now I'm not so sure." I squirmed to find a more comfortable position.

"The truth is, you're lucky you weren't more seriously hurt." His easy demeanor shifted and he addressed Jilly and Rick. "You'll excuse us so I can go over the test results with Willow and her father."

Jilly gave my hand a quick squeeze. "I'll be in the waiting room until you can have visitors again."

"Actually, you need to give Willow time to rest. She'll be receiving some meds that will make her tired," the doctor said.

"Hang in there," Rick said as he followed Jilly out of the room.

Doctor Tyler approached the bed. "That's better. Let's go over your test results."

Chapter 2

Four days later and finally free of the brace that secured my whiplashed neck, I walked into the school atrium carrying my lunch tray with my book bag over one shoulder. This spot belongs to us, the Capitol City Flyers.

The atrium is the primo lunch hangout at Capitol High School. Even in the middle of February, the atrium stays bright and warm. The glass walls enclose lush gardens complete with trees and park-like walkways. Some elderly Senator had an affinity for the east side of Madison and donated millions to build our state-of-the-art school. The atrium is one of many perks. Our auditorium is another.

While my school brags several winning sports teams and clubs, the Flyers are the school's crowning glory, the crème de la crème. The past three years we won state, and last year the National championships too. The Flyers received tons of media attention and pulled in huge donations to the school. That's why we command the coveted atrium.

"Willow, you're here!" Jilly popped up like a ping pong ball.

"Yeah, barely." I eased my aching body into the spot on the decorative park bench she offered. My muscles screamed as if I'd been pummeled by the football team, not suffered one measly fall. Granted, it was a horrible fall that I couldn't erase from my mind. I moved carefully to avoid jarring my tender back and shoulder as I leaned against the bench. The rest of the squad rushed over.

"Coming to school today seemed like a good idea this morning, but my painkiller wore off about an hour ago."

"Awesome, can I have some? " Kyle, my other catcher on the squad, joked. Kyle's short hair always curled tight at the sides, framing his quirky smile. "Maybe I could sell them. I need money to fix my car."

"No way. Those babies are edible gold. I can't wait to get home and take another one. I feel like I've been run over by a truck." I shifted the tray on my lap and tried to get comfortable.

"So what did the doctor say?" Rick asked.

"That I'll live," I joked. I didn't want to go into the details of my concussion and whiplash, or that the doctor said I was lucky to be alive. If Kyle hadn't made a last instant lunge to break my fall, I might have been toast. Charred-to-a-crisp.

"We need you for Sectionals. Can you compete next weekend?" Sydney, a pixie-haired blonde, asked."

Every team member stopped what they were doing and collectively held their breath. Normally, I'd say absolutely nothing could keep me away from competition, but every day since the fall I became less sure.

I've suffered tons of bumps and bruises during practice, but this time it was different. I hit hard; I almost bit the dust. Big time. My body hurt so bad I could barely raise my left arm above my shoulder. The thought of being launched skyward and doing a double twist flip seemed impossible.

"I don't really know," I said. "I go back to the doctor early next week. He said no practice until then." I took a huge bite of pizza so I couldn't say more.

My friends exchanged glances, but no one spoke. Every move was choreographed for maximum impact. Losing any piece of our complex puzzle would shift everything, not to mention I was their top flyer. I'd try anything, no matter how difficult. I know how much the team needed that wow factor to push our routines over the top and win. My role was kind of the sparkler on the top tier of the cake.

"You'll be fine. I know you will," Jilly said. "We don't even have to worry about it. We could win Sectionals on rollerblades and blindfolded."

"That I'd like to see," Kyle said.

"You aren't serious are you?" Carly, the only sophomore on the squad, asked.

He reached over and ruffled her hair. "You are so pathetic." Carly swatted his hand away and smoothed her glossy blond hair back into place.

"Hey Anna, Did you guys hear what happened at musical practice?" Jilly said, her eyes aglow with gossip.

"Yeah, Jessica Seymour brought pot brownies to rehearsal and got busted."

"No way!" Kyle said. "Why do I always miss the good stuff?"

I took another bite of pizza, relieved they'd moved on to a new topic.

Jilly leaned forward. "But did you hear the part about the big-wig director eating about six?"

"What! Are you serious?" Anna said.

"Yeah, Jessica thought it would be funny for the cast to get high. Apparently, the director is a total slave driver. She figured they'd float through practice. But before anyone realized, he saw the brownies and started eating."

"Oh my God! What did she do?" I asked. A few years ago, I took dance classes with Jessica. She danced great but was always getting in trouble. It seemed like a lifetime since those days.

"They didn't want him to eat too many, so most of the cast started to eat them too." Jilly cracked up.

"Alex Walker told me that after about a half hour, the director couldn't concentrate. He'd be talking, and then he'd start looking around the room in a daze."

"I heard he's totally hot!" Carly said.

"So, what did they do after he got high?" I couldn't imagine doing something so ballsy or stupid.

"Nothing! Who was going to point out that he was flying high on pot brownies?" Jilly replied.

"Can you imagine if we got Ms. Klahn high?" Kyle said. "We totally should."

That, I would love to see. Our coach, Ms. Klahn, acted like a drill sergeant. She pushed us super hard, but she knew her stuff. We couldn't have gotten to Nationals without her.

"Yeah, I dare you to try it," Rick said to Kyle

"And get kicked out like Jessica did? No way!"

"What? Jessica got kicked out of the musical?" I dropped my pizza and my jaw.

"Yeah, a janitor overheard Jessica bragging about the pot brownies, and he told the choir director, Ms.

Fuller. She threw a royal fit because she's in charge of overseeing the show rehearsals. Fuller reported it to the principal, and Jessica's out!"

"But isn't Jessica the lead?" I asked.

"Not anymore. They've been in rehearsals for two weeks. Now they've got to replace her."

"That ought to be a real cat fight. Can't you just see all the other girls hissing to take her part?" Anna said.

"You don't replace Jessica Seymour. There is no one in this city as good as she is—no one!" Jessica danced like nobody's business. We'd spent years dancing together until I quit the beginning of freshman year. The last couple of those years, I started landing the bigger solo parts and the leads in the dance competitions and programs. Jessica was not happy. I could only imagine how pissed off she was about losing her part in the show.

The bell rang. Everyone gathered their stuff and moved to the atrium doors. I groaned as I stood and eased my book bag over my shoulder. I picked up my tray and as I left the atrium, I couldn't help but wonder who would take her part in the show.

Chapter 3

A few days later, with my doctor's permission, I was back at the scene of the accident. My pulse raced out of control.

Same gym. Same mats.

Same skylights giving us a glimpse of the heavens.

The Capitol Flyers stood in formation, warmed up and ready to go.

"Ready and go!" Anna, our team captain, chanted. In unison, we moved through the routine with snappy arm motions, loud chants, and the occasional eagle jump. As we approached the first trick, a simple toe touch basket toss, I froze. Rick and Kyle stood in front of me, waiting for me to put my hands on their shoulders and feet on their linked arms. I didn't step forward. I stared at their waiting position, seeing only a sling shot of danger.

"Willow, come on," Rick urged.

I looked at him and hoped he couldn't see my fear. I didn't move.

"You can do it," Kyle said. "Let's go."

I turned to Kyle and his grin of encouragement. He waited expectantly, eager to vault me into space. I liked Kyle, and I wanted to trust him, but I couldn't. Not him, not even Rick, who had been one of my bases forever. I shook my head and stepped back away from the threatening catapult. The rest of the group had stopped the routine and watched the hold up. I was always the first one at practice, always eager to get started. Cheerleading was like playtime. Until last week, flying was my greatest thrill, and I couldn't wait to go again. I always pushed for more difficult stunts and higher launches.

Now the team stared in silence as panic squeezed my chest. I noticed Jilly and Rick share a glance.

Jilly stepped to my side. "It's okay, you can do it."

"No," I whispered, paralyzed, arms glued to my side and palms moist with fear. My shoulders hunched tight, my breath came in shallow bursts.

Jilly got in my face and spoke in slow quiet tones. "Let's just try it again from the top. Willow, it's just like getting on a bike."

Dread stalked me. I shook my head. "I can't do this."

"You just need a little time. You're still sore from last week."

She was trying to talk me off this ledge of terror, but it didn't matter what she said. I looked at each of their faces, first Jilly, then Anna, Kyle and finally Rick. My face turned hot in a flush of panic as the words I longed to speak wouldn't flow through the tightness in my throat. The squad surrounded me, sucking up all the breathable air. My chest tightened as they stared at my unusual behavior. They needed me for the next competition and I wanted to need them too, but they represented pain and fear and maybe even death.

I didn't want to fall again. I didn't want to die.

All it took to make me slam down into the mat last time was a simple distraction. How could I believe Rick and Kyle would catch me this time? Even if there were a dozen bases on a twenty-foot mat of feathers, there were no guarantees.

I took another step back and shook my head. I looked at Jilly and whispered, "I think I quit."

"No!" She reacted as if I'd slapped her .

"Willow." Jilly took my arm and spoke like I was a scared little kid. "It's going to be okay. You don't have to do this right now. You can try again later." She exchanged glances with the others."

"I quit," I said again and felt more secure saying the words out loud.

They stared, jaws open in shock. More kids squeezed closer as word spread.

"Come on, you're our Fearless Wonder," Kyle teased. He'd always been my biggest supporter, but his eyes looked worried.

"I quit," I repeated, more fortified each time I said the words.

"Hey, what's going on? I step out for two minutes, and it's a parking lot in here." The squad peeled apart to let Ms. Klahn into the middle of the circle. "Is there a problem?" she asked, her brow furrowed when she discovered all eyes on me.

I faced Coach. The rest of the squad no longer mattered. This woman taught me how to fly, how to reach for the stars and how to be the best I could.

I gulped. "I quit," I said quickly before I could chicken out of chickening out.

Our eyes met and locked. Ms. Klahn could always read my emotions like a Vulcan in a mind meld. She held my gaze and saw my panic and terror.

She knew. She saw it.

I would never fly again. Fear had this girl grounded. Permanently.

"Are you sure?" Ms. Klahn asked after a moment.

"Yes." My heart tried to pound its way out of my chest.

"I see." Disappointment colored her face as she contemplated the situation for several beats. She looked into my frightened, determined eyes, and I knew she realized she couldn't change the reality of the situation. She nodded in understanding. "You may go," she said softly.

Relief washed over me and took away the weight of the world that I hadn't realized I'd been carrying. The stark fear and panic I felt earlier evaporated. I exhaled a breath I'd been holding. My shoulders sagged in release.

"What about Regionals?" Anna blurted. "We can't win without Willow. She's the only one who can do kick triple twist basket."

"Looks like we'll have to get back to work and redo the routine then. Let's go. What are you all standing around for?" Ms. Klahn barked.

I sure ruined her day, but it couldn't be helped. This was about survival.

I walked through the throng of my friends and former squad members toward the locker room. Their eyes followed me, filled with a combination of shock, confusion and anger. Jilly ran after me.

"Willow, wait. Think this through. You can't walk away from cheer like this. Okay, you're not ready to fly again yet. You just need some time. We'll figure out Regionals, but we can't win State without you." Jilly pleaded. "Take a few days off, let your bruises heal. It'll be okay. You can be a base at Regionals, nothing hard. Just don't give up."

"Jilly, unless you plan on handing in your uniforms too, get back in formation," Coach yelled across the gym.

"The team needs you. You just can't walk away so easily. I need you!" Jilly pressed.

Easy didn't begin to describe the mix of my pain and emotions.

"Remember how we talked about Nationals, and that we were going to get our belly buttons pierced when we win?"

I grimaced. My belly would remain pure and unmarred as the driven snow. No more National titles, no more competitions and certainly no belly piercing.

"Come on, Willow. Work with me here," Jilly leaned in close to my face and pleaded

"No, you work with me! Nothing's going to change." I didn't want to hurt Jilly, but I wouldn't agree to something I couldn't do anymore. She just didn't get it.

"Don't say that. Promise you'll think about it for a while. It's the least you can do. This squad made a pact, and you were first to sign it. We had a deal."

Jilly was right. We'd all made a team pact. But everything changed the day I felt my body crunch into the gym floor. Pact or no pact, I wanted out.

"Even if I wait a few days, it won't change anything," I said.

"But you'll think about it?" Jilly lit up as hope fueled her fire of determination.

Crud. I wanted to be free of this, but I didn't want to

hurt my best friend either. "Fine, I'll think about it, but don't get your hopes up." Maybe Jilly needed time to accept my decision.

"Woo hoo!" Jilly leapt in the air. "You won't regret it. Everything is going to be fine."

"Jilly." Ms. Klahn yelled again.

"Go. They need you." I turned my back on my best friend and walked away.

Everything would not be fine. Not fine at all.

* * *

Normally, Jilly dropped me home, but waiting for her to finish cheer was the last thing I needed to do. So, I walked home in the early darkness of a late February afternoon. The long cold walk helped clear my head from all the drama. My shoulders even began to release some of the tension I'd been clinging to. I let it all go. Well, all but the niggling reminder that Jilly made me agree to think more about quitting before I made it final.

Now I had to figure out how to let Jilly down without hurting her feelings. Jilly was nothing if not persistent. That girl could maneuver people to do pretty much anything she wanted. She wasn't used to hearing the word *no*.

I crossed the street and jumped over icy patches on the frozen road. My toes were like icicles. Wearing flats with no socks wasn't the best idea, but then again, I didn't know I'd quit cheer today and have to walk home. I walked past a couple blocks of huge homes that overlooked Lake Monona and veered in a few blocks to the older homes built so close together that only a single lane driveway separated them. By the time I reached our house, my fingers felt like frozen sausages, despite how far I pushed them into my pockets. I ran up the ancient wooden steps, across the porch and through the antique front door into the welcoming warmth of home.

Inside, the aroma of cookies filled the house.

My fluffy dog, Twinkie, skittered around the corner and jumped on me. "Hey girl." I ruffled her ears. "Aren't my hands cold?"

Twinkie isn't her real name. When I got her for my eleventh birthday, I was still in my dance obsession stage and named her Twyla after the famous dancer and choreographer Twyla Tharp. Unfortunately, when my little sister started to talk, she couldn't say Twyla, so she started calling her Twinkie. Much to my frustration, it stuck. So my beautiful Twyla is a Twinkie.

"Mom?" I called.

"In the kitchen." Her voice echoed off the high stucco ceiling.

I dumped my school bag, balanced my coat on the entryway coat tree and wandered through the cluttered living room into the kitchen.

"I didn't think you were home until Thursday." I rubbed my arms to warm up.

"Surprise," she said and pulled a pan of white bean cranberry cookies from the oven. Even cookies were healthy at our house. "I'm here until Sunday, then I'm on the Tokyo route. What are you doing home so early? You're usually not home for another hour or so." She placed the pan on the stovetop to cool.

"Yeah, that's something I need to talk to you about." I stepped to the stove and opened the oven door. Hot air poured out, and I held my hands out to warm them as if it were a roaring fire. I inhaled the warm air. Twinkie lay in the corner and kept watch.

Mom faced the counter, dropping dough onto a clean pan with her fingers. She wore her light brown hair stuffed into a clip at the back of her head with loose strands hanging out. She wore an old faded denim shirt, loose sweats and Birkenstocks with socks.

"What's up?" she asked, rubbing an itch on her nose with her arm.

Inching backward for maximum heat exposure, I turned to warm my rear end. "I quit cheer today. Sort of." I added, since Jilly roped me into delaying the inevitable.

"Really?" Mom stopped messing with the cookie sheet and turned to me, her fingers covered in dough. "I thought you loved cheer."

"I did, but now I don't know. I think it's time to do something else." I rotated again in front of the open oven door like a rotisserie chicken in front of the oven.

"What's the 'sort of' part?" she asked with a raised eyebrow.

"Jilly. She kind of made me promise to give it a few more days before I make up my mind."

"You mean more time for *her* to change your mind?" Mom grinned and then plopped a blob of dough into her mouth.

"Pretty much." I turned and grabbed a warm cookie from the counter.

"Did you have a fight with Jilly?" She reached around me for the cookie pan from the stove.

"Why would you say that?" I took a bite of cookie.

"Considering how much cheer has been your life, it's a logical question. I would hate to see a pattern develop."

"There's no pattern and there's nothing to worry about. I think you've spent too many hours at 30,000 feet."

"I have and I'm sorry I wasn't here the day of your accident."

"It's okay. I'm fine."

"Yes, you are, but I hear your Foods grade isn't." She winked

"That little snot. Breezy is the world's biggest blabber mouth."

"How about your Dad? He and I have a secret connection with clandestine meetings and covert communication about our kids."

"Oh, I should have known. What else did he say?"

"That you have a C minus in that class?"

"What a narc! I told him not to tell. It's a dumb class and should have been an easy A."

"Haven't you learned by now that your father and I don't do secrets?" She held out a chunk of cookie dough. I swiped it up with my finger and ate it.

"So what's going on with you and the rest of the squad?"

"I don't know...nothing really."

"If you say so. I'd hate to see you quit for the wrong reasons. Are you warm enough yet? Because pretty soon the kitchen is going to be so hot this pan of cookies will bake without closing the oven door."

"Actually, I am. Thanks." I snapped the oven door shut, grabbed a handful of cookies, and left the kitchen.

Chapter 4

The next morning, I sat on the edge of our crowded bay window watching for Jilly. It was a tight fit among the bunch of pots and planters placed to catch the short winter sunlight. Every fall, my dad hauls in all the plants from the front porch and garden. It's a veritable potter's hell of scraggly looking cilantro, garlic, and sprouts. The plants looked pretty bad this time of year, but Dad insists on his organic garden.

Jilly pulled up in the beat-up Chevy her brother gave her when he left for college.

"Bye, see you tonight," I yelled to no one in particular and rushed out the door. Outside, frost covered the steps and sidewalk as the morning sun hadn't risen high enough to melt it. I hopped into the warm car and pushed my book bag on the floor.

"Sorry I'm late," Jilly said. "I changed clothes like five times. I couldn't make up my mind."

"Don't worry about it. I'm in no hurry to get to first block. I have a group project in Marketing. Jessica is in my group, and she's been a real bitch since she got kicked out of that musical."

"Oh my God, I heard her parents were so pissed about the pot brownies. Her dad is a cop, and he went totally postal." Jilly backed out of the driveway and onto the road.

"You have to admit, that was a pretty stupid thing

to do, bringing it to school."

"Well, she never was the sharpest tool in the shed," said Jilly. "Speaking of which, I've been thinking about your problem."

"Why does not being the sharpest tool in the shed make you think of me, and what is my problem?" I gripped the strap of my bag. I did not want to go down this road again with Jilly.

"You know, cheer. Quitting is not the brightest thing; plus, your quitting is a problem."

Great, here we go already. What'd that take? Twelve seconds?

"So, I realized that you're a little scared about flying again, which makes total sense. Heck, you bit the mat pretty hard. You should be scared."

I'm not scared, I'm terrified!

"And it was only a week ago, so you're probably still a little sore from the fall." Jilly tried to talk and watch the road at the same time.

"You want to see my bruises? They've changed from black and blue to green and yellow." I pulled my coat and shirt back to reveal my multi-colored shoulder.

"Ew! Does it hurt?" She cringed.

"Not anymore." I adjusted my coat back in place.

Jilly snapped back to her bubbly self. "So about cheer. I think we need to ease you back. Do some little stuff first. Do a scorpion, and then after a while a simple toe touch basket toss. Work your way back up to the hard stuff."

My chest tightened at the mere mention of stunts. What was wrong with me anyway? Why did I switch to panic mode every time I thought about cheer? But what I did know is that there was no way Jilly or the even the entire cheer squad could force me back in that gym. Not happening.

"You know, Jilly, I appreciate what you're trying to do, but I'm pretty much done."

Jilly delivered a stubborn glare. "No you're not! You promised to give it some time, and this is not giving it time. You can't just shut cheer out; shut ME out! You have an obligation to the squad and even the school. We need to go back to Nationals and defend our title. No one can fly like you! No one else can do half of those tricks!"

Jilly was right about the stunts. No one else had the nerve to even try some of them. Rick and Kyle have amazing power when they toss. Most of the girls are afraid of being teamed with them. The guys strength gave me more time to complete all the twists and flips. Most of the girls were too chicken to try. I chewed at my lip with a combination of guilt and worry about how I'd make sure Jilly didn't twist my arm and get me back to cheer.

"If we don't have you, we lose Nationals. Heck, we'll be lucky to get through Regionals on Saturday. We need you back as soon as you can."

"You'll win Regionals easy. The biggest competition is from West, and you'll wipe the floor with them." I tried to distract Jilly from her argument.

"Okay, this weekend shouldn't be a huge problem, but still, we can only go so far without you." Jilly pulled into the student parking lot where kids walked between cars toward the doors like a swarm of locust.

"So what are you guys doing to rework the

routine?"

"Anna is taking your place, but she won't do a Double Down Twist Cradle and her Rainbow isn't that good. I'm in her place."

"What? You're flying? Why didn't you tell me?" I couldn't believe it. Jilly was our best tumbler, so Coach never had her fly.

Jilly grinned as she pulled into a parking spot. "See why we need you back so bad? With me flying, I'm bound to screw it up."

"No, you're not. You'll do great." I grabbed my bag and got out. Jilly beeped the car locked. "I'm so proud of you, you're a flyer now." I bumped Jilly's shoulders as we walked.

"Stop changing the subject. You are coming back. Hear me! Take two more days off, and then you're back at practice putting the rest of us to shame."

Why bother arguing? I wasn't coming back. I didn't know how I'd eventually convince Jilly. There would have to be a really good reason, but what? What would make it impossible for me to do cheer, other than another accident?

* * *

During choir, Jilly wouldn't stop bugging me. She kept scribbling notes on our sheet music with all the reasons I couldn't quit. Ms. Fuller, our choir teacher, kept giving her the evil eye.

The bell finally rang and saved me from reading any more of Jilly's annoying scribbles. Our music looked like a graffiti rag with pencil scrawls in every space. Glad to escape, I grabbed my bag and headed for the door. Now I had to endure the entire squad in the atrium at lunch. Jilly made sure everyone knew I agreed to rethink quitting. But it didn't matter what they said or how much Jilly begged. I would never fly again.

"Willow, could I speak with you for a moment?" Ms. Fuller asked.

I spun around. Ms. Fuller never spoke to me unless it was to tell me to stop talking. She was probably ticked we were whispering and writing notes on school property. Jilly shrugged her shoulders, grinned and shot through the doors before she, too, got called back.

Thanks Jilly! What a loyal friend.

I stepped aside as the choir room emptied. If I was going to be chewed out, I didn't need an audience. Ms. Fuller stood at the piano and organized music.

"Come on over, and pull up a chair."

I obeyed, not liking the feel of this. Ms. Fuller sat down at the piano bench and turned to face me. She didn't look mad. Her grey eyes peered at me through her bifocals. She wore the same blue blazer she wears every Wednesday with grey slacks and brown shoes.

"I heard you quit the cheerleading squad. Is that right?"

"Yeah." Wow, news traveled fast!

"I'm surprised. I thought you loved cheerleading." She seemed to be analyzing me, and I couldn't imagine why.

"I do, I mean I did."

"You played a pretty big role in the squad, and I know they were making another run for Nationals. Are you sure you don't want to cheer anymore?"

I wondered who put her up to this. Ms. Klahn? Jilly?

"Positive," I answered without hesitation. I never wanted the sensation of free falling again.

"So there's no chance you'll be changing your mind and going back to the squad?" Ms. Fuller studied my reaction. Her forehead wrinkled in the spot between her eyes.

"Nope. I'm done. Cleaned out my locker and turned in my uniform." That part hurt more than I wanted to admit, but the relief far outweighed the pain. Jilly didn't know I'd done it, but she'd have to accept it. Eventually. "Can I ask why you're so interested in me quitting cheer?"

"Actually, I was getting to that." She smiled as if we were friends. "I'm sure you've heard there is an opening in the Tyson Scott Pilot Project."

"The what?" I asked, now more confused than ever.

"The musical is called Dream Chaser and its being brought in by the National Arts Board. You must have heard of it. They auditioned kids from all over the city. I talked about it in class a half dozen times."

"Oh yeah, you mean the one Jessica Seymour got kicked out of?" I didn't mention it happened because of pot brownies.

"I'm on the committee, and oversee the use of our school's auditorium for the duration of rehearsals. This is quite an honor for our school." She pushed up her glasses. "We're looking for someone to join the cast who can step in and hit the ground running. I only want to talk to people who are truly interested and available. It sounds like you're available, now the question is are you interested?"

"I don't know. I never thought about it before." This might be a way to make a clean break with cheer. Jilly would never stop bugging me unless there was no way for me to go back. If I could get in the chorus of this show, it would solve everything. "Isn't it super dance intensive?"

"That's right. Mr. Scott is bringing some of the most technical and innovative dance ever done at the high-school level. If this show is as successful as he hopes, it has an excellent chance of getting picked up for Broadway. We are fortunate to have a few members of Capital High in the show. It would be nice to have another student represent the school.

"I'm sorry, but I haven't taken dance since freshman year. I don't know if I could keep up." Dance had been my life for so many years, but after what happened, I dropped it and switched to cheer.

"Don't worry about that now. One step at a time. What I need to know is if you're interested." She waited for my answer as if she had all day.

I wasn't sure what to do. She'd caught me off guard. "It never really occurred to me."

Now that I thought about it, I did recall a couple months back when news of the show and the amazing Tyson Scott was all over school and the Madison media. News crews even reported outside our school about the amazing pilot program that would put our city on the map for more than the University and the Wisconsin Badgers. At the time, everyone on cheer watched with curiosity over all the attention. I heard a lot of the kids from my former dance school auditioned. They had to agree to quit all their other clubs and activities for the three months of rehearsals and shows.

"Do you have something to do with all this new time on your hands? Did you have anything else in mind?"

"No, it's still pretty new." It hadn't been twenty-four hours yet. I still couldn't figure out how she knew.

"Well, give it some thought and let me know." Ms. Fuller stood up as kids started to file in for the freshman Madrigal rehearsal.

"Okay. I'll think about it." Happy to get away from her prying, I slipped past the freshman mob. What an interesting idea. There wasn't much Jilly and the others could do if I committed to something else, like the show.

I went to the commons to grab lunch and join the others in the atrium. Unfortunately, because I arrived late, the lunch lines trailed on forever. I joined the back and waited an eternity to reach the food counter.

Usually I stand with half the squad talking and oblivious to everything else, but with no one to distract me, I actually noticed the surroundings of the cafeteria. Polished silver columns marked the edges of the huge room. A sea of round lunch tables filled the gleaming clean space. Bright light shone down and illuminated the students who gathered in their various clusters and cliques.

Now, as I looked at it, the groups were so obvious. The Cross Country team took up a couple tables. The guys were all lanky and lean. They had their own nerdy confidence that long distance runners seem to have.

The techies gathered in a far corner. These guys were mostly scrawny with pasty white skin. Some of the cheer guys loved to harass them.

On the side near the wide staircase to Level Two sat the show contingent. They consisted of kids who did theatre, dance, and music. There was an unspoken challenge from them to take the atrium from the cheer squad. I knew some of them from my early years of dance. It's funny how much life changes and evolves. I never even talked to those kids anymore. My memories of that time were bittersweet.

Beyond that was the atrium; I spotted my friends through the foliage. Jilly sat on one of the benches laughing.

Finally, I hit the front of the line. I grabbed my regular lunch: a slice of pepperoni pizza, and a chocolate milk. I took a bite, inched down the line to the cashier and slid my ID through the scanner to pay. As I made my way toward the atrium, a couple girls from the JV squad stopped me. If they were good enough, eventually they'd make varsity.

"Hey Willow, is it true you quit cheer?" asked Kelli, a short sophomore with a bob of brown hair.

"Uh, yeah."

"I told you," Kelli said to Jenna who perched next to her at the table. "That is so huge! I can't even believe it! Why'd you quit?"

I hadn't thought about other kids asking.

"Jenna, stop being so nosy," Kelli said.

"What? I'm just asking." She turned back to me. "I heard it's because you got hurt really bad, and your parents made you quit."

Their overeager underclassmen pupils focused on me. How little they knew. My parents never make me do anything. Or, for that matter, never forbid anything either. If I told them I wanted to shoot bear in The Yukon, they'd buy me a hunting license and put me on a plane.

"No, nothing like that. I just lost interest." Which technically was true, but still a lame answer.

"I heard she chickened out," a blond said from the other side of the table.

"I gotta go." I turned my back on them, not willing to listen anymore. Let them gossip. That's half the fun of cheer, talking about everyone else who wasn't lucky enough to be one of us.

I mean them. If this was what the saying meant about a taste of your own medicine, I didn't like it. Having people gossip about me to my face, let alone behind my back, sucked.

I took another bite of pizza when the warning bell rang. Crap. So much for lunch. At least it saved me from facing Jilly and the squad of inquisitors. I dropped my tray at the kitchen window and grabbed my pizza and milk to finish on the way to class.

Chapter 5

After school, I walked in the front door to discover a huge drop cloth on the living room floor and a giant canvas stretched across the room. Dad and Breezy stood on the drop cloth throwing handfuls of paint at the canvas.

Another average day at the Thomas house.

"Hey Willow, what are you doing home so early?" Dad asked.

"I'm not doing cheer anymore. Remember?" He must be the only person who didn't care one way or another.

"That's right. You feeling okay about that?" He paused with the paint long enough to give me one of his obligatory concerned dad looks.

"Yup. It's all good," I said, only a little bit surprised at how easy it was to walk away from cheer. Knowing I'd never have to be airborne again gave me great relief.

"Hey, Willow, wanna throw paint with us?" Breezy stood barefoot, wearing a stained smock and a paint smudge on her cheek.

"No thanks, I'll pass, but it looks great!" The bright blotches looked like a nauseous dragon horked colors.

"Thanks!" She beamed.

"Willow, before you go, Breezy took a message for you. It's on the fridge."

"Who called?"

"You have to go read it," Breezy yelled. "Geez! That's why it's called a message. So I wouldn't have to tell you."

I found her message taped to the fridge with grey fingerprints smeared on it. I could barely read "Call Miss Ginny." The phone number was illegible, but I knew it by heart. Miss Ginny owned the Davis Dance Academy, my old studio. I wondered what she could possibly want after all this time.

I grabbed my cell phone and went upstairs to escape the flying paint. I dialed the number and asked for her.

"Hello, Willow!" The cultured voice of my former dance teacher rang out.

My heart ached a little as her voice immediately took me back to the many hours I'd spent with this woman. "Hi, Miss Ginny."

"Thank you for calling back so quickly. I knew you would. I called because I need you to stop by the studio this evening. I have something to discuss with you."

"Sure, I guess." I hadn't stepped foot into the studio for about three years. I couldn't even make myself visit; it was too hard for me and for her when I quit, and my presence in the studio would've broken both our hearts.

"Wonderful. I have a class now, so I must go, but swing by around seven o'clock; I have a break between classes then."

"Alright, I'll be there."

"It will be so good to see you. It's been too long since I've seen that beautiful face. I have to get back to class, so goodbye for now."

The line clicked off. *Great*. What was she up to? I'm barely out of cheer, and Miss Ginny is trying to recruit me back to dance? I wasn't sure it was something I wanted to do. For just a second, I'd like to relax and take a breath, but I wouldn't let her down, I'd be there and on time.

At the allotted hour, I pulled our aging Prius into the crowded parking lot of Davis Dance Academy. Parents sat in their cars with the engines running as they waited for their kids to finish class. My mom and dad were part of this crowd for ten years, dutifully picking me up four nights a week. Dance had been my passion, my whole world, my identity. It broke my heart to quit, but at the time, it seemed like the best choice.

I squeezed the car into a spot with the right side parked up on a snow bank. This left the car hiked at an angle. Parking was not my strength, especially when winter snow crowded all the spots. Unexpected emotions clouded my eyes as I grabbed my bag and approached the doors. Three years was a long time to stay away from what had literally been my second home.

The heavy front door still stuck when I pulled it open. Three young girls rushed past, twittering away with dance bags over their shoulders and their winter coats hanging open to the frosty elements. Inside, dozens of girls loitered in their leotards and tights. Many took up camp in the corners, changing shoes or doing homework between dance classes.

"Willow is that you? I don't believe my eyes!" Miss Kathy, one of my former teachers, rushed over and hugged me. "Look at you! You're all grown up."

I suppose I had changed a bit since freshman year. I hugged her back, filled with nostalgia.

"What are you doing here? Are you coming back to

dance with us?"

"Miss Ginny asked me to come in. I'm not sure why." I glanced around the lobby. Dance pictures and posters lined the walls.

"I'm sure it must be something important for her to call. She's in Studio C. Go on over. I hope this means you're coming back. We could use more dancers like you. I've got a class, but don't be stranger." Miss Kathy rushed off.

A crush of pint-sized dancers squeezed past as I made my way to Studio C. Miss Ginny stood near a large stereo, organizing CD's, garbed in her standard studio uniform of pink tights, black leotard cinched at the breast and her trademark chartreuse wrap. Mirrors covered one wall and ballet bars lined the other three. The worn wood floor reminded me of my endless hours spent practicing.

She turned and spotted me. Warm kinship shone in her eyes. "Willow," she said like a melody. Miss Ginny offered a warm smile that felt like a welcome home after a long journey. Her lips were stained red and her bright eyes rimmed with black liner. She still wore false eyelashes, as if she were about to step out under the bright stage lights.

"Come let me take a look at you," she said, back in her business mode. "Take off that coat."

I grinned at my former mentor, tossed my coat aside, and stepped before her.

"You're taller," she stated as she examined me.

"Yes, that happens." I fought the urge to hug her.

"How are your parents?" She gripped my biceps and triceps. "Look at these muscles. Tsk."

"Same as usual." I bit back a response about the muscle comment. Cheerleading demanded a lot of strength.

"Are they still blending tea?"

"Oh yes, and they've expanded to some new flavors."

"And your sister? I haven't seen her in my studio." She continued to examine me, nodding approval.

"She's a free spirit, but maybe someday." Breezy didn't seem like the dancing type. Drama, yes, but the discipline of dance? I didn't see it.

Miss Ginny harrumphed.

"You quit that cheerleading thing," she stated, but arched an eyebrow like it was a question.

"Yes, just yesterday." Here it was again. Did everyone in the entire city know I quit?

"Good," She said with satisfied finality. "You must go home and stretch out those muscles. Don't worry. They will be long and lean in a couple of weeks. Have your father teach you some yoga."

"Yes, ma'am, but Miss Ginny, will you please tell me what this is about?"

"Tyson Scott needs a new dancer for his pilot project Dream Chaser. Of course, Jessica threw her opportunity into the toilet as she often does. A talented girl with no drive. What a waste. Now everything is a mess. He must find another dancer immediately. He has all my best dancers, but he doesn't have you." She drilled me with a look like a nun at a Catholic school. "I told him you can step in immediately."

"What?!"

I *had* thought about it since Ms. Fuller mentioned the

idea this morning, but step in immediately? Let's slow this train down.

"Is there a problem?" she asked. "Tyson needs a dancer, and you need to dance. You're done playing cheerleader, so what else are you going to do?"

"I don't know if I have time to do a show right now."

"Nonsense. Of course you do. Tyson is a former student of mine. He is a brilliant choreographer with the most innovative mind to hit Broadway in twenty years. This show will put Madison on the map as an excellent location for the arts." She paused and peered over the top of her glasses. "If his show garners the critical acclaim it deserves, great things will happen to all involved. You must be a part of it."

"Yeah, but..."

"No, no. No more disagreements. I want you to go home and do some warm ups. Practice your last competition routine, the one you performed at the Joffrey summer workshop. Play some classical music, and for goodness sake, stretch out those muscles. This is a once in a lifetime opportunity, and you will not be left behind! Do you have a problem with this?" Her head held high and her posture perfect, she awaited my answer like a ticking bomb.

"No, ma'am." What was the point in debating? When Miss Ginny got something in her head, she always got her way. Except when I quit dance. That was the hardest thing I'd ever done, much harder than quitting cheer, and Miss Ginny took it personally. But it had nothing to do with her.

"Excellent. Be ready to audition for him after school

tomorrow. It's in the Capital High Auditorium. It will be a private audition before the full cast rehearsal."

My eyes bugged out. An audition tomorrow! I needed time to prepare. It had been three years since I last danced. Miss Ginny assumed too much if she thought I could be polished enough for an audition by then!

"Now what is this? You can't expect to just walk in and get the part."

"But I need a lot more time!"

Young students wandered in. "I wish I had time to work with you now, but the night is filled with classes. Here is a DVD of your last competition routine. The one you took first place with. Do you remember?"

"Yes, of course." How could I forget? I practiced each number until I knew it inside out and backwards. And once I knew a routine I never forgot it. I was a freak that way.

"Good. Now go home and work this number until you have it the best you can. You won't be anywhere near your former skill level, but it should be enough." She placed the case in my hand. "You have a lot of work to do, off you go. I will see you tomorrow." She smiled with satisfaction.

Dumbfounded, I left the studio. As much as I couldn't imagine doing a dance audition after going cold turkey, the thought of having a concrete reason not to go back to cheer — ever — gave me a renewed determination. Plus, the idea of being part of something great kindled a tiny flame deep inside.

* * *

I sat in the cold car still in shock. Now I had the perfect out. Try out for the show and never go back to cheer. I turned the key. After a slow turnover, the engine rumbled to life. This was what I wanted, wasn't it? A guaranteed reason to never fly again. Just the thought of walking into the cheer practice gym scared me.

But could I dance well enough to get a part? I used to dance four or five times a week and compete on the dance team. How much had I forgotten? Could I do those leaps anymore? Could I do a double switch leap or a quadruple fuette turn? Miss Ginny was right, I had the short tight muscles of a cheerleader. My long lean dance muscles disappeared soon after I quit.

The air blasting out began to turn warm. I rubbed my hands together in front of it. Doing the show would solve some of my problems, but not my biggest one; convincing Jilly that I really had quit. The two of us had been tighter than the Kardashians ever since cheer camp that first summer. We roomed together, ate together, guy watched together, and harassed the underclassmen together.

Her uncle owned a gymnastics gym, and we spent all our free time perfecting our tumbling and stunts. We even learned how to fly together. While Jilly could fly, she didn't have the flair or fearlessness I did. Boy, had that changed. My dad calls us Thing 1 and Thing 2. Somehow I needed to soften the blow to Jilly. She wasn't going to like this.

I put the car in reverse and backed off the frozen mountain of snow. Once I was on level ground again, I left the Davis Dance Academy behind and headed toward Badger Twisters gymnastics school where I got to know Jilly that summer three years ago. Distraught after quitting dance, I gravitated to gymnastics, Jilly and I hit it off immediately. Because her uncle owns the place, we were able to spend every spare moment screwing around on the trampoline, learning cheer tricks, and jumping into the huge cushioned pit. Now Jilly works there.

A few minutes later, I ran through the icy cold air to the warm inside lobby. I unzipped my coat. Chairs lined the sides of the room for waiting parents. Bright lights illuminated the cluttered lobby and the sound of kids working echoed off the high metal ceiling.

One wall had dozens of cubbies to store street shoes, coats and gym bags. The other wall held a long counter for registration and concession sales. Jilly worked, selling red licorice to a couple of middle school girls.

"Hey," I walked over, not sure how to break the news.

"Oh my god. What are you doing here?" Jilly lit up like the Las Vegas strip.

"I was in the neighborhood and thought I'd stop by." I leaned one arm on the counter.

"Good thing. I've been so bored. I was about to hang myself with the climbing rope."

Jilly glowed with happiness. She always wore her feelings on her sleeve. There was no mystery in Jilly's emotions. If she felt it, you knew it, which made being in a fight easier, or maybe not. Sometimes it would be nice if she'd hide her anger.

"Good thing you didn't. That would have scared the little kids."

"Probably. Popcorn?" Jilly asked.

"Awesome."

Jilly opened the popcorn machine, filled two bags and handed me one.

"Thanks." I put a handful in my mouth.

"So why are you here tonight? Oh my god!" Jilly dropped her popcorn on the counter. "You changed your mind. You're coming back to cheer! I knew it!" She bounced up and down in her cheerleader way.

I scrunched my face. "Well, actually no."

Jilly sobered. "What?"

I took a breath and decided to just dive right in. "I was over talking to Miss Ginny, my old dance teacher."

Disbelief shown on Jilly's face, as if I just violated some sacred oath.

"She called me," I defended. "She asked me to come see her."

"What for?" Jilly sounded innocent enough, but I was pretty sure she knew I hadn't met my former dance teacher just to catch up on old times.

"Well, she heard I quit cheer."

Jilly gave me a pissed off glare.

"Don't look at me, I didn't tell her. Heck, I didn't tell anyone, but the whole world seems to know."

"So?" Jilly asked, waiting for the bad news.

"So, she wants me to try out for that pilot project. It's called Dream Chaser. There's a spot in the chorus since Jessica got the boot."

Jilly's jaw stiffened and her lips pinched tight. She grabbed a dishrag and began to wash off the scratched countertop.

"I told you. I didn't call her. She called me." But I

knew Jilly didn't care.

Jilly scrubbed harder. Finally she tossed the rag aside and crossed her arms. She turned to me, her shoulders set. "Just say it."

"What?"

"Just say what you came here to tell me." She glared.

Just as I opened my mouth to speak, Jilly interrupted. "But let me point out that you promised to take some time before you made it final."

I started to talk.

She interrupted again with her hands firmly on the counter. "You promised."

Jilly was acting unreasonable, but still I felt like a jerk. I shrugged my shoulders and said, "I have to."

Jilly turned away in a huff. "Oh please."

"Miss Ginny is really important to me, and she asked me to try out." I realized I was just making up excuses for Jilly, trying to avoid the real reason I quit, but I was too scared to keep flying.

"I don't know if I'll even make it. I haven't danced in forever. I'll probably suck." I prayed I wouldn't. I didn't want to embarrass Miss Ginny or myself.

"Not likely. You're good at everything." Jilly cocked her head to the side. "This is so crappy. You aren't even giving me a chance. You're scared. You fell. That's fine, but give yourself some time to get over it. It'll go away."

"Scared because I fell? That's a little mild, don't you think?" I glared at Jilly.

"It felt more like a full body slam into the gym floor head first. You may not think that's a big deal, but when you're free falling from twenty feet in the air, it hurts! A lot!" I pushed my hand through my hair as I recalled the horrible memory. Suddenly I felt out of breath, and my pulse raced from thinking about it.

Jilly had the decency to look guilty. "I know. It's just that I don't want you to quit. You're half the reason I love cheer so much. Plus, without you it won't be fun anymore." She looked at me with the saddest eyes.

"Sure it will. You and Anna will become BFFs." I teased, trying to make Jilly lighten up. And it worked, a least a little.

"You're such a jerk." She tossed popcorn at me and grinned.

"And we'll still see each other all the time; just not at cheer. Like I said, I don't even know if I'll make it, but I have to give it a shot." I drew circles on the surface with my finger. The more we talked about the tryout and show, the more I realized I really wanted it.

"This rots big time. You shouldn't run away just because you're scared."

"I'm not."

Jilly pierced me with a look that said she knew otherwise.

I squirmed. A group of kids came with money in their hands. "Well, I should get going." I pushed away. "I'll see you in the morning."

Jilly didn't say anything. She just shrugged, then turned to scoop more popcorn.

Chapter 6

The next day, all through fourth block, I was freakin'
out. The history teacher droned on about the Vietnam
War, then left us time to work on the next day's
homework. I drummed my pencil on the table to the beat
of my erratic nerves.

On the way to school, Jilly made it clear that if I
went out for the show it would be slamming the cheer
door closed forever. But that was exactly what I wanted.
During lunch everyone in the atrium barely spoke to me.
It's like I became some evil traitor just because I refused
to cheer. Okay, fly. An involuntary shiver shook me at
the thought of it. No. I needed to make sure no one
asked me to cheer again. That door needed to be locked,
barricaded, and welded shut.

But to do that, I needed to get that open spot in the
show. All the best performers from the entire city were
in the show, and Madison has some awesome dance
schools. I grew up dancing with a lot of them, and then
turned my back on all of them when I took up cheer. I
didn't relish the idea of trying to rejoin their clique. I
didn't even know who the understudy was for Jessica.
Probably McKenna or Chloe. They were the next best
dancers that I knew of. At least they were three years
ago.

With any luck I could join the chorus. But my dance
skills had rusted with lack of use. Last night, when I dug

through the back of the closet for dance shoes, I came across the box packed with my old dance trophies and awards. At one time I'd been an awesome dancer for Davis Dance Academy. Last night, that box mocked me.

After pushing all the living room furniture out of the way, I stayed up past midnight working my old routine. By the time I went to bed, I could do it as well as I used to do a triple flip.

The bell rang and startled me. The pencil I'd been drumming flew across the row and hit a kid on the head. He turned and raised an eyebrow at me.

"Sorry." I scrambled out of my chair and picked up the accidental weapon. I gathered my books and stuffed the pencil down the wire spiral of my notebook.

The crowded hallways suffocated me as I fought the combination of dread and adrenaline for my audition with the famed director. After I stuffed my books in my locker, I grabbed my old dance bag with the frayed sides.

Unsure of where the kids in the show changed, and not wanting to run into any cheer kids in the locker room, I used the girls' bathroom closest to the auditorium. In the handicapped stall, I stepped out of my street clothes and pulled on tights and a leotard. The lycra snapped tight against my skin, making me aware of every muscle. It reminded me to suck in my gut and stand straighter.

Afraid to step out of the stall as a few girls still moved in and out of the bathroom, I did a few pliés and stretches in the confines of the space. I felt like an idiot, but it was better than trying to warm up and have someone see me. What a fraud I was—hiding in the bathroom.

I checked my phone; it was almost time. I pulled on a pair of soft workout shorts and rolled down the waistband. Then I pulled on a pair of loose sweats and a t-shirt and put my shoes back on. The bathroom became eerily quiet as most kids left for the day.

I went to the sink and looked at the scared pale face in the mirror with long brown wavy hair pulled back tight. This would not work. I slapped my cheeks and bounced on the balls of my feet a few times. Better. I could do this. It was this or cheer; and cheer was not an option. It would be like riding a bike.

I hoped.

I took a deep breath. Shut up, suck it up, and go deliver the goods. With a nod to the mirror, I went to the auditorium.

From the main doors at the back a sea of darkened seats led to the empty, brightly lit stage. I performed on this stage for choir plenty of times, but never dancing and certainly never alone illuminated by all these bright lights.

At the front of the room, a man, who must be the director, spoke to Miss Ginny. Cripes! Miss Ginny must have wanted to make sure I showed up. I stood a little taller and forced an easy smile on my face as I approached.

"Ah, there she is," said Miss Ginny. Kindness shone in her eyes. She reached for my hand and gave it a reassuring squeeze; she felt like a lifeboat in a storm.

"Tyson Scott, I'd like you to meet Miss Willow Thomas."

He seemed way too young to be a Broadway director. A shadow of dark beard covered his chiseled face and his expertly styled hair came right off a magazine cover. He looked like New York. He smiled wide and friendly. He was hands-down the hottest guy I had ever seen.

"Hello, Mr. Scott. Nice to meet you." I found it hard not to stare.

"Please, call me Tyson. My father was Mr. Scott." He held out his hand and we shook; his firm reassuring grip matched his intelligent sapphire eyes. I noticed his quick assessment and wondered if I measured up.

"Nice to meet you, Willow. What a great name."

"Thanks. My parents like to be different. They're kind of modern day hippies. They named my little sister Breezy."

"They sound like people I'd like to meet."

He watched my posture with an expert eye. I stood straighter.

"Your name has come up from a couple of different sources, and I've been hearing great things about you."

"Really?" I felt lost in the presence of this hugely charismatic man.

Miss Ginny beamed with pride as if I were some sort of prized show dog.

"Why, of course," Miss Ginny said. "You were always my star pupil. I had so much hope for you, and then you abandoned me and quit dancing."

Star pupil? She sure knew how to lay it on thick.

Miss Ginny nodded. "Tyson, you will see. She is a fabulous dancer."

"I have no doubt," he said. "In all these years, you have never steered me wrong. No, that's not entirely true. There were a couple costumes you forced me to wear that had no place on a young impressionable boy."

"Ha, you were never a boy. You were always a man struggling to break out into the world."

Suddenly, I recognized him as the boy in many of the old photos in Miss Ginny's office. One of the costumes made him look like a life-size piñata.

Tyson hugged her. "Miss Ginny taught me everything I know."

"Nonsense, I taught you everything I know. You took your skills to New York and became an icon."

He smiled and shook his head; the admiration they shared for each other was clear. "You took all my bouncing-off-the-wall energy and channeled it into something great." He smiled at her, and Miss Ginny blushed. It touched my heart.

"Having the lead removed from the show by school officials wasn't in my game plan. You aren't in the habit of creative baking are you?" he asked me as his eyes danced.

"Me? No way. I definitely do not bake." I was practically flunking Foods class. My dad on the other hand, might very well bake special brownies now and then, but I didn't think this was a good time to mention it.

"I'm down a dancer, and, from what I hear, you know a thing or two about dance."

"Yes," I hesitated. "To be truthful, I haven't danced in a long time." I didn't want him to be disappointed. Dance was a discipline, and I'd ignored it for so long.

"And why was that?" he asked.

"I took up cheerleading."

"Really? Did you like it?"

"Actually, I did." His sincere interest surprised me.

"She was a flyer, the girl they toss in the air. She helped them win a national title last year," Miss Ginny said.

"That's great! Quite an accomplishment."

"Willow doesn't do anything half way," Miss Ginny added.

"I understand you left cheerleading? What happened there?" Tyson asked finally getting down to the dirt.

I took a deep breath and figured I might as well put it all on the table. "There was an accident. I fell and got hurt. My heart just isn't in it anymore."

"I see." Tyson nodded, his eyes met mine, and I wondered if he knew that fear made me quit. "How are you feeling? Has the doctor cleared you for activities?"

"I'm good. It's all good."

"Glad to hear it. So what do you think of our little show?"

"I don't really know much, other than it's a lot of dance."

He laughed, revealing straight bright teeth. "Yes, it is that and so much more. I like to think of it as a fusion of art, but let's not get ahead of ourselves. Let's see if you still know how to dance, shall we?"

"Okay."

Here we go. It's now or never.

"Did you bring something to dance in?"

"Yes, under my sweats."

"Do you need time to warm up?" he asked.

"No, I'm already."

"Willow is always prepared. You will see," Miss

Ginny chimed in. "I brought the music from your last competition solo. You remember it."

She wasn't giving me any chance to back out.

"I hope so." I glanced at Tyson, worried. He grinned, amused by Miss Ginny's subtle manipulation. "I'll give it a try," I said.

I took off my sweats and t-shirt then squeezed into my ballet slippers. My feet had grown since I last wore them. Miss Ginny spoke in soft tones to Tyson as I took the stage front and center and waited for the music to begin. I took a couple of breaths to relax, and then said a silent prayer. *Please let me be good enough to get in and not embarrass myself in the process.*

I stood alone. Solo. The way I'd felt since the fall.

Moments later, the sound of music filled the air. With no time to think, I began. At first I felt stiff from nerves as I struggled to remember the dance, but then muscle memory set in and I got lost with the music. I danced and twirled, my body moving to the music as fluid as water in a spring stream. With my back arched and toes pointed, I let the past week dissolve and lived for this moment. I worked to make every turn tight and straight. I pushed each leap higher and made the floor rolls as smooth and effortless as possible. I let my tensions go and felt the grace and power of the moment. The more I danced, the more the memories flooded back. My love of movement and art returned like an old friend.

The music ended, leaving me in the closing pose. Adrenalin pumped through me. I'd forgotten what a high I got from dance and how the energy and emotion fulfilled me. My eyes watered and threatened to embarrass me. Cheer was regimented and precise, not an artistic release. My body buzzed with the passion I'd locked away.

"I see you haven't forgotten after all, but, of course, one never forgets their true calling, no matter how far away they run," Miss Ginny said and then addressed Tyson. "She's rusty, but that's to be expected. Give her some time, and she'll be back in perfect form."

I swiped my wet eyes.

Tyson watched with his arms crossed and head tilted to the side in thought. A smirk lit the corner of his mouth. He nodded to himself and then leaned over and spoke with Miss Ginny.

As I worked to recover my breath, I looked anywhere but at the two holding a private pow wow to decide my fate. Before I danced, I wanted this so bad so I could escape cheer for once and for all. But dancing full out stirred my memories. Dance is such a joyful place. When I dance, nothing else matters. It's as if I existed in a perfect world of free flowing grace and joy. Now I wanted to be a part of this show more than I've ever wanted anything. I didn't care how small the part. And if I didn't get in, I'd talk to my Mom about taking classes again. I was coming home.

Tyson and Miss Ginny looked up. "Willow, that was very nice," he said.

I sighed in relief and walked to the steps at the side of the stage.

"Hold up, please. I'd like to see you try some new choreography."

"All right." I looked to Miss Ginny.

Tyson turned toward the back of the dim

auditorium. "Eli, are you back there?"

"I'm here." A low voice answered from the darkened seats.

My gut clenched at the sound of the familiar voice from my past.

Eli Cooper.

The reason I quit dancing.

"Come on up and teach Willow the first combinations of the dream sequence," Tyson said.

I shielded my eyes from the bright stage lights and watched a shadow appear from the darkness. His lanky form grew larger, like a mirage in the desert. As he ambled down the aisle past Tyson and Miss Ginny, the light caught his blond hair. He needed a haircut. It still curled up at the sides. He leapt on stage like a jungle cat and walked toward me. He averted his gaze and stopped a few feet away.

I bit at my lip. Why hadn't I thought about Eli? Of course he was in the show; he would have the lead. This would be his nirvana, working with a Broadway director. The hope of reaching his dreams. Eli had talked about working on Broadway so many times over the years. That was before I walked away from Eli and dance on a warm fall night.

I peeked at him.

He glanced back from behind a swipe of hair.

My old friend.

Chapter 7

We hadn't been this close in nearly three years. Not since I dove head first into the life of competitive cheerleading and never looked back. And I never looked back so that I wouldn't have to face Eli Cooper.

Eli went to East High School, lived in upscale Maple Bluff, played soccer, studied dance, and probably performed in every show that ever came along. After I bailed out of dance, I picked up new friends, all cheerleaders, and never went to our old haunts again. Partly out of respect for Eli and partly out of embarrassment.

"Hey," he said and looked away.

"Hey," I answered.

The awkwardness between us stood as thick as the Berlin Wall. Except I didn't see it coming down anytime soon.

Eli looked down at me by several inches. We used to see eye to eye. I didn't expect we'd see eye to eye on much anymore.

"So you're going to do the show." A statement, not a question. His eyes finally settled on my face.

"Maybe. If I'm good enough." I shifted from one leg to the other.

He stared for a couple of seconds. "Don't be stupid." He looked away again.

Apparently I hadn't avoided him long enough. He

obviously wasn't ready to make nice. Not sure what to do or say, with my arms wrapped around myself I gazed at the curtains, the stage floor, the piano. Anything I could look at except him.

"I don't see any dancing!" Tyson called from the auditorium seats where he chatted with Miss Ginny. "Five minutes, then I want to see what you can do."

"Got it," Eli said in a resigned voice.

Geez, I wanted to walk away right now. *Remember, Willow, you need this to get Jilly off your back!*

He turned to me, his chin set and eyes steely. "Let's go." We moved stage left, and he walked me through the steps. " One, two, touch, turn, step, step, leap." It didn't take long until I felt the rhythm of the moves. They were tricky, but Eli was an excellent teacher as we marked through the steps again and again. But he was careful not to get too close, or god forbid, accidentally brush against me. Working alongside him felt surreal as we tried to ignore our awkward separation.

"You guys ready?" Tyson asked.

"As ready as I'll ever be," I answered.

Eli walked away to give me center stage.

"Eli, stay there and do it with her," Tyson said.

He sighed, nodded and took his place a couple feet to my right. The music came on and in unison we performed the thirty-second sequence Eli taught me moments before. The loud pounding energy of the music made the moves easier, more fluid and meaningful.

"Not bad," Tyson said. "You're a quick study. I know you just learned this, but let's have you do it a couple more times so you can really get into it. I need to see your heart and soul, not just the steps."

Each time we moved through the steps, Eli and I became more in sync. Yet each time we moved through the steps, it became more obvious how out of sync our lives truly were. He ignored me as if he were dancing alone, but still kept his moves perfectly in time with mine.

His cold shoulder made it easy for me to focus on the routine. I completed each turn with fluid grace, hit each step with precision timing and pushed my physical and emotional limit to the edge.

Tyson Scott studied us closely, his arms crossed, with one hand rubbing the dark stubble on his chin. We waited, heaving from the exertion of the full-out dance, for his next direction.

"Miss Ginny tells me the two of you danced together competitively."

I nodded and glanced sideways at Eli for a split second. We danced together for years. Our numbers were some of my best memories.

"Did you do any lifts?"

"Yeah, some," Eli answered, his body angled away from me.

"I'd like to see a few."

"We haven't danced together for years. I don't know if I remember," I said. God, did he really expect us to touch each other? Hadn't Miss Ginny told him we weren't exactly friends anymore?

"Of course you remember," Miss Ginny interjected.

I looked to Eli for support. He didn't even want to look at me, so surely getting close enough to do a lift was out of the question.

"I remember. I can do them," Eli said in icy

challenge. "But obviously she doesn't, so I'll pass."

So this was how it was going to be. *Fine.*

"I just want to see what you can do together. Nothing fancy. I realize I'm throwing Willow into the fire here, but the show is heavy in partner work with a lot of lifts and tricks."

Eli crossed his arms over his chest and huffed. "Seriously, if she screws this up, I'm toast!"

Good, he didn't want to do it either. For once we were on the same side.

"Eli, do you have a problem executing a lift with Willow?" Tyson asked. "Is there something I need to know?"

"Nope. Hey, it's your show, man."

"Great. So show me what you can do. I'd like to see a lift into first arabesque."

Eli stepped closer. "Let's get this over with." His cold dark eyes bore into me.

"Whoa! Could you slow down a sec?" I said under my breath, stalling. "Are you sure you can even lift me anymore?"

I really needed a second to figure out if I had the guts to do this. It was a lift. A toe dipped back into the water I feared most: midair. He could drop me. I could get hurt.

Was I willing to do this? Or maybe the question was could I? I couldn't make myself do a toss that day in practice. I might freeze up again. A shiver ran through my body and I shuddered.

How could I get out of this.

He cocked his head to the side and put his hands on his hips. "Yeah. I can lift you. The question is can you jump high enough? Oh. That's right! You're a cheerleader. Of course, you can jump really high."

"I'm not a cheerleader anymore," I snapped back in a loud whisper.

"That's right. You quit. What happened? Your partner get a little too close for comfort?" This time, when I really wanted him to look away, he kept his eyes glued to mine.

I wanted to slug him, but Tyson watched, intrigued by our exchange. Miss Ginny looked ready to blow. Everyone was waiting for me. Irritation stiffened my spine, and I made my decision.

What the heck! A lift was nothing like a toss in cheerleading. I would never be airborne or free falling. Eli's hands would always be on me. Of course that was another problem, but one worry at a time...

"Whenever you're ready," Tyson called.

"Yes, sir. I'm ready if he is," I said through clenched teeth to Eli.

I moved into first arabesque, standing on my right foot with my left leg lifted high, foot pointed, and arms extended in first position. Eli stepped behind me, placed one hand under my thigh and the other on my waist. He lifted me straight up with ease, his arms extended over his head.

His effortless strength surprised me, but his confident hold brought back memories of years together when we would rehearse together for hours on end. Eli had always made me feel safe when we danced. We were inseparable best friends. While still the lean dancer of our youth, Eli now possessed strong muscles hidden well beneath his T-shirt. After holding the position for a couple of beats, he returned me back to the floor with gentle grace.

"Good. Now an overhead lift," Tyson prompted.

This one would be harder. I'd be over his head, with my back arched, facing the ceiling. I glanced at Eli. He cocked his head in annoyance. Eli stepped behind me his hands on my hips. I could feel his breath on the little hairs of my neck. His familiar scent reminded me of days long past.

A light squeeze of his hands on my hips told me he was ready. I took a breath, pliéd, and leaped. He lifted me straight up and over his head, his body braced beneath me. With my arms extended and toes pointed, I held my body taut. He balanced me with ease.

Tyson nodded approval. "Very nice."

We'd hit to post perfect, and I readied myself for Eli to release his arms and swing me down. But he didn't.

I held my body taut and waited for his transition, which continued not to come. *What the heck was he trying to prove?* In cheer, my positions were always upright, which was much easier for the lifter and the liftee. Holding this position was much harder than it looked, but I refused to break it before he did.

Eli's arms gave the slightest of twitches, and I knew he was getting tired. His damned ego had stepped into the middle of my tryout.

"You can let me down anytime," I seethed.

"What, you tired?" He shot back. Eli lowered me to the floor with care.

I sneered.

Tyson chuckled. "Ah, not only do we have history, apparently we have chemistry too."

"What. Ever." I folded my arms across my chest and looked away. Eli turned and faced the opposite direction.

As I glanced to the side of the stage, I was horrified to discover half the cast. Curiosity shone in some of their eyes, while others glared at me with blatant hostility.

Oh crap!

How long had they been there? My eyes darted away to avoid making eye contact. Would they welcome me if I made the show? I'd be the new kid, an outsider.

Tyson faced away from the stage, talking with Miss Ginny and Ms. Fuller, who had just arrived. I tried to ignore the whispers spilling over from the crowded backstage.

"Willow, please move center stage. I'd like to hear you sing."

My head snapped up. Sing? I looked to Eli, I don't know why. I guess an old reflex. He whistled like a missile soaring through the air and then hitting the ground. He watched its imaginary progress and made an explosion sound.

Tyson stepped to the edge of the stage. "Eli, you can take a seat. Thank you."

Eli smirked and left me.

Alone.

Tyson Scott wanted to hear me sing. It hadn't even occurred to me, which was so stupid. Of course I'd have to sing. This was a musical!

Now don't get me wrong. I love to sing, but in that "sing into a hair brush in the privacy of your own room" kind of way.

My previous annoyance with Eli evaporated and

panic replaced it.

"Right now? You want me to sing right now?" I swallowed.

I glanced from Tyson to Ms. Fuller and then at the growing group of cast members off stage. I swallowed again, my throat closing up.

"Yes, that's the general idea of an audition. Everyone else already has already been through this process."

Ms. Fuller nodded like a bobble head doll.

"In fact," he said, "why don't we get everyone hiding backstage to come out and take a seat. You can show us all what you've got."

Tyson smiled in a way he probably thought would put me at ease, but there is no relaxing when you're about to be forced into the vocal equivalent of standing on stage naked. I could cheer in front of a stadium of fans and dance in front of a packed audience, but when it comes to singing alone, I get stage fright.

Now, Eli's voice is another story. He's good enough to cut CDs. He's taken voice lessons for years.

The kids from backstage came into the light like munchkins in the Wizard of Oz and found seats. Ms. Fuller stepped forward and handed me sheet music. "Why don't you sing this. We worked on it in choir today." She gave me a "you can do this" nod. Another copy of the music sat open on the piano. How convenient.

I accepted the music, but felt like a mouse trapped in a corner by a really big cat. Make that several really big cats. Tyson Scott looked on without a care in the world. Eli relaxed in the front row, his legs stretched before him, waiting for me to fail.

As I gripped the music, my hands began to shake. My throat now dry as a sandy beach on a hot day.

"Ready?" Ms. Fuller chirped from her perch on the piano bench.

Never! When would anyone ever be ready to sing alone in front of this mega important Broadway guy, let alone all these strangers in the cast who looked ready to lynch me for intruding on their private party.

"I guess," I squeaked, realizing my deodorant no longer worked.

The rest of the cast watched my slow torture from their cushioned seats. I recognized a lot of them from my former dance life. Some watched with supportive smiles, but some didn't seem happy to see me. Definitely not the positive reception I'd hoped for. Was this show really worth it, even if it let me escape cheer once and for all?

Ms. Fuller began the intro. Tyson's eyes settled on me; he smiled. I took a deep shaky breath and stared at the music.

I missed the entrance.

"Let's try that again," Ms. Fuller said with patience. I heard a few kids snicker from the safety of their seats. Ms. Fuller's head snapped around to drill them with her evil eye. I appreciated the gesture of support.

"Sorry," I said. What did they expect? I never claimed to be a singer. I just wanted a small part in the chorus.

"You know what?" Tyson walked to the piano, "I think we should start with some simple scales. I know we've put you on the spot here today. You didn't audition the first round of cattle calls, so today must be pretty nerve wracking."

"Yeah," I said, relieved he seemed to understand.

"By the way, why didn't you audition the first time around?" he asked.

"Oh, I was already on the cheerleading squad."

"Ah, that's right," he nodded. "Now, let's have Ms. Fuller run you through some warm-up scales."

My nerves flared again, but not as bad as before. Ms. Fuller played the chord and gave me the beat with a nod of her head. I opened my mouth and sang low, moving up the scale and back down with each note. Each set started a note higher, and I sang my way up the scale and down. Each scale sounded stronger, and I felt better even though my legs shook. Then my voice broke on a high note. I cringed and stopped.

"Let's hear that song now," Tyson said.

I opened the music again, my nerves only a tiny bit calmer.

Ms. Fuller played the intro again. This time I came in on time, but I sounded breathy and quiet. When I got to the high note, my voice cracked, and one of the kids snorted.

Eli was right, crash and burn. My hopes were going up in flames. The director wandered the carpeted area in front of the stage as he listened; his face a blank mask, making it impossible to read his thoughts. When I finished, he walked to the piano and spoke privately to Ms. Fuller.

Unsure what to do, I closed the music and held it behind my back. I shifted from leg to leg and tried to pretend they weren't talking about me, or that Eli and the others weren't still staring.

"Thank you, Willow," Tyson said.

I swallowed, embarrassed and ready to go home and hide in my room with Twinkie. With the music limp in my hand, I waited to be excused.

Tyson turned to the peanut gallery. "Okay, you've been idle long enough. Let's get Chloe and McKenna on stage with Willow."

Chloe and McKenna's heads snapped up. They were as surprised by the request as I was. They took the steps on stage and looked at Tyson.

"I'd like to see the three of you do the dream number. Just the first segment," he said to Chloe and McKenna. "Willow, that's the sequence Eli taught you earlier."

I wracked my brain to pull the sequence forward. I'd just barely learned it twenty minutes ago, and now I had to be compared to Chloe and McKenna. I stepped to the side to allow them space on stage. Chloe, a super tall blonde with a pointy nose, stood center stage and ignored me; I knew her from dance with Ms. Ginny. Chloe had been Jessica's understudy before the pot brownie incident. That meant that she was now the lead. I had no idea what role McKenna played.

The music played, and we ran the number. Thankfully, my nerves hadn't wiped away my memory of the steps. Tyson watched, deep in thought. He sat and mulled for a minute and then asked to see it again. Now that I was dancing again and not singing, I embraced the situation and flowed through the lyrical steps, forgetting about the girls who danced at my side.

"McKenna, you may take a seat," Tyson paced and rubbed his chin. He turned and focused on Eli, who slunk low in his seat. "Eli, hop up on stage with them too."

Eli eased out of his seat with his head low and lumbered forward. He leapt onto the stage and took up McKenna's former position.

"Stand between them, please," Tyson directed.

Eli moved center stage. At least now the scrutiny was on the others too! We stood like specimens under a microscope. It was nice not to be the only one up here, but what was going on? Did he want to see if we could work together as dancers?

"Let's see that sequence again."

Eli groaned.

At least I wasn't the only one tired of this process.

"Last time, I promise." Tyson clicked on the music, and the three of us danced again. I became one with the music and the graceful flow of the moves. I loved the dance and wished I knew more. After performing the dance so many times, I knew I'd delivered my absolute best.

We waited, out of breath, as Tyson looked us over. I couldn't imagine what he was thinking. Either I was good enough to make the show or not. I'd been afraid my long break from dance would ruin my audition, but I had proved myself wrong. It all came rushing back to me, like ice skating did each December. Granted, my singing sucked, but that shouldn't keep me out of the chorus. I hoped.

Miss Ginny and Ms. Fuller watched but didn't interrupt or try to sway his decision either way. This was Tyson Scott's show and Tyson Scott's decision.

"Thank you, that should do it. Willow, please come

down. Everyone else, up on stage for vocal warm-ups."

Finally! I took a quick peek at Eli, but he'd turned his back on me and talked to Chloe.

I joined Tyson. So this was it. Moment of truth. I tried to act cool and not reveal my jumble of nerves. Miss Ginny nodded her approval, but said nothing.

Tyson led me away from the kids who were supposed to be filing on stage, but instead were holding back to hear what he said.

"That was a nice audition. You have great technique."

"Thank you." I wished he'd get to the point. Up close again, it was hard not to feel intimidated. He had this chiseled jaw. I never understood what that meant until I met Tyson. He carried himself with amazing confidence. God, it would be great to be in his show.

"I'll give you a call tonight, and we'll talk." His exceptional eyes softened.

"Okay," I said dumbfounded. That was it?

Tyson turned and rejoined the group. So, no concrete answer. He said he'd call, so I must be in. But if I was in, why didn't he just tell me so I could join today's rehearsal? I turned and walked out of the auditorium. I knew that the eyes of all the cast members followed me out. Was this my walk of shame? I didn't think so, but they probably did.

Chapter 8

"Why doesn't he just call and put me out of my misery?" I said from the couch where I tied the fringe of the afghan in knots.

Dad handed Breezy a puzzle piece. "He's probably some sadist who likes to make teenagers suffer."

"He's probably still at rehearsal putting them through boot camp." Mom looked up from her Sudoku book.

"Or maybe he's scooping their eyeballs out with a melon baller," Breezy said making ghoulish expressions

"Did you hear that? She is totally warped. Dad, aren't you the least bit worried?"

"Breezy, are you warped?" Dad asked.

"Totally." She pretended to remove her eye with an imaginary melon baller.

The old fashioned wall phone rang!

Everyone froze and looked across the room.

"I got it!" I leapt off the couch and raced across the room.

Dad blocked my way like a basketball player. "Are you sure? I can get it."

It rang again.

"Dad, not funny." I stepped left to go around.

He moved left with me and kept my path blocked. "What, I just want to help." He smirked.

"Step aside old man and don't make me hurt you." I

gave him the evil eye and moved right.

The phone rang again.

I dodged past, but he grabbed me around the waist and swung me away from the kitchen, like he did when I was a little girl headed to the kitchen for a cookie.

"Daddy, stop it!" I squealed. "It's my call. I have to answer it. Mom! Make him go away." I broke free and ran to the phone, beating Breezy by a hair. I answered just as it rang again.

"Hello?"

"Hi! May I speak to Willow?" the low smooth voice of Tyson Scott asked.

"This is Willow." My entire family stood next to me like a bunch of puppies waiting for a treat. Go away, I mouthed and waved at them.

"Is it him?" Breezy blurted loudly.

I covered the mouthpiece with my hand. "God Breezy, yes. Now go away. All of you." I glared at Mom and Dad but they didn't budge. Why did my family have to be so weird? I stretched the long spiral cord to the other end of the kitchen and turned my back.

Tyson laughed on the other end. "Sounds like you have a little sister."

"Yes, I'm sorry, she can be a total demon." I looked back and stuck my tongue out at her. Breezy fell backwards as if hit by an arrow in the chest.

"No problem. Growing up, I was the annoying little brother."

I couldn't imagine him as annoying or as a little brother. He was so cool and collected like he had been born a really awesome guy. But whatever his childhood had been, I wished he'd get on with it and stop with the small talk. I turned to lean against the kitchen counter, but saw Mom pantomiming and asking what was happening. I glared and turned back around.

"I wanted to tell you how impressed I was with your audition today."

"Really?" Yes! I clenched the phone. Now say the words. Tell me I'm in.

"Yes. I would never guess you've been away from dance so long. You have excellent technique. But more than that, you have amazing stage presence."

"I do?"

"Yes," he chuckled. "When you dance, everything else disappears. You become one with the music. So many kids your age still perform like little rockettes with cheesy smiles. You dance with a passion I don't see very often. Especially in someone your age."

"Wow." I didn't know what to say. Tyson Scott, a Broadway choreographer, loved the way I dance.

"So please tell me this means I'm in the show." I couldn't bear to wait for him any longer. A noise sounded behind me. Breezy, Mom and Dad were sneaking up like they were on a black ops mission.

"Yes, you are in the show," he said and I grinned and bounced up and down. "However, there is a little more to it and I want to run it all by you before you say yes."

"Okay." I stopped bouncing. Why couldn't it be only good news? Why did there have to be a "but"?

The phone cord went taught. Mom tugged on it to get my attention. She gave me a thumbs up and a thumbs down choice. I returned the thumbs up with a grin. They fell over themselves on the floor in silent cheers. I rolled my eyes.

"When you came in, I was looking for someone to join the chorus. As you know, we lost Jessica and Chloe is the understudy. However, once I saw you dance, combined with the physical match up and chemistry of you and Eli, I'd like to cast you as the lead, Lauren.

My eyes bugged out and I'm pretty sure my heart stopped. I looked at mom in shock. The silent cheering ended as they stared. I couldn't begin to respond.

"Willow? You still with me?" I detected humor in his voice.

"Yeah," I uttered.

"There is one catch though. Your vocals aren't where we need them."

What an understatement. I pictured Eli's crashing missile gesture.

"You have a beautiful voice. Your choir teacher Ms. Fuller agrees. But you lack experience and confidence. So I've arranged for you to take some crash course voice lessons from an old friend of mine. She is an excellent teacher and is willing to rearrange her schedule to squeeze you in if you take the part."

"Are you sure I can do it? I'm not much of a singer." Hugest understatement of the year.

"Listen, we have singers who also dance and dancers who also sing. The role of Lauren is for a dancer who also sings. I wouldn't cast you in the role if I didn't believe you'd be able to get up to performance level in time for opening night."

I couldn't believe my ears. All I wanted was to get out of cheer, and now not only was I in the show, he was offering me the lead. My annoying family started whispering questions. I stepped past them and went to the hall pantry and closed the door. I sank down to the floor and leaned against Twinkie's twenty-pound dog food bag.

"So, you're saying that if I agree to voice lessons I have the lead?" A sheen of perspiration appeared.

"That's right. However, I want to be sure you understand that it won't be nearly as easy as it sounds. We're almost three weeks into rehearsals and you'll have a lot of catching up to do. As Lauren you will have rehearsal six days a week. It will be a grueling schedule, but I spoke to Miss Ginny and your cheerleading coach, Ms. Klahn, and they both assure me you have an amazing work ethic and are one of the most dedicated kids they've worked with. We all believe you're up to the challenge. So if you take the part, you're going to spend a lot of time looking at my ugly mug."

Now *that* I could do. "May I ask you a question?"

"Sure, always," he replied.

"What about Chloe and the other girls in the show? I can't imagine they'll be too happy to see me take over Jessica's spot. Maybe it would be better if I were just in the chorus." I really didn't want to start with the cast hating me. That would be a big problem. Huge.

"Listen, I realize this is a youth show, however, it is also a professional production. My baby. I am the director, writer, producer and anything else you can imagine. There are a lot of people who invested a great deal of money to make this project come to fruition. There is an expectation that this show make the theatrical world sit up and take notice. I will not allow anything to jeopardize this opportunity. You are hands down technically and artistically superior to any other girl in that show. In fact, it was a blessing in disguise that Jessica left. You outshine her on the stage and are a much better match for our leading man."

I swallowed down my shock. He thought I was better, no, superior to everyone else in the show? The cast consisted of the top kids from every dance school in the city. Was he out of his mind?!

"Oh."

"With that said, don't expect to hear praise from me again. I'm a slave driver."

I couldn't imagine Tyson being mean, but who knows. Ms. Klahn could be a real bitch, but she always got results.

"So what do you think? Did I give you a good enough sell or do I have to beg?"

"No, no begging necessary. If you think I can do it, I definitely want to." My heart pumped a Latin beat. This was really happening!

"Excellent. Then I'll see you tomorrow after school. Be ready to work your tail off."

"Thank you. Thank you so much. I will."

Tyson clicked off, leaving me alone in the dark with a huge grin and the curly phone cord wrapped around my hand about five times. I stood, unwound the cord and opened the door to find Mom, Dad, Breezy, and Twinkie sitting on the floor. Mom stopped. She had been dabbing shaving cream on Breezy's face.

"So?" Mom asked with a blob of shaving cream on her nose. "What happened?"

Grinning, I reached over them, knocked Breezy in the head with the cord as I hung up the phone and yelled, "He wants me to play the lead!"

"What!" They jumped to their feet and we all screamed and cheered. My dad did his happy dance; he calls it "happy feet".

Breezy launched herself at me, wrapped her arms around my waist and pressed her foam covered face against my belly.

"Breezy!" You just messed up my shirt!"

Mom shook her head. "Breezy, you need to be more careful." Then Mom took my face with her foamy hands, a sneaky look in her eye. "You know how much Willow hates getting messy." She smoothed my hair down with her sloppy hands.

"Mom!"

"You got the lead!" she squealed like only a proud mom can do.

Dad grinned, holding the can of shaving cream. He squeezed some into his hand and held it out. I swiped it. "Yes, I got the lead!" I grinned at mom, then smooshed the whole blob on top of her head and smeared it around. Twinkie jumped on us and barked.

From there the celebration turned into a world-class, knock-out, drag-out Thomas family shaving cream fight. Afterward we sprawled on the kitchen floor looking like a shampoo commercial gone wrong. The empty shaving cream can rolled in the corner next to Twinkie. Thank god Tyson didn't know about my odd family. He might think twice about giving me the lead.

I had the lead! Yikes, how weird was that? I barely knew anything about the show.

"I'm hungry," Breezy said.

Dad skimmed sloppy cream off Mom's arm. "How

about ice cream?"

"With chocolate sauce and peanuts," Mom added.

I squeezed foam from my hair onto the floor. "And whipped topping!"

"Eww." Mom said.

"Look at Twinkie. Something's wrong." Breezy said.

Twinkie looked stiff like a taxidermied dog. Her frozen body fell sideways against the cupboard door and slid onto the floor.

"What's wrong with her?" I rushed to her side. Her body began to shake, a little like when she had dreams in her sleep, only now it was more rigid jerking and her eyes stayed open.

Dad tried to pet her, but his hand bounced off her jerking body. "I think she's having a seizure."

We surrounded her and watched her body twitch.

"Daddy, Mommy, make her stop," Breezy cried.

I bit my lip and looked to Mom.

"I can't," she said. "Someone grab me a towel."

I pulled the hand towel from the rack next to the sink and handed it to her. She placed it under our precious dog's head. Twinkie's stiff jaw froze halfway open, like she had lockjaw. The seizure continued, and Breezy started to cry. Mom hugged Breezy; her eyes met Dad's.

Finally the seizure stopped and Twinkie lay limp. Suddenly she took a huge breath as if she'd been holding it all that time. Twinkie's eyes moved. "Hey girl, are you okay?" I scratched behind her ears where she liked it best. She lay there another minute, then gave a short whine.

"That's a good girl." Dad pet her and Breezy leaned

over and hugged her around the neck.

"What's wrong with her?" I asked.

"I don't know, but I think we'd better get her to the vet tomorrow," Dad said.

"Poor baby," Mom said. She got up and grabbed a spoon and the peanut butter jar. She scooped out a big dollop and held it out to Twinkie.

"Are you sure that's a good idea?" I didn't want to do anything to make her worse.

"She's scared and hurting. I don't think a little peanut butter is going to make whatever she has worse." Twinkie's tail flapped against the floor as she licked the peanut butter.

Later that night, after showering off the shaving cream, I lay in bed with wet hair. My skin felt especially soft from all the cream. I couldn't go to sleep. My mind jumbled with thoughts of Twinkie, me having the lead in Dream Chaser and the huge relief that cheer was now over for good. All three of those things scared me. I needed to tell Jilly my cheer life was officially over. I would have called her tonight, but Twinkie's seizure freaked me out too much. And then I thought about performing opposite Eli in the show and that freaked me out even more.

Chapter 9

"So?" Jilly shot at me, as I climbed into the car the next morning.

"What?" I knew darn well she wanted to know about the audition.

"Oh please, the audition! Tell me everything, don't leave anything out." She nearly bounced out of her seat.

I sighed. Jilly could be so intense and she wasn't going to like what she heard.

"Were you scared? Was it really hard, did you screw up?" she asked in rapid succession.

I pulled my seatbelt across and clicked it. Jilly backed out of the driveway and toward school.

"Yes, I was scared. Terrified was more like it. Much worse than cheer tryouts." For cheer, all you had to do was yell loud, jump high and plant a smile on your face. Then again, there were also the gymnastics, the lifts and the tricks. So maybe cheer wasn't that easy either.

"Really, how?" she snapped her head back and forth from watching the road to watching me.

"Well, first off the director is so hot that...oh my god! You should see him!" I couldn't believe I'd get to see him almost every day.

"I heard from Jessica that he used to model. We'll have to Google him," Jilly said.

"Anyway, it was so intimidating to audition in front of this great looking guy, and he's not even that old. He looked about twenty-eight, but I'm sure he's older."

"So, did you bomb?"

"What?" I asked.

"Did you screw up? You haven't danced in forever, and then they make you audition with like five minutes warning!"

She seemed anxious to know if I tanked.

"No, actually I did pretty good."

Jilly looked disappointed.

"But then he made me sing. In front of the entire cast! I thought I'd die!" I left out the part about Eli. It was just too complicated to explain.

"Ouch."

"Yeah. I wouldn't say I bombed it, but it sure wasn't good either. My voice cracked, and not in a good way." I quivered at the memory.

Jilly bit back a smile as she turned a corner.

"Hey, it's not funny. I was trying really hard."

"I'm sorry, it's just the idea of you on a stage all by yourself singing. Can't picture it."

Twenty-four hours ago I couldn't picture it either, but Jilly would have to picture it soon, because that is exactly what was going to happen. Crap. Tyson's court-appointed voice teacher better be a genius.

"So the dancing was good, the singing bad. When do you find out if you made it?" she asked as she turned into the school parking lot.

"I already did." *Here we go.*

"What? You let me sit her and blab on and you already know." She pulled into a spot in the third row and threw the car into park. "Well? Spill it."

Why was I afraid to tell her? She was my best friend

and would get over it. Hopefully by lunch. I looked her straight in the eye. "I made it."

Her demeanor shifted right away. Not in a huge, "you're a bitch" way, but more of a subtle "can't see it, but can feel it" way.

"Oh." She turned off the car and dumped her keys into her bag.

We sat there in silence. I wasn't sure if I should keep talking, maybe tell her about Twinkie's seizure and get a little sympathy.

"So are you going to do it?" Her voice sounded monotone as if she didn't care which way I answered.

I stumbled over my words. "Well...yeah. I am."

"What about cheer? You know we can't get to Nationals without you," she said through tight lips.

"Jilly, I quit cheer."

"You said you'd think about it." She crossed her arms.

"I did," I said, but that was a lie. I never once thought about going back. Just about how to put more distance between me and the high-flying team.

"No. You didn't. You just said that to get me off your back!" She got out of the car and slammed the door behind her.

I got out and ran after her. "I can't do cheer any more. I'm sorry!"

"That's not true!" She turned to face me with angry tears in her eyes. "You can do anything you want! You just don't want to do cheer! You'd rather be in a show with all your old dance friends!"

"This has nothing to do with the my old dance friends. Would you get off my back," I snapped.

Jilly clicked her remote at the car; the horn sounded. "Fine. Consider it done." She stormed away and didn't look back.

Not a great way to start the day. And it only got worse from there.

In first block, Jessica, aka pot girl, cornered me.

"I hear you got a special tryout for Dream Chaser."

"Yeah." I didn't feel like talking about it any more than that.

"Don't even think you're going to steal the lead from Chloe. She's my understudy and she gets the lead. Not you or anybody else." If looks could kill, Jessica's would have just struck me dead.

"Isn't that up to the director?" Part of me wanted to tell her that he had already given me the lead, but I wasn't ready for the world to know.

"Yes, and he's the one who made her *my* understudy. You trashed dance freshman year. Don't think you can barge back in and take over."

Thankfully the bell rang, and she had to go sit down, but I felt Jessica's eyes lasered at the back of my head all through class.

By lunch it seemed the whole school knew I auditioned. I never got so many nosy looks. Jilly skipped choir and wasn't at my locker for lunch, so I guess she was gonna be pissed for a while. I went through the lunch line alone and got my pizza and chocolate milk. Chloe and McKenna from the show walked by and looked the other way. What. Ever. I took my tray to the atrium. I reached for the door and saw a note taped from the inside.

Written on notebook paper it read. "CHEER

SQUAD ONLY!"

Subtle.

I spotted Jilly and the rest of the squad inside with their backs to the door. Gee thanks! A couple of them peeked at me then looked away.

Great. So where was I supposed to eat? I took my tray back into the crowded cafeteria. I didn't notice anyone staring, but it felt like they were. I slid my milk into my book bag, grabbed my napkin and pizza and left the tray behind. I walked down the long hall at the back of the school, past the shop classes, to the girls' bathroom no one ever used. I ate my lunch sitting on the toilet in the handicapped stall and wondered how Twinkie was doing at the vet.

Chapter 10

The auditorium was empty when I walked in after school. I guess I was a little over eager to show up so early. Rehearsals didn't start until five o'clock, so that kids from the other high schools had time to get there. Tyson said there were thirty-two cast members from six different Madison high schools. He cast the best singers and dancers the city had to offer. So why did he give me the lead? Maybe the brownies he ate had more than pot in them.

"Oh good, you're here." Tyson walked across the dimly lit stage still wearing his black leather jacket, with a scarf thrown around his neck and carrying an overstuffed shoulder bag.

His hair looked all tousled. He sauntered across the stage as if he didn't know how good he looked. He gave me a warm smile that reached his eyes. That man sure knew how to put people at ease.

"I'm really early. I hope that's okay."

"I wish all my cast members were so enthusiastic." He trotted down the steps and over to the piano. He dropped his bag onto a long table, removed his jacket and tossed it over a front row auditorium seat. "Somewhere in this mess I have your paperwork." He rummaged through his bag and pulled out various folders and binders.

"Ah ha, here it is." He grabbed a large bundle of

papers and removed the rubber band around them. "Come on over and let's review it."

"Wow, that's a lot of stuff."

"It is. We're treating this project as a professional show including all the waivers, rules and agreements."

"First off is your participation agreement. Read through it tonight, sign it, have your parents sign it and bring it back tomorrow. Here is your bio form. Fill it out and return it to me by Friday. Next is your commitment agreement. It includes things like you agree to be on time, attend every rehearsal, obey all rules, you won't cut or color your hair, no sky diving or snow boarding, etc."

"I don't think sky diving will be a problem." Free falling. Not gonna happen.

"Good. You'd be surprised at the crazy stunts people pull when they are committed to a show. Our goal is to keep the cast intact and uninjured."

Thank God! Finally someone was going out of their way to keep me safe. Yet each item he reviewed felt like another shovel of dirt burying me deeper. What the heck had I gotten myself into?

Next, he reviewed the rehearsal schedule. He set it up efficiently with no time wasted. Every other day the entire cast rehearsed, the opposite days were principals only. Each rehearsal was detailed with blocking, dance, vocals, etc. It covered the next six weeks, including when to be off book, costume fittings, the move into the Overture Center and more. He even penciled in my voice lessons. I heaved a sigh.

"As you see, we have an intense schedule. You have the unfortunate position of playing catch up on the past weeks. There's no time to teach you separately what you missed, so you'll need to learn it on the fly. Here is a cast list, maps to some of the off-site locations you'll need to know, and, finally, here is your script." He presented it like a coveted gift.

"So you wrote this?" I held the thick, bound script with care.

"Every word. Except the music. I wrote the lyrics, but collaborated with a genius friend of mine on the music."

"This is amazing. You must be so excited." I now realized how hard he must have worked to make this happen.

"It's my baby. And this project, bringing in high school students to perform it, is a huge opportunity. Not to mention a risk. The goal is that when the show goes up, the powers that be—investors and industry people from New York—fall so in love with Dream Chaser, that they snatch it up and give it a home on Broadway."

"And you're trusting a bunch of high school kids to be good enough?" Holy crap, this man was nuts.

"Yup. By tapping into talented youth, untried and unpolished, I plan to feature the combination of vulnerability and heart. That's where you, Eli, and all the others come in."

I must have looked terrified because Tyson laughed and patted my arm.

"Don't worry, you'll be fine. You've got a great director to help you." He grinned.

"If you say so." Trusting a bunch of kids to help him with his dream was insane.

His cell phone rang. "I've got to take this call, so

why don't you look over the paperwork until we're ready to go."

"All right." I gathered up all the papers, found a seat further back in the auditorium and reviewed the details of my life for the next month and a half.

Deep doo doo. That's what I was in.

Twenty minutes later, kids began to filter in, dumping their coats and bags in the auditorium. Unsure what to do, I stayed where I sat, mostly out of view at the far end. A couple kids noticed me, but said nothing as they greeted others. .

A few minutes later Tyson spoke up. "Everyone up on stage. Chloe, you can lead warm ups today."

"Sure." She flashed a thin-lipped smile and strutted her ultra slim body on stage; her long blonde hair flailed behind.

I heaved a deep breath. This was it, now or never. I stepped into the aisle, walked past Tyson at his director's table and joined the others taking the stage.

"Oh yes, before we get started, I want to introduce the newest member of the cast," Tyson said. "We are fortunate to have found Willow Thomas to help us out."

All eyes stared at me. There I was, feeling naked and on display again.

"Many of you will know Willow from here at Capitol High or from the Davis Dance Academy. Willow will be filling Jessica's old spot in the role of Lauren."

The stares turned into daggers. I heard a couple gasps and then complete quiet. The silence felt like shock waves that reverberated in the hollow space as the other kids sized me up. They probably wondered who the hell I thought I was to march in and steal the lead. I gave a weak smile, not wanting to look cocky. Chloe glared and others whispered.

"So, if you don't know Willow yet, please introduce yourselves. I trust you will all make her feel welcome and help her get up to speed." Tyson seemed oblivious to the hostile situation.

No one said a word. Not the girls I used to dance with, not the couple of guys from Capital High.

Not even Eli. He stood on the far end of the stage and stared the opposite direction.

I swallowed my pride and found a spot in the back to warm up where they couldn't gawk at me.

That was the highlight of rehearsal. From there everything went downhill. Tyson had them review dances they'd been working on in an effort to help me catch up. No one slowed it down or called out the moves. Like a fish out of water, I floundered, trying to figure out the sequences with no instruction. The rehearsal turned into an eternity of humiliation. Chloe didn't help matters any by sneering at me and spitting mean words under her breath. I guess I should have expected it.

At the end of rehearsal, as I headed for the steps down to the seats where I'd left my stuff, Chloe blocked my way with her skeletal frame.

There was no way around her, so I figured I might as well let her vent her frustrations. I didn't blame her for being mad.

"You think you're hot shit because Tyson gave you the lead, don't you?" she seethed. The combination of her sharp bone structure and anger turned her ugly.

"No. I didn't want the lead." And I meant it.

"Oh right. Well, let me warn you. Don't plan on stealing anything else," she said, her face all pinched.

"What are you talking about?"

Others brushed past slowly, so they could hear the dirt.

"Don't be an idiot. Eli's interested in me, so don't think you can prance in here and play all sweet and take him away." You had your chance with him and blew it a long time ago."

"You're insane." I tried to pass her, but she stepped in my path like a schoolyard bully.

"Keep your slutty little cheerleader paws off him."

She got up in my grill, which really pissed me off.

"I don't want Eli, you can have him." I spat back a lot louder than I meant to. I moved to go around her, and there was...you got it...Eli.

Crap.

He took one look at me, shook his head and walked away. The only good thing about my day; I wasn't at cheer practice.

I went and grabbed my stuff. With my coat on and bag in hand, I watched the other kids file out in small groups. Some stayed back to joke with Tyson at the piano. Eli was nowhere to be seen.

So that's how it was going to be. I turned and left the way I came in.

Alone.

Chapter 11

The walk home sucked. The frigid air numbed my legs. The cold turned my jeans into stiff sand paper that rubbed my legs raw. Each block the temps plummeted lower, as did my excitement for the show. My arms were frozen under the wool of my peacoat. I couldn't feel my toes anymore. My cheeks chapped from the wind and snot froze above my lip.

I wanted so bad to call Jilly and tell her what a bunch of jerks the kids in the cast were, but Jilly is really good at holding a grudge. As much as she'd love to know how awful it was, I knew she wasn't ready to give me the time of day.

By the time I dragged my frozen body up our porch steps, every bit of me screamed in icy agony.

The second I stepped inside the warm sauna of home, Twinkie jumped on me and nearly knocked me down. "Hey girl, how you doing? You look good to me." I ruffled her fluffy ears, then slid out of my shoes and rushed over to the wood burner in the living room and opened the door. A blast of hot air whooshed out, and my body shivered to release the bone deep chill. I sat on the wood floor in front of it; Twinkie lay down next to me.

"What a good dog." I sank my cold hands into her thick fur.

"Willow? Is that you?" Mom yelled from the

kitchen.

"Yeah, what's left of me anyway."

"Come in and get some dinner. I made African peanut stew, your favorite."

"I'm too cold to move, can you bring me some?" I yelled back.

"Okay, but only because I love you and need you to pick out a really nice nursing home for me some day."

"Really?" I said to Twinkie. "What do you say we put her in a commune or a sweat lodge?"

"I heard that!" she yelled but still brought in a big bowl of steaming stew and a plate of homemade bread with honey butter.

"You are amazing! I take back every horrible thing I've ever said to you."

"I know. You forgot to address me as Supreme Goddess of Exquisite Beauty." Mom handed me the soup bowl and set the plate down next to me on the floor. Twinkie sniffed at the soup.

"Yeah, that too!" I held the bowl, letting the heat thaw my hands, then took a bite.

"Did you walk home?" Mom sat on the couch.

"Mmhmm," I grunted, my mouth full. Mom made the best African stew. She put peanut butter in it. Granted it was organic low fat peanut butter, but it rocked.

"Why didn't you catch a ride with someone from the show?"

"Let's just say the other kids aren't too excited about me showing up and taking over the lead." I dipped a hunk of buttered bread into the stew and then my mouth. Heaven and warmth raced to my stomach.

"Oh. Jealousy is such a useless emotion," Mom said in her singsong way.

"It didn't seem too useless from where I stood. It's a real pain in the ass." It hurt to experience them turn their backs and ignore me.

"Aren't some of the girls you used to dance with in the show? Like McKenna and Chloe?"

"They were there, but they acted like we never met." I dipped and stuffed more stew.

"What a shame. Those kids are really missing out." She gave me her sympathetic mom look.

I don't think they felt they were missing out on anything. They seemed thrilled to keep me out of their loop, maybe even empowered by it.

Twinkie laid her head on my lap, and her eyes begged for food. "Not yet, I'm still eating." I angled my bowl away from her, but on second thought took a spoonful and poured it on the hardwood floor next to us. She lapped it up, her tail wagging.

"What did the vet say about her seizure?"

"Because of her age, the vet doesn't believe its epilepsy or a genetic seizure disorder. He said that with a six-year-old dog it could be a fluke and never happen again or might occur again in days, weeks, or years."

"So we just wait and see?"

"Pretty much."

I took a last bite of my bread and stew and gave the bowl to Twinkie to lick clean. I lay on the floor next to her and watched. "That was awesome. I am so full."

"I hope you saved room for dessert," Mom said.

I rolled my head her direction, now warm, full and content next to my dog. "Dessert?"

"How do chocolate zucchini brownies sound?"

"Not as good as Better than Sex Cake."

"Sorry, no refined sugars in my house. And would you like to share with me your personal knowledge about sex?"

"No, I think it's best to keep you in the dark on my sexual escapades, but I will force myself to eat your brownies." I grinned.

"You are not funny!" Mom tossed a pillow at my head.

Later I showed Mom all the paperwork for the show then called Jilly from the pantry. She didn't pick up.

I went up to my room, thinking about how I'd be walking to school tomorrow, when I found a bouquet of paper flowers from Breezy. She drew little smiley faces on each one. I couldn't help but smile.

Twinkie lay on my feet while I snuggled under a quilt and read the script. I couldn't put it down. Tyson was a genius, and I couldn't believe he'd given me the part of Lauren.

After that I did a little yoga. Miss Ginny was right. I needed to transform my body from a cheerleader back to a dancer. Empowered after good food, a good script and a good stretch, I crashed into bed and hoped for a better day tomorrow.

Chapter 12

School went pretty much the same. I barely made the first bell, because I didn't leave the house soon enough. Dad drives Breezy to her Montessori school on the north side of town, so he couldn't drop me off, unless I wanted to get there at 7:30 a.m. Not.

During lunch, I decided to check the auditorium. It was empty, no class. So I ate my standard lunch of pepperoni pizza and chocolate milk while soaking in the vibes of the stage.

When I finished eating, I went up on stage and tried to mark through the dances I'd tried to learn through osmosis at rehearsal yesterday. Some of it I remembered, but other parts were totally gone. I felt stupid not knowing the dances the rest of the cast did. I needed to get a leg up so they'd stop treating me like I'm an idiot.

It felt pretty good to practice. Tonight I wouldn't have to deal with the whole cast, only Eli and Tyson. *Yikes*. Eli was another topic I was dancing around. But why should I put it all on myself? He didn't have to be such a jerk. He totally ignored me yesterday, which wasn't exactly a vote of confidence, and it sure didn't inspire everyone else to accept me.

The afternoon went by quickly with Foods Class and a movie in History. When I got to the auditorium, Tyson and Eli were already there. Eli glanced up and nodded. No smile, no hello. Still, at least he'd acknowledged me. I guess he figured he had to work with me, so he better be civil. Smart boy.

"Hey Willow." Tyson always looked glad to see me. It sure was a nice switch from the cold shoulder everyone else gave.

"Hi."

Tyson wore grey sweats and a black t-shirt that fit him oh so nicely.

"You two ready to dance?" He rubbed his hands together and his eyes lit up like a little kid on Christmas morning.

"You bet." How could I not, when he was obviously excited. I couldn't wait to get started.

"Sure," Eli said. He acted nonchalant, but if I knew Eli, he was as excited on the inside as Tyson acted on the outside.

"Today we're goin' ghetto." Tyson made some funky hand gestures and bobbed his head like an inner city gangsta.

I looked at Eli with raised eyebrows. He shook his head and grinned at Tyson's gangster act. "All right," I said, a little skepticism crept into my voice.

"You'll get used to it," Eli said as we followed Tyson on stage.

"I thought we'd work on something new so Willow doesn't feel behind in every aspect of the show," Tyson said.

"Thanks, it is a bit overwhelming." Major understatement.

"Today we're going to do some hip hop." Tyson aimed a remote at the docking station and hip-hop music blared. "We're gonna start out with some easy warm-up moves. Just follow me. When we get to the hard stuff, we'll stop and work through it."

So Eli and I stood behind Tyson as he swagged through some hip-hop basics, putting us all in the mood. It was really weird to watch our awesome director go all ghetto. He hit every move hard and sharp. Nothing sloppy.

Eli even lightened up. After a while, he shared looks with me when Tyson would do some move like a snake up. It seemed so out of character to see Tyson roll his body that way. The longer we were thrashing and tutting, the more I relaxed. It's funny how you forget all the crap in life when you're in a good mood from dancing. I swung my attitude like nobody's business.

After we warmed up, Tyson slowed it down and fed us the steps one chunk at a time.

It had been so long since I'd learned a new dance like this. Yesterday didn't count, since I was trying to figure out what they were doing with no clue what the steps were. Today, I had an amazing choreographer feeding me the steps.

"Make sure the knee pops when you twist left," Tyson said.

Next to me, Eli focused on Tyson's every word. At least we had one thing in common now; we both wanted to do it right. Not to mention, I wanted to prove to Eli that I could keep up.

An hour later, drenched in perspiration, I hunched over to catch my breath.

"Let's take five. That's a really good start," Tyson said.

I moved to the side of the stage, grabbed my water

bottle and collapsed. Tyson grabbed a couple things from his bag, climbed back up on stage and joined me. Eli dropped down next to us with a satisfied sigh. Tyson ripped open a bag of pretzels and pushed it toward us. "Help yourself."

Eli grabbed a handful and stuffed them in his mouth. I didn't realize how hungry I was. I should have brought a snack; my slice of pizza wasn't enough to hold me over. I took a handful, too, though I tried to eat them without looking like a caveman. "Thanks."

As we relaxed and caught our breath, Tyson looked more like a college student than a big-time choreographer. His brown hair curled in a loose mass. He leaned over and lay on his side, propping himself up on an elbow. His long legs stretched out and crossed at the ankles. I wondered if he really was gay like Jilly said. Not that it mattered; he was still amazing to look at. I wish I could tell Jilly about it.

Eli was almost the polar opposite of Tyson in coloring, but he looked just as great. He leaned back on his hands next to the pretzel bag, a bottle of purple Power Aid at his side. Blonde hair covered his forearms. That hadn't been there when we were kids. He wore a loose East High School Athletics t-shirt with grey sweats and sneakers. His blonde hair stuck up in front where he'd pushed it off his forehead when we finished. He looked laid-back, relaxed, as if he had no idea how good he looked. Knowing Eli, he probably didn't.

I couldn't believe I was rehearsing for a big show with these two great-looking guys. Hanging out with them was crazy fun. The only change I'd make is to have Eli forgive me and stop with the cool indifference.

"So how do you like the number so far?" Tyson asked.

"Awesome," Eli said.

"I love it! It's so different from what I learned yesterday. I can't wait to see how it all fits together," I said. But dealing with Eli's cold shoulder threw a wet blanket on the fun.

"I've been working on this show for years. It's already been work shopped in New York. What we're doing here in Madison is like an out-of-town tryout. Most Broadway shows begin with that type of tryout, before they open in New York. That's when last-minute changes are made, so the show is perfect by the time it gets to the Broadway."

I nodded and took more pretzels.

"And because I'm going about it in my psychotic Tyson Scott kind of way, you can expect small changes and tweaks up to the end. I need to make sure it feels absolutely perfect. We've got some influential people flying in for opening night. Including a casting director." He eyed Eli. "You still interested in meeting with him?"

"Hell, yeah!" Eli said.

Okay then. No pressure. I glanced at Eli. While his body language was calm, I could tell by the way his eyes darted into the distance, that he was worried about impressing Tyson's big wigs. As long as I'd known Eli, he dreamed of not only making it big, but getting out of this town and away from his parents.

"Are you sure putting it on with high school kids is the right thing to do?" I asked. He was crazy to leave it in the hands of a bunch of teenage dancers and drama kids.

Tyson grinned. "Absolutely. There is nothing more fresh or more powerful than the energy of raw talent discovering themselves and performing at their best. You guys have so much potential, it's bursting from you."

I raised my eyebrows in doubt.

"I know you may not believe it now, but you will. For example, look how fast you two are picking up the hip hop. This is complex choreography and you two are so hungry to learn it and get it right. Your energy is what powers me."

Now I was in bigger trouble. It took every ounce of concentration to make it look easy. If he was counting on us to get his show on stage and make it a success, I better figure out a way to step up my game.

"On that note, let's get back to it. We need to finish this number and then move on to the second dream scene before we call it quits tonight.

By the time I walked home, it was almost eight o'clock. My body was so hot and sweaty that I didn't feel the cold for the first half of the walk. I left my coat open the first few blocks; my head buzzed with excitement and steps from the amazing rehearsal. Tyson had worked us hard and taught us as much as our brains could hold. By the time I got home, I was sufficiently cooled down and glad to step inside. A note from Dad said he and Breezy were at a movie. So I gave Twinkie a couple treats, wolfed down the leftover stew, then went to my room to mark through the three dances we'd learned. I wrote down everything I could remember in a notebook. I needed to work every trick I could think of if I was going to survive learning a whole show in such a short time. Panic reared its ugly head a couple times, but I blocked it out.

"Whatcha doing?" Breezy barged in as I did some risqué hip thrusts.

"Breezy! You ever heard of knocking?"

"It looks naughty." She plopped on my bed to watch.

"I'm trying to remember the dances I learned so far." I pointed to the door. "Now get out."

"It looks like you're demented."

I crossed the room and stood in the open doorway. "Breezy, out."

"I wanna watch; it looks funny. Do some more."

"No. I'm done for the night."

"Come on," she whined.

"I'm going to bed. You should too."

Breezy pouted her way off my bed and left while trying to imitate the hip move.

I shook my head. When she tried the move, it looked stupid. I hoped I didn't look so lame.

Chapter 13

I woke up Saturday morning and could barely move. As I sat up, every muscle screamed in pain. It hurt so much I couldn't even manage a real scream. I tried to stand up, but my muscles were so tight and sore I had to put my hands on my thighs and push myself up.

"Ow!" My voice came out high and meek.

If I didn't know better, I'd say someone came into my room in the night and beat me with a baseball bat. I didn't want to move. If I moved, it hurt. How was I going to survive rehearsal? It was the whole group again. At the beginning of cheer camp, we were always sore, but nothing like this.

I took a couple of ibuprofen and then let the shower water run super hot, hoping it would warm up and loosen my rusty muscles. How could I not realize I was out of shape? With all my time working out with cheer, I thought I was in shape, but obviously not. Cheer used a ton of strength, balance, and a lot of short staccato moves. Tyson had given us every move under the sun in his choreography. No wonder the man looked like a god. His body must be rock solid.

Thinking of cheer reminded me that today was Regionals. The team would already be in Watertown. A pang of longing hit as I thought about the excitement of competition; especially as you climbed the ladder closer to State and Nationals.

I could picture Jilly, Rick, Kyle, and the team warming up and hanging out in the staging rooms before they were queued to perform. The energy would hum as everyone counted down the minutes. The girls' hair would all be pulled back into the world's perfect ponytail, not one flyaway hair to be seen. Their performance make up would be flawless, including false eyelashes, glitter, and rosy cheeks. When our squad took to the gym, the entire crowd would jump to their feet. The Capitol Flyers were the national champs, and everyone bowed down in awe.

Except for me. I ran the other way. So I rinsed the shampoo from my hair and blocked off thoughts of cheer and Jilly and the gang.

After a marathon shower that used up all the hot water, my muscles screamed a little less loudly. When I went downstairs, Dad sat with a cup of tea listening to National Public Radio. Twinkie lay on the rug in front of the fireplace; her tail beat when she saw me. Dad glanced up.

"You're walking like an old man."

"I feel like an old man." I shuffled to the kitchen and grimaced as I reached for a bowl, the container of granola, and milk. I brought my breakfast into the living room and sank into the couch, blowing out all my breath instead of crying in pain.

Dad looked over his reading glasses. "Hard workout?"

"Yeah, the worst," I said. "Actually, it was amazing, but the aftereffects are killing me."

"A cup of herbal tea should help your sore muscles."

"I don't think a tanker truck of herbal tea would make much difference at this point." I took a huge mouthful of granola.

"And some yoga wouldn't hurt either." He raised his cup and sipped.

"Fine, Doctor Nut Case. Let me finish my breakfast first. Can I take the car later?"

"Sure, I've nowhere to go today."

So after I ate and sort of crawled off the couch, Dad put on some eerie Indian music and we did some yoga. It just about killed me, but at the end, my aching body felt better.

I drove the short distance to school. Light snow fell, not enough to add up to much, just a light dusting to clean up the black sludge that had accumulated on piles of plowed snow. Inside the auditorium, I dropped my bag with the others. Most ignored me, but Sophie, a girl I used to dance with, nodded my direction, and McKenna glanced at me then quickly looked away. Chloe sneered, with her face all pinched up. She made a huge production of swaggering on stage for warm ups.

Eli looked my direction.

"Hey," he said, which wasn't a total snub, but he didn't smile. He turned and joined some guys and a really pretty girl I didn't know.

I put on my invisible suit of armor and followed the stragglers on stage. Taking the steps killed my sore thigh muscles, but after warm up and two more ibuprofen, it wasn't so bad. Tyson had us run through the numbers I'd tried to learn the first night. The rest of the group looked pretty good, while I struggled to follow, always a half beat off. I stood in the back, but still Chloe and some of her posse would turn and scowl. When she wasn't targeting me, she flirted with Eli. He talked with her and even laughed a couple of times, but I'd say she acted a little desperate.

After an hour, Tyson called a ten-minute break. By then I was kind of pissed off I couldn't nail the dance. I didn't want to ask Tyson to slow it down. As everyone left the stage for their bags, I approached Sophie.

"Hey Sophie," I said.

She paused, turning to look at her friends leaving her behind. "Yeah."

"I was wondering if you could run some steps with me?" I tried to keep the desperation out of my voice, but I knew that if I didn't get some help, I'd be the joke of the production.

"Um," she looked to the rest of the cast grabbing their water bottles and chatting and then back to poor pathetic me. "Sure, why not." She smiled a little.

Thank god!

We moved to the back stage area, so the rest of the cast couldn't watch me struggle.

"I really appreciate this," I said.

"No problem," Sophie said. "I sure wouldn't want to be in your shoes, trying to catch up and learn everything."

"I don't want to be me either," I joked. At least I wasn't being launched skyward at the cheer competition right now, hoping my bases kept their concentration and didn't drop me.

"What do you need help with?" she asked.

"Everything. If we could just mark through the steps real quick that would help so much. I'm trying to figure out exactly what we're supposed to be doing. I'm kind of getting it, but I want to know exactly what the step is supposed to be."

"Okay."

Sophie marked through the entire number. A light bulb went off in my head. Now I knew for sure what the steps were supposed to be, instead of guessing that I had the right sequence or the right beat.

"You should go take a quick break before we get started again," I said.

"Yeah, I've gotta pee." She grinned.

"Thanks so much, I feel like I get it now."

"Any time. Listen. I know Chloe and some of the others are pissed that you got the lead, but I just want the show to be good. If Tyson thinks you're the one, that's good enough for me."

"Thanks. I hope Tyson made the right decision too." Sophie not only helped me learn the dance, but her kindness was the shot in the arm I needed. Maybe I'd end up with a friend in the show after all.

Sophie left and I stayed backstage and marked through the steps a couple more times before Tyson called everyone back. When we ran it again, I no longer stumbled or did it half assed. I got it. At one point, Tyson smiled my direction. He must have been relieved that I finally knew what I was doing. That made it one number down, how many more to catch up?

Next, we spent two hours with Ms. Fuller on vocals. I was terrified she'd make me sing my solo, but lucked out that it was only the chorus numbers. Afterward, the girls were dismissed so Tyson could work with the guys on one of their numbers.

We'd been seated for vocals so long that when I stood up, my muscles had cooled down so much they basically locked up. I thought I'd die, going through this again. I edged my aching body to my bag and popped a couple more ibuprofen, a girl's best friend, and moved to my next scene of torture. Voice lessons.

Even though Tyson gave me directions, I Google mapped it. He spent the past ten years in New York; Madison roads could have changed. I took the Beltline Hwy across town with a pit stop at Arby's for a big cheddar and curly fries. I couldn't imagine how many calories I'd been burning, and Mom's cooking was too healthy to put fat on anyone.

This woman lived in Timbuktu. It took half an hour to get across town to my voice teacher's house in Middleton. I easily found it, a refurbished Victorian in an older neighborhood. I parked on the street, grabbed my music, and slowly climbed the steps to her house. Now that I stood outside her stained glass front door, the reality of why I was here hit me straight on. Crap. This woman was supposed to teach me how to sing. On stage. In front of a thousand people.

Double crap.

I rang the doorbell and waited. A tiny woman, who appeared to be in her late thirties, yanked the door open.

"Hi, you must be Willow." She smiled at me with optimism. Little did she know how much work this would take. I nodded. She must have been a former beauty. She was still pretty, but her face looked like she'd lived a little hard or maybe worshipped the sun too much.

"Come on in. I'm Gloria."

I stepped carefully onto her entry mat, not wanting to track snow in her house and have her mad at me right off.

"Just kick your shoes off and hang your coat on the rack." She indicated the old-fashioned coat rack in the corner. "We'll be working in here."

I obeyed and followed her into a front room with a huge picture window looking out onto the street. The sparse room held only a love seat with embroidered pillows edged with lace, a couple of floor lamps, and an upright piano, which faced the wall.

"Have a seat." She motioned to the antique love seat. I sat down and gripped my music like a life preserver. She pulled the piano stool over, sat down, and faced me, her hands placed on her legs. "So you're Tyson's dance prodigy?"

"Excuse me?" Dance prodigy? She must have heard wrong.

"Tyson raves about you and says you've saved the show."

"Oh, I don't know about that." What exactly had Tyson told her, and what had he been smoking?

"I'm so glad to meet you and happy to help out. Tyson and I go way back to when he first got to New York. Back then, when I wasn't in a show, I gave voice lessons. It was a great run, but then I met my husband, and we didn't want to raise a family in the city."

"Oh," I said, not sure how to respond.

"I still do shows on occasion. Mostly opera as guest performer."

"Wow, that's impressive." Except that it made me feel even smaller.

"Enough about me. Tyson tells me your vocals could use some help, and that your biggest issue is lack of confidence."

"Yeah, singing isn't really my thing. I mean, I'm in choir, but I'm no soloist."

"Well, let's warm up and see what you've got." Gloria wheeled her stool back to the piano. "You can stand here next to the piano. Leave your music on the stand."

Standing there in front of her without music, my hands started to shake. I don't know why I was so nervous, maybe because I hated the idea of singing in front of people. She better be able to cure me of that, too.

"We'll start with some scales." She played a chord and then her fingers punched out each note. She sang with me the first run, which was horrifying because her voice was totally perfect. It reminded me of the time my parents took me to see Wicked at the Overture Center. The singers were so amazing. Their voices were clear and pure and filled the entire theatre. Gloria's was just like that.

She hit the next chord and let me sing this one on my own. The decibel level in the room dropped to almost none.

"This time give me more. Louder. Sing from your belly button."

Huh? I didn't know how to sing from my belly button, so I sang as loud as I could. We changed from ahs to oohs. She didn't look at me as I sang; she just listened, staring off into space. She made me sing higher and higher until my voice cracked.

"Sorry."

Gloria sat deep in thought for another minute and then looked at me. "You have a lovely voice, you just don't know how to use it."

After that she had me hooting like an owl and skipping around the room to shake off my nerves about singing. She had me lie on the floor with a book on my stomach to learn how to breathe and then do a bunch of other insane things.

An hour later, I left, feeling more confused than ever, with a bill for fifty dollars and a schedule for three lessons a week until further notice. Major crap. My parents weren't made of money. I didn't even know if the lessons were going to help.

Dejected, I drove back across town and wondered how Jilly and the cheer squad had done. I hadn't talked to her in a couple days and I really missed her, but that didn't mean I missed cheer. Not at all.

Trying to learn all this show stuff was a steep price to pay to get out of flying. I really wanted to go home and crawl under an afghan with Breezy and play cats cradle. Instead I drove straight to Miss Ginny's. It was already getting dark out, but the lights were on.

Once I was inside, she gave me a big hug. "Good to see you!"

"Is it okay I showed up?" I didn't want to intrude.

"Of course. You are always welcome here." She beamed. "I'm surprised you're here so late. You must have had a really long day!"

"I have, but I need to get this right or I won't be able to sleep tonight." After the voice lesson, my ego was bruised, my body ached, and I was dog tired. Part of me wanted to cry, but instead I sucked it up, changed into dance clothes, and met Miss Ginny in the largest of her six studios.

I stretched out, warmed up, then slowly worked through each of the dances I'd learned so far. Miss Ginny helped me break them down and polish each step.

"Willow, chin down. Relax your shoulders."

I made the changes.

"Much better."

She corrected my turn out and extension. She watched like an eagle and had me repeat the leaps and spins until they felt natural and second nature.

If there is one thing I love, it's dance. I guess I forgot that for a while. Now that I was back, and immersed in it, I realized how good it felt to move around the floor. Even after a crappy day like today when I was so exhausted I could fall asleep in a chair. So I didn't sit down. I kept going. I was determined to catch up and to get it right. I didn't believe what Gloria said about me saving the show, but I was sure going to do everything I could not to ruin it. Even if that meant pushing books up with my stomach from Gloria's floor and spending extra time on my form with Miss Ginny.

Finally, we'd covered every number I'd learned so far.

"Good work. You should be pleased with yourself," Miss Ginny stated in her matter-of-fact way.

"Thanks." I slouched unable to hold good posture for another moment. "Thank you again for letting me come and practice. I really needed it."

"I'm so happy to see you in the lead role. As I said before, my door is always open to you. I want you to come here anytime you need to." She walked me out to the office area. "In fact, I want you to take this and use it anytime you need."

She took my hand and placed a key in it. "Just be sure to lock the doors after you're inside for safety and turn the lights off when you leave."

I stared. "Are you sure?" The studio was her life. I'd never heard of her giving anyone a key, but knowing I could come here by myself and run numbers without worrying who watched would be heaven. No more being ridiculed by an inquisitive eight-year-old sister or a judgmental teen terror named Chloe.

"Absolutely." She smiled like my grandma does when she see me. "I have the utmost faith and trust in you Willow."

"Thank you. I'll be very careful with it." Her confidence helped wash away the ill taste of my struggles with the show. I hugged her with the key held tight in my fist.

Chapter 14

You know how sometimes you're stuck in a dream and you can't wake up? Or you know you're dreaming, but you're kind of awake at the same time? That was Sunday morning. I dreamt that I was dancing, because, gee, I sure hadn't done much of that in the last couple of days. But in this dream, it was the day before opening night and I didn't know any of the steps, so I was trying to fake it. But I stood front and center, and Chloe kept laughing at me.

I had this fake smile plastered on my face like little girls in a beauty pageant. Grin so big your fillings show, and then the audience will like you, right? Then Eli grabbed my arm and shook me because I kept messing up, but I couldn't stop dancing. As Eli kept shaking me, I heard Breezy.

"Wake up, Willow, wake up."

In my dreamy haze I wondered why Breezy was onstage during the show. Then Dream Eli looked at me like he wondered why I was sleeping on stage during our dance.

"Willow, Twinkie had another shaky thing." I heard Breezy's distant voice cry.

I kept trying to dance, but my arm hurt from Eli and Breezy hitting me. Then I realized Breezy was actually hitting me.

"What!" I startled awake so fast, I wasn't sure where

I was for a second. Then the fuzziness cleared, and I saw Breezy on the edge of my bed with a worried face. No Eli.

"Twinkie did that shaky thing and pooped and everything."

I blinked a couple times to clear away the cobwebs. "Oh no! Is she okay?" I jolted up in bed. My voice sounded low and rough like sandpaper. Not sure if it was from my owl hooting yesterday or just waking up.

"The shaking stopped, but she's just lying there in my room, staring at nothing." Breezy's lower lip quivered.

I bolted out of my warm bed and rushed to her room. My muscles played a repeat of yesterday. I ignored it the best I could and did kind of a speed-limp walk. Dad kneeled on the floor next to Twinkie, who lay stretched out on her side. When I got to her, she looked at me and wagged her tail.

"There you go. See, Breezy. She's going to be all right." Dad pet Twinkie's side.

Breezy stood behind me, keeping distance between her and our mysteriously sick dog.

"Has she had any others?" I asked under my breath. Dad gave a slight nod. I chewed at my lip.

"Looks like Twinkie and I are going for another check-up, aren't we girl," he said in a cheery voice for Breezy's sake.

Breezy wrapped her arms around my neck, her head plastered to mine. I reached up and patted her arms. "Don't worry," I said. "The vet will get her all fixed up."

"Promise?" Her voice squeaked with emotion.

"I promise the vet will do everything he can to make

her feel better," Dad said.

Her little head nodded against mine, her arms still wrapped tight around my neck like a rubber band around a newspaper.

"And we better call mom, too," Breezy added.

"Yes, that's a good idea," Dad agreed.

"How about pancakes?" I suggested, knowing it was the quickest way to release the static cling of Breezy.

"Really?!" She lit up.

"Sure, we'll make this a special day."

"Good plan," Dad said. "This afternoon, after I get back from the vet, I have to go down to the Memorial Union for an art show. How about you take Breezy sledding? We got a fresh two inches last night."

"Yeah! Can we? Please." Breezy bounced behind me.

I gave Dad the evil eye. Smooth move. Taking Mini Me sledding was the last thing I wanted to do, next to, say, singing a solo in front of hundreds of people. But on the bright side, it was definitely a step up from flipping around in the air for cheer.

"Fine," I groaned. "But not right now. Later, when I'm awake." And hopefully in less physical pain.

We destroyed the kitchen making pancakes, which I was able to do only because it was an Amish pre-made mix and Breezy helped. Then I did more yoga in hopes of stretching out my sore, knotted muscles. This time Breezy joined me.

Dad came home with Twinkie. He said the vet gave him some pills to help control the seizures and that Twinkie should resume normal activities.

Breezy wouldn't let the sledding thing go, so finally

I gave in and bundled her up.

"We should bring Twinkie, too," she informed me.

"I'm not bringing a dog to the sledding hill. She'll get hit by some out-of-control kid on a snow board." I hauled a sled out of the basement.

"No, she won't. I'll take care of her. She's had a bad day and needs to be cheered up" Breezy stuck her hands on her hips, which looked funny in her puffy snow suit.

"Breezy, it's a long walk with you, a sled, and the dog."

"Walk? You want to go for a walk, girl?" Breezy patted her legs.

Twinkie jumped up and nearly knocked Breezy over.

"You want to go sledding don't you?" Breezy let Twinkie lick her face, which always grosses me out.

"Come on Willow, she wants to go." Twinkie's tail wagged like mad.

"Fine, but you have to hold her leash on the way there and back."

"Goody!" She hugged Twinkie around the neck.

So I pulled on my Dad's old winter coat, Mom's Sorel's and a pair of mittens from the bottom of the mis-matched box of winter stuff.

I trudged six blocks to the sledding hill between Lake Monona and Atwood Avenue. Breezy sang De Colores, a Spanish song she learned at school; Twinkie trotted along happy as a clam.

Eli and I used to love to sled. We started coming here right after we met during the third grade; it felt like yesterday. We never went home until we were so cold we could barely hold the sled rope through our frozen mittens.

But now sledding is a pain in the ass. So is Eli.

The hill was packed; nothing like a couple inches of fresh snow to bring out every grade schooler in the city. Within seconds of arrival, Breezy spotted a friend from school and took off.

I pulled down Dad's coat so it would cover my butt and sat on it in the snow to avoid getting my jeans wet. Twinkie lay next to me and watched the kids, her head on her paws and her tail wagging. I put my boot on the end of her leash to keep her near me.

While Breezy squealed and yelled at me to watch, my mind wandered. Things look so different when you're older. This hill used to be huge, but now it wasn't big at all. Funny how perspective changes when you grow up. It used to be a wide-open expanse, but now all the trees and bushes were overgrown, and a gas station and convenience store stood next to a new apartment building and a video rental store.

Twinkie stood up and started to whine.

"What's the matter girl?" I ruffled her fur.

She started pacing and acting strange. I leaned forward to pet her. "Are you okay?" Her eyes looked wild and frightened.

"It's okay, you're fine." I shifted to get closer to her. My boot came off the end of her leash about the time she decided to bolt. She took off like a shot down the hill toward the buildings and the road.

"Twinkie!" I yelled, already on my feet after her. "Breezy, stay here with Ally, don't you dare leave!" I shouted as I skittered my way down the hill.

Twinkie ran into bushes then darted around the

front of the video store and disappeared.

Please don't run out in the road and get killed.

"Twinkie! Here girl," I yelled and ran to the video store. They had huge evergreen shrubs that covered both front corners of the store. "Twinkie! Twinkie!" I yelled, feeling kind of stupid as people who were returning their movies gave me odd looks. I searched through one group of bushes. Nothing. "Twinkie!

"I saw a dog run around the corner of the gas station," said a woman as she climbed back into her minivan.

"Thanks." I took off that direction.

"Twinkie!" I yelled again when I reached the gas station, now out of breath. Where the heck had she gone? I stood there, looking around, and wondered what to do. She'd never run off before. What if I couldn't find her?

"Twinkie!" I yelled. This could not be happening. Cars kept pulling in and out; she could easily be hit.

A couple guys walked to their car. "Twinkie, Twinkie," they mocked in high-pitched voices and laughed.

Jerks.

I gave them a dirty look then noticed a sporty blue jeep parked at the pump. Eli leaned against the gleaming vehicle, looking really good. The collar of his coat was flipped up and his hair was blowing in the wind. Then he raised an eyebrow and cocked his head. He had been watching me make a fool of myself. He shook his head and chuckled.

"Need some help?" He stood there all cool and arrogant. I wanted to smack him.

"No, I got this," I said, disgusted.

"Whatever you say." He turned and got into his overpriced wheels and drove off.

Asshole. I guess our truce only existed during rehearsals.

I turned to look for Twinkie, too embarrassed to scream her name again. I walked around the side of the gas station. Nothing. I went around back and found her in the snow by the dumpsters. She was having another seizure.

I ran over and knelt in the snow in front of her while she spasmed out of control. Her mouth was locked open, and her eyes looked like a marbles.

"Oh girl, I'm sorry." I reached to pet her; her body was rigid as it convulsed over and over. Helpless, I covered my mouth and watched my beautiful dog trapped in her own body.

It lasted a couple more minutes then slowed to a few twitches and stopped. Seconds later, she gasped a huge breath, and I realized she couldn't breathe during the seizure.

"Oh sweetie, it's over now. It's over." I lay in the snow next to her and spoke quietly in her ear and petted her. She didn't move other than her heavy breathing. Her eyes didn't budge either. "It's okay, girl," I soothed.

Finally her tail gave a little twitch. Thank goodness.

* * *

That night, while I worked on memorizing lines, Dad came in and sat down.

"So what did the vet really say this morning?" I patted the floor and Twinkie ran to me as if nothing had happened.

"Where's Breezy?" He glanced around.

"Upstairs, taking a bath."

Dad took his coat off and hung it on the hook inside the door. "Because of her age, the vet is pretty certain it's a brain tumor."

I crouched down and hugged Twinkie close. My eyes got watery.

"He gave us stronger meds to keep the seizures at bay, but eventually they'll increase until the meds don't work." He sat on the couch with a sigh.

"Then what?"

"We have a prescription of valium. Apparently a dose of it will shut down her nervous system enough to stop the seizures."

"Can they make it go away? What if they're wrong?"

"The vet says the tests to confirm the tumor would cost over a grand, and there's nothing he could do about it anyway. Basically we just hope the tumor is slow growing, and she gets as much time as possible."

My dad looked really sad; and that was something new for me. He was always the rock in the family and could handle anything. I moved next to him on the couch. I wanted to cry. "I don't like to see her suffer."

"Me either," he said.

I put my head on his shoulder, and we watched Twinkie chew on her new peanut butter rawhide. My heart squeezed with emotion as I tried not to imagine life without her.

Chapter 15

Monday morning after choir, I tried to corner Jilly. The day I told her I made the show, she'd moved to a seat two rows behind me, which seemed pretty grade school to me.

There was so much we needed to talk about, and, bottom line, I missed her. I didn't want to lose her friendship. As Jilly put her music folder away, I rushed to intercept her outside the choir door.

"Hey." I got in her path to stop her.

She glared at me with a prissy expression.

"I was wondering if we could talk at lunch?"

Jilly turned her head and walked past. Apparently she wasn't done giving me the silent treatment. Tough! I caught up with her.

"Listen, I know you're still mad at me, but come on. You can't stay mad forever."

"Wanna bet." She didn't even look at me, just kept walking fast.

"Okay, so you need more time. I get it, but I wanted to say congrats on Regionals. That's so awesome! I wish I could have been there to see it."

She slowed to a stop.

"Really? You would have been there if you hadn't quit! Give me a flippin' break. You didn't want to be there. You wanted to hang out with your new dance friends."

"That's not true. You're my best friend." I fixed her with a stubborn stare. She knew it was true but obviously wasn't ready to let it go.

"Oh, I heard you got the lead. It must be nice to get everything you want all the time."

"That is not true and you know it. Now, come on Jilly, spend lunch with me." I pleaded and was pretty sure I cracked through her tough girl façade.

"I can't do lunch. Everyone in cheer is still pissed at you. And honestly, so am I. I don't think they want to see you." Jilly glared at me and then seemed to soften a bit. "I guess I could get together right after cheer practice," she mumbled under her breath.

"I can't. I have rehearsal." I hated to point it out, but that was my new reality.

"Of course you do," she said in a snotty way. "After you're done I'll be at work, so come by there."

"I can't." I cringed inside. "I have voice lessons."

Jilly huffed and crossed her arms. "Fine. Tomorrow night then."

I hesitated to answer. I didn't want to make things worse. "Tomorrow night rehearsals go late."

Jilly's face got all pinched up, and I knew this wasn't going to work. "Wednesday?" she asked, irritated.

I bit my lip. "Rehearsal and voice again." I couldn't believe how hard it was to find a time we were both free. Dream Chaser rehearsal was sucking my life dry and with her cheer and work schedules I now saw it wouldn't work.

"You know what? Never mind." She brushed past.

I didn't bother to follow. What was the point? I didn't have time to hang out with Jilly or anyone else for that matter. I wondered if she'd be willing to see me when the show ended.

* * *

Rehearsal that night was all about lifts. Okay, not really, but it felt that way. There was this contemporary number, kind of lyrical. It was the "falling in love" scene. With Eli. Who I knew still sort of hated me. Maybe hate is too strong. But he doesn't like me. At all!

So we learned this beautiful lyrical dance where Lauren and Zach fall in love. It's very graceful and heaven-like, except it didn't feel like heaven. Nope, much more like hell. My own private living hell.

Tyson stood with us, describing each step in detail. "Good, now after the chassé, Willow turn out, do a gran jeté, and as you leap, take his left hand. Eli, put your right hand on her hip and extend it lifting her up over your head." The idea of leaping into Eli's arms posed a couple of problems.

My first problem was Eli. I'm sure the last thing he wanted right now was to touch me, let alone lift me. He still avoided speaking to me at all costs, unless we were learning a dance together.

My next problem, also Eli. I know we used to do this stuff all the time when we were kids, but now he's older and taller and, I have to admit, smells good. Maybe not too good now, after an hour of rehearsal, but earlier when we stood close, I noticed he smelled like shampoo or shaving cream or something. Back when we used to dance together, he didn't shave. Back then he smelled like a kid who drank a lot of Sunny D, not a guy who showered daily and wore deodorant.

My final problem wasn't Eli, it was me. This wasn't cheer, and I knew Eli wasn't going to launch me in the air, but still, terror overwhelmed me at the mere thought of being aloft. What if he couldn't lift me, what if he tripped and dropped me? I could envision a neck brace in my future. None of this had bothered me during auditions, when we did those two basic lifts, but that happened so fast I didn't really have time to think about it. But now? Not so much.

Tyson walked through the moves and explained how it would work.

"Willow, once Eli has you up, put your arms in high third and scissor your legs open. Eli, you're going to move stage left then rotate her and release her by rolling her forward to the floor."

The three of us marked the moves. I reached over our heads for Eli's left hand while he crouched down a bit with his hand on my hip. Then I was supposed to jump, and he was supposed to lift me over his head! One handed!

Like *that* was going to happen.

Tyson corrected our hand placements and the angle of my body. "Good. Now Willow, for practice sake, jump as high as you can. Eli, see how you'll need to get under her right away to get the right angle. Push with your legs as well as your arms."

Eli stood behind me, just inches away. He held my hand firmly. His other hand rested on my hip. His long fingers curled around to my butt.

Why did I eat two slices of pizza today plus fries? I never ate that much at lunch, but today I figured I needed the energy to get through all my rehearsals. Bad idea.

Eli's eyes focused in serious concentration. "Ready?"

"On three," I said. So standing in place with no space to step or run into it, I counted. "One, two, three." I gripped his hand and did the best standing high jump I could despite being at a sideways angle.

Eli bent at the knees and tried to get under me. Tyson moved in to support Eli, but I didn't have enough momentum and Eli had the wrong hand placement, so partway up, I started tumbling down. Into Eli's unwilling arms.

"Umph."

With one hip against his chest and my head dangling near his knees like a monkey, I caught the safety mat with my hands. I think Tyson had an arm around my waist, and I kneed both of them with my flailing legs. It's horrifying to have some famous choreographer have to catch your ass, especially when it's in the most unflattering position, and you're wearing sweaty dance clothes. But I'm not one to shy away from a challenge, so I sucked it up and tried to erase the image from my brain for all eternity. Hopefully Tyson was gay after all. It somehow seemed less embarrassing.

"Good try," Tyson said.

Eli shook his head and looked away with a sigh.

I felt like a cow.

"Each time you try, you'll get a better feel. Let's try it again," Tyson encouraged. "Be sure to hold your whole body tight. It will help Eli lift and balance you."

So we got back in position and tried again. This time I jumped crooked, and Eli had to step backward to keep me from going over his back. We fell onto the mat with me on top. I think I damaged Eli's big fat inflated ego as well as his manhood. A couple more tries ended with me landing all helter skelter, him grabbing my boob a couple times, and my legs in awkward places like around his neck.

"Tyson, I'm too heavy. He can't lift me. Maybe if I ran into it," I offered, out of breath and trying to find a way to make it work. I wasn't overweight, but he was a lean dancer, not a weight lifter like the cheer guys.

"If you jumped higher and didn't make me do all the work, it would go a lot better," Eli blazed and wiped off his sweaty brow.

"Hello, I'm a cheerleader. Nobody jumps higher than I do."

"*Was* a cheerleader. You quit. Remember?" Eli said with a snide look.

Tyson rubbed his stubbly chin, deep in thought. "All right, I think I know what the problem is."

I sat on the mat all slimy with sweat; Eli didn't look any better. His hair stuck out all screwy from my missed leaps.

"Lifts are all about trust. And for whatever reason, neither one of you trusts that the other can do it. You just need a little confidence in each other." Tyson reached out a hand to each of us and pulled us to our feet.

"Do you trust me?" he looked directly at me.

"Yeah," I hesitated, wondering what Tyson was getting at. Why wasn't Eli included in this?

"Do you think I could do this lift?"

"Well, sure, of course." The man was a dancing god. I had looked him up on the internet and found amazing pictures and videos of him in action. Tyson could do absolutely anything!

"Okay, let's go. You and me, right now." His eyes glint in challenge.

Holy crap. I thought I'd have kittens right then and there.

"No way!" It was one thing to screw it up with Eli, but with the director?! Uh huh.

"Why not?" He laughed.

Eli grinned. A first since we'd been thrown together. Of course, he didn't believe I could do it. Neither did I.

"What if I hurt you?" I certainly didn't want to damage Tyson's man parts. Or what if it got out that even the great Tyson Scott couldn't lift me? Oh my God!

"You're not going to hurt me. And even if you did, I'll recover. I've been taken down by far better than you. So what's the matter? You scared?" He raised one eyebrow slowly in challenge.

Shit. I couldn't believe this: Tyson Scott lifting me!

Resigned, I stepped next to him, a sheen of perspiration covered my hands and face.

"Want me to spot?" Eli offered, having way too much fun at my expense.

"No, I've got it." Tyson reached his left hand over to me. "Ready?"

"I guess." I blew out a breath and concentrated. *Don't screw up. Don't screw up.*

"One. Two. Three," Tyson counted off.

I jumped.

And, like magic, rose high above his head. With Tyson's hand planted solidly on my hip, he moved across the stage with me floating above in perfect position. He did the choreographed turn then twirled me to the floor as if we'd done it a million times. I stood breathless, shocked and not feeling at all like a cow.

"Oh my God, that's the most amazing thing I've ever done!" I couldn't control my grin. Was there anything this guy wasn't good at? Tyson laughed. Eli, speechless, looked impressed.

"Okay, you saw how easy that is, and now you know how it should feel and where to put your weight. Eli, now do you believe she can do it?"

"Yeah."

Hard to argue.

"Good, now come here. You're going to prove to Willow that you can lift her."

Who's in the hot seat now? I pointed at Eli and laughed.

"What?" he walked over. Confused.

"You said you believe Willow can do this. Now she needs to believe you can. So take your shirt off."

I bit back my laughter.

"Why?" Eli looked super uncomfortable.

"You need to prove you have the strength to lift her."

"Yeah, but..."

"Dude, lose the shirt." Tyson commanded.

Eli shook his head in annoyance then reached back and pulled his grey t-shirt over his head and down his arms. He tossed it to the floor.

Yowza! No more laughing from me. Eli's sweats hung low on his hips. His flat stomach had that washboardie, six-pack thing going. *Who knew?*

"Take a close look," Tyson said to me. "See those

arms? Eli flex your arms for her."

"Aw come on man, this is humiliating." He shook his head.

"Show the lady your guns." Tyson tried not to laugh, but I knew he wanted to.

Eli rolled his eyes, but raised his arm and flexed. Whoa! A huge bicep appeared. Where'd that come from? Eli never had muscles before, but then again it had been a while since I had looked. I had no idea he'd been hiding all that under his t-shirts.

"Willow, come here and feel his arm."

"No, it's okay, I can see from here."

Tyson gave me his *"I'm the director, so do what I say,"* stare. Eli's face turned pink. Seeing how uncomfortable it made him made it all worth it. So I stepped up and felt his arm. Rock solid, strong, steady. Who was he? Where was the boy I used to dance with and dare to play Ding Dong Ditch?

"Do his arms feel strong enough to lift you?" Tyson asked.

Speechless, I nodded.

"Look at his chest and shoulders too. Those are the muscles that are going to lift you and lead you around this stage for every beat of every song."

Eli was built. After all our work for the past hour trying to get the lift, his muscles sculpted nicely across his chest, shoulders and back. He didn't look puffed up like the guys from cheer who spent hours in the weight room until they resembled the Hulk. Eli was a well-trained athlete. A thoroughbred. Then another thought struck. Please don't make me feel up his chest. Now my face turned pink.

"Nothing like the bloom of youth to make my day!" Tyson grinned and rubbed his hands together.

Eli and I looked every where but at each other.

"Now that you both know the other is fully capable of executing this lift, let's try it again."

"Can I put my shirt back on?" Eli reached for it.

"No, I think you should leave it off 'til you get this right." Tyson grinned some more. I don't know who was more embarrassed, me or Eli. Tyson had a definite evil streak.

Eli shook his head in resignation while I avoided looking at him. I know I should have been totally checking him out, which I sort of was, but yikes. He stood right next to me, half naked.

Eli held my hand and placed his other firmly on my hip. As we prepared to start, I whispered, "Please don't let me fall." If I was going to put all my trust in him, I needed reassurance.

His eyes flickered from guarded to soft. "I promise," he said.

And then he winked.

That was always our sign. We used to communicate across a dance studio with looks and gestures. Whenever I was nervous or upset, he'd wink, and I knew everything would be fine. It caught me off guard that he remembered.

I jumped, he lifted, and up I went. He kept a strong grip on my left hand and a solid hold on my hip. I held the pose while he moved across the stage and we did a pretty decent release.

Oh yeah! Eli's former embarrassment about dancing shirtless must have fed his adrenaline. His knowing wink had fed mine.

Tyson whistled low. "Nothing like a little motivation." He tossed Eli his shirt, which Eli couldn't seem to put on fast enough. It left his hair ruffled as he pulled the close fitting shirt into place. I hadn't realized how good looking he'd become. I didn't know what to do with that, so I pushed it out of my mind.

Thankfully Tyson moved on, and we worked the rest of the number, including more tricky, but awesome lifts. Tyson kept talking about this being a dance of love and passion, and told us that we needed to show it when we danced. There were a lot of close romantic moves where Eli holds me, and we're supposed to look longingly at each other.

I blocked out Tyson's words. I was not ready for that. Dancing together I could handle, and I thought we did a pretty good job managing to do the lifts together, but acting romantic was hitting too close. The guy didn't want to hang out with me, how was I supposed to pretend he wanted to kiss me.

Pretending to be in love would be too dang embarrassing. The way Eli acted around me was so confusing and I couldn't begin to figure out what he was thinking. Ignoring whatever emotions I was having about him seemed the best way to go.

As Eli and I practiced the number, we faked the romantic emotions and never actually looked in each other's eyes. I figured we'd save that for the show, but definitely not now!

Tyson let it slide. Thank God. I could only deal with so much in one day. But then I knew something was up, because Tyson kept biting the inside of his cheek, the way some people do when they are trying hold something back, like a laugh, which is exactly what he was doing.

"You want to share with the rest of the class what's so funny?" Eli asked.

Tyson folded his arms across his chest and grinned. "I'm just trying to figure out how to break this to you."

"You already made Eli dance with his shirt off. What could be worse?" Big mistake. I never should have opened my mouth.

"It's actually not worse, depending how you look at it." He started to chuckle then caught himself.

"Well, what?" Eli asked.

Tyson tried to keep a straight face, and bit the inside of his cheek again. "You kiss."

Eli and I looked at each other, then snapped our heads away at whiplash speed.

"That's it. You kiss. The dance ends with a kiss." He looked from one of us to the other and chewed on his cheek again.

Oh shit. I didn't think anything could possibly be worse than falling over not one, but two guys, discussing my weight or being forced to feel up my former best friend's biceps? But a kiss!

A huge silence filled the theatre. Bigger than an elephant in the room. Bigger than a monster truck. Kind of like if a giant shark tank from Sea World sat on the stage between us.

The only time Eli and I had ever kissed was the day I quit dance and pushed him out of my life.

Not good. I sighed. But this was theatre. It wasn't real life. So we had to do a stage kiss. Awkward, but it meant nothing. If Eli could man up to plant one on me, I could meet him halfway.

"No problem," Eli said, as if he'd only been asked to do a triple time step, but his jaw was set and his arms were crossed tight over what I now knew were rock hard pecs.

Shit. He better not even think about tongue action!

"Great. Then let's get on with it," Tyson said, still grinning.

Now? Didn't I get a chance to shower and brush my teeth first? Or at least get some gum.

"You just finished your last move. Eli, take her face gently in your hands, lean in and kiss her." Tyson said it like he had just asked us to shake hands.

We looked at each other, both pretending it was no big deal, but clearly neither of us was hyped about the kiss.

"Any time now." Tyson chimed.

Eli shot him an evil look and then turned back to me. I pretended I didn't have a care in the world and avoided meeting Eli's eye as long as possible.

He stepped closer, bursting my personal space bubble. He took a bracing breath, slid one hand past my neck. Eli's fingers splayed through my hair and cupped my jawline. His other hand brushed past my chin, and his thumb touched my cheek. He held me. Our eyes met.

Holy crap!

Then he pulled away.

I didn't know if I should be relieved or mad.

Tyson broke into laughter.

"What's so damn funny," Eli demanded.

"I'm sorry, that's not fair. It's just that I remember

my first stage kiss, and it was horrible, so I know what you guys are going through. I've waited a long time to watch someone else suffer like I did."

I shifted from one leg to the other. Let's hurry up and get this thing done! What was I supposed to do? Tell Eli to man up or I'd plant one on him myself?

"Come on, let's just get it over with," Eli said.

"Fine," I snapped.

Before Tyson could intervene with more snarky commentary, Eli came at me like a missile on a target. I squeezed my eyes shut and we did it.

Yup.

Way awkward.

Eli's lips were tight and flat, and mine were, too. We just sort of pushed our mouths together and called it a day. Nothing soft, nothing pleasant about it.

When we were done mooshing our faces, I looked away, afraid to see the disappointment in Eli's eyes. It was the world's worst kiss. I haven't kissed much, but I'm pretty sure this one was the most horrible kiss on record. Does MTV give out worst kiss awards? It was like when I was in middle school kissing my arm for practice.

Tyson burst out laughing, which really added a nice touch to the moment. "You guys suck! I mean really suck!"

I crossed my arms, but really wanted to curl up in the fetal position under a blanket. We were trying to be civil with each other and that kiss was so embarrassing. But if we were going to stay mad at each other, that made it all the more embarrassing.

I don't know what Eli thought, because I refused to

look his direction. What happened to his first try? I would have liked to know how that one felt. He appeared to have the goods to deliver a hot kiss, but what I got sure sucked. Not that I wanted a hot kiss from him. I didn't know what I wanted from him. Yes I did. I wanted friendship.

"I'm sorry. But you guys crack me up. Have I told you two how much fun I'm having working with you?"

"Yeah, we're totally feeling the love," Eli muttered.

"Okay, seriously. Nice try." He chuckled. "No. Actually that was terrible, but at least you put it out there. You get points for that. If you want to be serious performers, you need to reveal your vulnerable sides. The audience can tell if you're just going through the motions or if you really mean it."

"Listen up, here's the best advice I can give you. Jump in the backseat of Eli's car sometime and practice. That way no one's watching and it's just the two of you. You can figure out whose nose goes this way and whose head goes that way. Have a couple of beers and go at it."

We stared at him like he was growing a horn from his forehead.

"Scratch that. I keep forgetting how old you are. No beer. Making out, okay. Beer, not okay."

I swallowed. Eli shook his head toward the floor with a smirk. "Tyson, you are insane."

"It's a tried and true method. What can I say?" Tyson said. "Some very enjoyable moments as I recall."

Eli looked at me with his hands tucked deep in his front pockets. "What do you think?"

I swallowed again. Alone with Eli. With our sole purpose to be locking lips. Déjà vu. My eyes darted from

Eli to Tyson and back again.

"Um. I have a voice lesson. I have to go." And I all but ran from the theatre. What a chicken. I drove across town to skip around the room and breathe properly for Gloria, but all I could think about was figuring out how to kiss Eli.

Chapter 16

Since Capitol High got out a little after three, I always showed up early to practice. I still needed to do everything possible to catch up.

Eli showed up early today too, but kept his distance.

"Hey guys, let's work your duets while we're waiting for everyone else," Tyson said from behind the piano.

I can't tell you how much I didn't want to sing that duet. It's like my stomach dropped out of my body. I'd only had two voice lessons so far. I didn't even know the song yet.

Eli stepped up to the piano, biting back a smirk, he glanced up past his blonde bangs with one of those, *'this oughta be good'* expressions. I guess he was still annoyed I ran out yesterday. Plus, despite our years apart he knew me well. Singing wasn't my thing. Dance, yes. Singing, no. In choir, I'd be one of the last people Ms. Fuller would give a solo to. Ever. Gloria keeps telling me I have a voice the size of a lion, but that I'm using it like a kitten. Whatever that means.

So here's the thing about Eli. He's really talented. I mean, like, amazing. He doesn't just dance, but he sings and acts too. He's been doing it since he was little. You name a show, and he's probably been in it. And the way he sings is just not fair. It's like he was born with these amazing pipes. And he knows it.

He also knows that I don't love to sing. Well, that's not true. I love to sing, but alone in the shower. Is there stage fright for singing? I have it. Choir is fine. I'm with sixty other people, but God forbid if someone could actually pick my voice out of a crowd.

I grabbed my music and lay it open on the piano. Tyson played the intro. He gave me a reassuring smile, then nodded to Eli for his entrance. Eli sang the first verse, his voice strong and pure like the deep water of a dark lake. I swear he was ten times better than the last time I heard him. It was eighth grade and his voice teacher had a concert of all her students. Eli sang last and brought down the house.

Crap. The next verse was mine. Well, sink or swim. Tyson gave me my cue, and still I was late. I sang the lines, and I was mostly on key, but it sounded breathy and weak. I wanted to crawl under the piano.

But Tyson smiled, the poor man, stuck with me pretending to be a singer. Eli, on the other hand, didn't hide his feelings. He raised his eyebrows and shook his head. After that, I didn't look at him.

The third verse we sang together. It's hard to sing and stay on beat with someone else when you don't look at them, but I just wanted it over. Eli brought out the big guns and showed off his beautiful baritone vibrato. Like we didn't already know. I swear the stronger he sang, the worse I sang.

"Good job, guys. Let's run it again, this time just the third verse. Willow, I need more from you. Get your gut behind it and give me some volume."

I knew Tyson must be disappointed, or more likely, panicked. Maybe he should recast the lead again.

We sang it again. Tyson watched me and nodded a lot in a vain effort to make me feel I was okay. The whole time I felt Eli's eyes bore into me. The rest of the cast started showing up, but Tyson still made us run it a couple more times. Instead of getting more comfortable, I was mortified as other cast members watched. They didn't even whisper to each other, they just stared at me as my voice came out breathy and flat. I wanted the floor to open up and swallow me, because there was no way to get out of this situation with dignity.

When we finished, my face was hot with humiliation. I closed my music and focused on a stain on the carpeting.

"Tyson," Eli whispered. "I don't think this is going to work."

Gee, Eli, thanks. What a slap in the face.

"It'll come. Willow, just keep up on your voice lessons, and you'll do fine," Tyson said.

I nodded, avoiding eye contact.

Tyson stood and walked away from the piano. "Five minutes and I want everyone on stage for warm ups."

"Unbelievable," Eli muttered.

My jaw quivered and my eyes welled up. I dumped my music with my stuff and hightailed to the back stage area where I could escape for a minute without an audience to ridicule me.

I hated feeling sorry for myself, but sometimes it's just too hard not to. I went past the curtain lines and sat out of sight against the cement wall of the theatre. I tried not to cry, but my teeth started to chatter like one of those wind-up toys. I huffed a few big shaky breaths to keep the tears at bay.

What did I get myself into? I heard the others find spots on stage. I huddled further in my dark corner as a big warm tear rolled down my face. I stared up into the dark of the rafters far above the stage, wishing I could escape and go home. Another teardrop slid down my face. As I brushed it away with my arm, I saw Eli standing about twenty feet away, watching, his expression unreadable.

We looked at each other across the space; that twenty feet could have been twenty miles. I clamped my jaw shut and wiped my face with my arm. Eli turned and walked the other way.

Chapter 17

After a couple minutes, I pulled myself together and joined the others. At least we were working on dance, and dance was something I could do.

Unless, of course, I didn't know the steps yet, and everyone else did.

I was soon ready to strangle Chloe. If she "tsked" one more time, whispered behind my back, or commented that I was a half beat off, I was going to deck her! The rest of the cast wasn't much better. They huddled in their little clusters and whispered. I was still an outsider.

I tried to silence them with a few well-placed glares, but it didn't help.

We ran the number again. Honest to God, I tried, but it didn't show. I had no idea what the hell I was doing. I'd only worked on this number once before, and they'd had it for three weeks. The stress of singing, crying, and knowing I was the outcast kept me from pulling my shit together.

"Cut. Start again, please," Tyson called from his post near the piano apparently unaware of the cast of bullies.

The rehearsal accompanist played the intro once again. I went back to my starting position, which, of course, was front and center. We started, and things went pretty well for about twelve bars. Then my mind went fuzzy on what came next. Passé, contract, chassé, attitude, step, pencil turn, coupé left. No, right!

Shit.

"Cut!" Tyson yelled.

Eli aimed an irritated look my direction.

"Oh my God, why the hell is she even here? She doesn't know a coupé from a jeté," one complained.

"I bet Tyson wishes he never cast her," said another. "She sucks."

"Did you hear her sing? She can't carry a tune."

"I heard they're sending her to voice lessons, but she's so bad the teacher quit."

"When is he going to kick her out?"

I refused to look and give the tormenting bastards the satisfaction of seeing my agony. Inside I seethed. Not like a teapot on the stove, but more like a commercial sized pressure cooker where the lid is clamped on and it's building up power. That was me. Trapped in a pressure cooker with no place to vent.

"Tyson?" Chloe said, "How many more times do we have to run this for her? Aren't we falling way behind?"

Outraged and humiliated, my body shook with anger. I clenched my jaw and bit back my venomous thoughts. If I spoke my mind, it would be a horrible display I knew I'd regret.

"Take five," Tyson said, distracted. Eli joined Tyson at the table.

"How'd she get the part anyway? She can't sing, and she's messing up all the dances," one of the girls said.

"I heard she fucked Tyson," Chloe announced.

I spun around and pierced Chloe with a glare so strong it should have melted the thick makeup off her zits. My hands fisted at my side, that pressure cooker reaching explosion level.

"What?" she acted all innocent. Some gasped at her nerve.

Instead of slamming my fist in her face and gouging her eyes like I wanted to, I gave up. Enough already. I could take no more. So I marched my lousy dancer self down the steps. Tyson and Eli glanced up, like something important just happened and they'd missed it.

Someone's water bottle lay on the floor. I kicked it so hard it slammed against an auditorium seat, split and sprayed water.

"Where are you going?" Tyson asked.

"Outside." I kept walking.

"Why?" he asked, confused.

"I'm gonna try to get run over by a car." I stormed past.

"She's kidding, right?" Tyson turned to Eli.

"Bye bye," someone on stage said. The peanut gallery on stage snickered.

Assholes.

The air in the auditorium suffocated me. I needed to escape its smothering effects, so I shoved through the doors to the hallway that led to the parking lot. Halfway down the hall, who should I run into but the whole damn cheer squad.

"Hey guys, look who's here. It's twinkle toes the dancer," Marcus said stepping in my path.

"What's wrong, Willow, you look upset. Isn't the ballerina thing working out?" Rick taunted. Jilly jabbed him in the ribs. Marcus blocked my way, so I bulldozed by.

Screw 'em.

I knew they were still ticked that I quit cheer, but grow up already and get over it!

I slammed out of the school, walked through the parking lot and just kept going. I didn't know where, but I had to get away from everyone and all their shit. I aimed for the lake and stormed that direction. After crossing the road, and trudging through snow, I found a bench that overlooked frozen Lake Monona. Numb with rage, I sat. I didn't know how to cope anymore. Everything was going wrong. I'd given it every ounce of effort I had, and it wasn't working. What more could I do? No one was happy. Not Eli, not Jilly, not the cast, not the director, and certainly not me.

I don't know how long I stared out at the winter night, trying to swallow down the pain. Lights twinkled from homes across the lake. I gazed transfixed at their starry glow and glazed over.

"Willow!" It sounded faraway and muffled, like it was coming from underwater.

"Willow!" Louder this time.

I snapped out of my trance-like-state enough to glance back and spy Eli in his Jeep at the side of the road. What the hell did he want? I ignored him.

A minute later, he trudged up, hands deep in his coat pockets, his breath coming out in white frosty puffs.

"What are you doing out here?"

"Escaping hell. Why are you here?"

"I was driving around trying to find you. Someone said you walked outside. Come on, let's go. It's freezing out here." He bounced up and down to stay warm. "Aren't you cold?"

"No. Actually I don't feel anything."

And I really didn't. Even though I wore only a t-shirt and dance pants and sat on a frozen bench surrounded by snow.

Eli sat down next to me. "Ignore them, they're just pissed you got the lead. They'll get over it."

This was the most Eli had talked to me since the show started. "Yeah, when pigs fly."

"It's not so bad. You can take it."

I looked at him. "They hate me! The cast hates me! The cheer squad hates me. And you. Well you barely tolerate me." He had the decency to look guilty as charged. "When did you turn into such a jerk? And by the way, I never asked for the lead. I never wanted the lead. A measly little part in the chorus is all I wanted."

"Then why did you take it?" he asked.

"Have you ever tried saying no to Tyson?"

He shook his head.

"Well I did, and see how it turned out."

"So you took the lead; now stop being such a baby." He stood up. "Come get in the Jeep and I'll take you back. If you sit out here much longer, your toes will freeze off and then you really won't be able to dance. Or do you plan on quitting this too?" he asked with a raised eyebrow.

Eli knew how to hit low and hard. "No thanks. I'd rather walk." I got up and stomped away.

"In that case I'll give you a head start so I can run you over."

I couldn't help it. I cracked a smile.

"I saw that. You almost laughed," he called after me.

So I flipped him off, and it felt really good. But then

he made a point of following me the whole way back, which made me want to slash his tires. By the time I got back into the school, my anger had cooled off enough to realize I really was cold.

"I'm gonna hit the bathroom," I said. "I'll meet you in the aud."

He nodded.

In the bathroom, I turned on hot water and ran my hands under it until the temperature reached scalding.

When I entered the auditorium, I heard Tyson talking to the cast who sat in a half circle on the stage floor all looking downcast.

"This is NOT a high school show," Tyson lectured in a tone I'd never heard from him. "This is a professional production of a Broadway-caliber show. Each one of you was selected because of your exceptional talent, which is extraordinary for your age, and I expect you to act with maturity and professionalism."

He ranted and paced in front of them, so I stayed at the back of the house.

"I see what's happening here and I don't like it. We don't have time for hissy fits and juvenile jealousy. You should all know by now that everyone in this show is replaceable. Don't push me; you won't like the result."

The man was pissed. I couldn't see even a glimmer of his normal easy-going personality.

"Willow is the female lead of this show. You need to accept that fact or find the door. Jealousy is ugly, and I won't let it infect this show. You should be helping her, not standing in her way. If she fails, you fail. I expect cooperation and teamwork from each and every one of you."

His hands on his hips, he stared them down. "Is that clear?"

"Yes," they muttered.

"I understand your childish desire to initiate the new kid, but the hazing is done. Over. I don't want to see or hear one more thing unless it's positive. But let me tell you. *Your* hell week has just begun."

Without turning around, he asked, "Willow are you ready to get back to work?"

"Yes, sir." I answered from the back, feeling more isolated than ever. They'd really hate me after getting their asses chewed.

"Then let's go." He left the stage. As I passed him, his face was serious and stressed, but he smiled quick and whispered, "Hang in there kid." So I guess we were okay.

The rest of rehearsal developed into the most quiet and intense I'd ever experienced. At least I didn't have to suffer anymore muttering or snide comments.

After practice, I swore I'd never let them catch me unprepared again. After walking home and eating dinner, I drove to Miss Ginny's and practiced alone for three hours.

Damn them all.

Chapter 18

The next day I wanted to thank Tyson for sticking up for me, so I brought in a pan of my Dad's special brownies. Not *that* kind of "special," but the kind he was allowed to send to school without getting arrested.

I plopped them on the table next to Tyson. He'd been going over notes in his binder. He looked at the brownies for a couple seconds and then at me and again back to the brownies. He considered the contents.

"Are these what I think they are?" He made this big production of crossing his arms over his chest.

"Depends. What do you think they are?" I cocked my head.

He looked closely at the brownies and back at me. "Are you trying to get kicked out too?" He arched a brow and tried to stare me down, but I wouldn't look away. I'd played this game too many times with my Dad. And won.

Eli walked up. "Are those your dad's special brownies?"

"Yup," I said.

"Oh, then they're fine." Tyson relaxed and reached for one.

"Have you met her dad?" Eli said.

"No, why?"

"He's an artist, wears a pony tail and grows his own herbs," Eli said.

I folded my arms across my chest and raised an eyebrow at Tyson.

"Oh." He pulled his hand away and eyed me again.

Eli grabbed two and took a bite. "They're awesome, try one."

Tyson looked at me again. "Nice try."

"Looks like someone has trust issues; you should work on that." I smirked.

"Hey, you had that look again. I knew to be leery," Tyson said.

"What look? I don't have a look."

"You know, that look in your eye that practically screams that you're up to something, or know something no one else does."

"I don't look like that."

"Sure you do." Tyson said. "Doesn't she?" he said to Eli.

"All the time."

I couldn't imagine what they were talking about. My mind is like a huge vacuum of random thoughts. Mostly about how to survive the stuff thrown at me every day. And I never know something no one else does.

Tyson helped himself to a brownie and took a huge bite. Eli glanced at me and hid his smile. Tyson chewed for a few seconds then looked at me, his eyes wide.

"What's in these?"

"Cayenne pepper." I grinned. "It's supposed to heighten the senses, or so I'm told."

He grabbed his water bottle and took a huge drink. "Not bad actually. I'd like to meet your dad."

We had a much better rehearsal. I enjoyed today because I got to work with Jason, the guy who plays my ex-boyfriend in the show Victor, aka the stalker. This was my first principal rehearsal with anyone other than Eli, so I hoped it meant no practicing the kiss.

Jason had brown hair cut really short and a wide mouth that's always smiling. He's kind of tall, but a really good dancer. He goes to Memorial High School on the other side of town and studies dance at the Diamond Dance Institute. He's very sweet, and nothing like his creepy character.

The show is a series of dreams by this guy Zach. His dreams start turning to reality, starting with his dream of meeting Lauren. At the beginning of the show Jason's character, Victor, is normal, but as the show progresses Lauren and Zach fall in love. Then Victor turns jealous and keeps bothering Lauren. He shows up in some of Zach's dreams and then appears in the last one and tries to kill Lauren, which is what cues Zach that she's about to die.

So Jason and I learned this cool chase scene. Then Eli and Jason had a fight scene; it's aggressive and violent with lots of kicks and punches. I especially enjoyed when Jason missed and hit Eli square in the jaw. Sorry, but it was nice to see Eli get clocked.

We blocked out all the scenes with Jason, which was great because I felt the scenes of the show fitting into place.

During a break, we sat at the front of the stage drinking water and eating more brownies.

"So how come you haven't given us the actual death scene yet?" Eli asked, his hair all ruffled up. I wanted to reach over and smooth it down, but he'd probably chew my arm off.

Tyson finished his brownie. "I'm still working out the details."

"Don't you need that figured out by now?" I asked. "I mean the show is less than three weeks away." I said.

"Don't remind me." He said. "I've got it figured out, but I'm still working through logistics with the Production Designer and union workers. I can tell you it will involve special effects."

Jason, Eli, and I shared a look of excitement.

"Do I get to shoot them?" Jason asked.

"Or how about a stabbing? Then I can die long and slow." I could picture myself taking the stab and crumpling to the floor.

"Or a hanging," Eli said with a little too much enthusiasm

I bet he'd love to see me dangling from a noose. Tyson seemed to be enjoying our guesses.

"I know, how about a poisoning? Tyson, another brownie?" I pushed the pan his direction.

"You guys aren't even close, I can tell you this much. You fall to your death from a bridge."

My breath caught, and I froze. "Really?"

"How's that work? Is there a mat on the floor?" Eli asked.

"No, that's old school. It'll all be done with lighting effects. Wait till you see it. It will be spectacular."

"Thank God! For a minute I thought I might hyperventilate," I said as my heart rate slowed.

"I want to fall too," Jason said.

"Sorry, but you do get to push her off?"

"What?" My head snapped around. "But you said it's an illusion. There's no actual fall."

"That's right. Just a fall from standing to the floor. No worries." He smiled.

"I can handle that," I said.

"Can I push her?" Eli asked.

I threw a chunk of brownie at him. He caught it in his mouth.

After I got home that night, I called Jilly again, making sure it was when I knew she could answer, but, of course, she didn't.

"Hey Jilly, how's it going? I really miss you and I hope you'll stop being mad pretty soon cuz life sucks when I can't talk to you. I did this funny thing to the director with brownies that I wanted to tell you about, so call me...please.

Chapter 19

My days were jam-packed with dancing, memorizing lines and voice lessons. They flew by. Now Gloria made me sing to a volume monitor, to help me learn how much power I needed to belt out my songs. First, she turned on music to a normal volume, and we checked the monitor. Then I sang, and we compared the difference. As usual, it sucked in the volume department. She said I have plenty of stamina and breath control from dance. Now I just need to learn to redirect it.

Gloria brought her daughter in with all her stuffed animals and made me sing to them like they were the audience. I felt like a fool, but at least they couldn't judge me. I actually felt better about the singing after that.

Any time I found an extra hour, I worked at Miss Ginny's. At home, my History book stared at me, so I threw a pillow on it. Writing a five-page paper about the political unrest during Vietnam ranked low on my to-do list; right behind making up two missed cooking days in Foods. I hate cooking. Foods class was another bad decision.

After Tyson's big blow up, the cast became uncomfortably helpful. It's like in grade school when you have a fight with someone on the playground, and the teacher makes you work together so you learn to get along. Not fun, but marginally better than before. Chloe kept her distance and her mouth shut, which made my life so much better. Eli lightened up too. Sophie and Jason were the only two I trusted to be nice all the time.

The show delivered a beating to my body. Between learning lifts, practicing the fight scenes and tripping over Eli too many times to count, my body became battered like a bruised pear.

"Let's see it again from the top," Tyson called from the front of the stage. "Five, six, seven, eight."

As a unit, we ran the combination again. Step, kick, three and four, turn, turn, leap.

Tyson pushed us through the arduous steps again and again until he liked what he saw. He snapped his long fingers, creating a strong sharp beat.

"Mike, arms lower, chin up." Tyson called as his eagle eyes caught every detail.

Snap, snap, snap, snap. His fingers kept a staccato rhythm.

"Brenna, this is not Zumba; a little less bounce please."

"Willow, shoulders down. Thank you." Tyson continued to monitor us like a drill sergeant in basic training searching for a flaw.

"Maria, focus. You keep missing the down beat."

Maria glanced up and stumbled the next step.

"And six. And seven," Tyson barked. "Step, lunge, and hit and hit."

The number ended and, out of breath, we waited for Tyson's next command.

"Liz, you're off again. Find the count."

On stage right, a couple of kids were screwing around.

"Do I hear giggles?" Tyson asked, unable to see

where it was coming from. "Jason, did you just grab McKenna's ass?"

A peal of laughter erupted. Chloe, Sophie and Troy tried to keep a straight face but failed miserably

"This number is like a big warm cup of vomit! Focus people, we have a lot of work today! Again! Five, six, seven, eight."

We ran it again, but Tyson became more frustrated than before.

"People!" he exclaimed. "Is anyone listening to the count?"

Someone in the back farted. Probably Jason since he had a huge grin and McKenna stepped away from him.

"Alright kids. Take five." Tyson left the stage dejected.

I wanted to feel bad for him, but instead was relieved for the break. Some went for a water break, while I lay on the stage staring up at the curtain pulleys and catwalks high above. When Tyson gave us five minutes, I always took full advantage of it to relax. Most of the others gathered in their tight little cliques. By laying down at the back of the stage, it put me in my own zone and I didn't have to feel ignored by the others.

"I'm telling you, he's gay," said McKenna from her cluster of friends sitting center stage.

She and Chloe were back to the debate of Tyson's sexual status. I angled my head to eavesdrop.

"No way," said Chloe. He's too damn hot to be gay," she said in a low throaty voice.

"That doesn't mean squat. He could be a total player and still bat for the other team," McKenna said.

"Most creative guys are gay," added Jason.

These guys haven't met my dad. He's the most talented and creative person I've ever known.

"I'm telling you, the guy is not gay!" said Troy, a great dancer who always wore tight tank shirts.

"Who's not gay?" Tyson's voice sounded close. I fought back a laugh from my supine position.

"Oh, ah, hi Tyson," McKenna stuttered.

I craned my neck to watch them squirm.

"No one!" said Sophie with panicked eyes, afraid Tyson would find out she was debating his sexual preference.

"We're debating if you're gay or not," Troy blurted out. The others gasped.

Tyson's eyes lit with surprise, but then his expression changed to a smirk, and he laughed. "So what's the consensus?" He didn't appear bothered.

"It's split pretty even," Chloe said, which I thought was ballsy to say to his face.

Tyson nodded. His eyes swept over the group as the rest of the cast gathered around to listen.

"I keep telling them you're straight, but they won't listen," Troy said.

"I am? And how do you know that?" Tyson challenged with a look of innocence.

Every eye on stage bounced from Tyson to Troy to see the outcome of the debate. Eli watched with open amusement.

"Because I'm gay. And I can spot gay a mile away!" Troy said with cocky pride.

"I didn't know you're gay," Sophie interrupted.

"How could you not know?" Jason said to Sophie as if she just walked off the short bus. She shrugged, still digesting this new information.

"So, Tyson, are you straight or gay?" Chloe demanded, as if she were in charge and she deserved an answer regardless of his feelings.

"And why is this so important?" He smiled, relaxed and unruffled despite their grilling. He actually seemed to enjoy the conversation.

"It's not. We were just curious," McKenna said to soften Chloe's rudeness.

"Good, because I'd hate to know my sexual preference could change our working relationship." He pinned McKenna and her posse with a friendly stare.

"Oh no, it never would!" she said, and the others bobbled agreement.

"Good to know." He turned to go.

"But you didn't tell us which way you swing!" Jason said.

"No, I didn't." Tyson grinned.

"Come on, man, you gotta tell us," Jason begged clearly bummed he hadn't gotten the goods.

"Alright, I'll tell you this much."

Everyone literally leaned in. They pretended they didn't care, but they were all dying to know!

"I'm in a committed loving relationship."

"See, I told you he's gay! He said committed relationship. That's a gay term!" McKenna said as if she won a bet.

"That doesn't mean anything. It just means he's with someone." Chloe shot her down.

Tyson watched with a goofy smirk. "Break's over! Back to work!"

A collective groan sounded out of disappointment at

not getting the dirt and knowing we had a long rehearsal ahead.

Later, after my body felt beaten to a pulp, I dragged myself out of the auditorium to the bright Ex hall when I spotted Rick.

"Rick, wait up!" I called. He didn't appear too happy to see me. Everyone on the squad had been avoiding me like the plague.

I hiked the strap of my bag higher on my shoulder and rushed over in case he tried to elude me. I could never seem to corner him or anyone else on cheer.

"We need to talk," I huffed when I caught up with him.

"Hey, Willow." His eyes wandered anywhere but at me.

"How's it going? What have you been up to?" He looked like he'd bolt like a deer in hunting season.

"Not much. I've been pretty busy." His grey eyes examined the trophy case across the hall.

"I know everyone's avoiding me because I quit cheer, and I'm sorry about that. But I could use some help with Jilly." I moved and blocked his view. More kids left the auditorium from rehearsal.

Rick turned and leaned his hand against the wall and stared at the high ceiling as if checking for water spots. "You can do whatever you want with your life." He adjusted his arrogant chin.

"Don't be this way. Can't we talk?"

"We are talking." He shrugged.

Normally, I would refuse to push so hard, but my whole life felt off balance. I needed something concrete. I needed my friends back. The show kids wouldn't accept me. My grades were in the toilet, and something was seriously wrong with my dog. Oh yeah, the whole Eli situation still sucks.

I moved into the space between him and the wall where his hand rested. "Won't you please look at me?" I let him hear the pleading part of my voice. "Don't I at least deserve that?"

He glanced at me, so much in his eyes he wouldn't reveal. Was it guilt?

"Rick, it's not your fault I fell and it's not your fault I quit cheer?" I tried to read his thoughts.

A loud squeal erupted across the hall by the aud doors. Rick and I looked over. Mike, from the show, carried McKenna piggyback.

After the group passed, I saw Eli. He stood watching me with Rick. To Eli, I'm sure it looked like Rick and I were all cozy.

"You'd rather be with them than us," Rick said, interrupting my thoughts.

"No, it's not like that." And it wasn't.

He glanced around and then leaned his round face close to my ear. "Listen, I'm really sorry I screwed up your catch, but Jilly is still pissed and there's nothing I can do about that. I gotta go." He pushed away from the wall.

So there it was. Rejected again.

"I guess I'll see you around."

"Sure. Whatever." He shrugged and ambled away.

I looked up and noticed Eli was gone. The wide hallway now void of people other than the night janitor. And me.

Alone again.

Chapter 20

"It's time to bring your performance emotions to the next level," Tyson explained. Today he wore his hip hugging jeans and a fitted black t-shirt that stretched nicely over his toned upper body. It doesn't matter if he's gay or not, he's damn fine to look at!

"You can be technically perfect and still deliver a flat performance. I want you both to think about what it is you want to accomplish in each song, lyric, and dance. The way you deliver each line or dance move needs to show that goal."

When Tyson explains things he becomes so animated. It's easy to see how passionate he is about theatre.

"Find a personal experience that fits the arc of the story you are telling. In this case, a dance. Know where the shifts in the story are, and change the tone of your performance each time you reach one." He swung his hands in the air as he spoke.

Eli and I soaked in every word of his sage advice while still managing to mostly ignore each other.

"This dance is about the love of these characters, Zach and Lauren, the challenges they face and how they are going to deal with it. Can they overcome their problems? They want to be together, but Zach's constant paranoia about Lauren's safety is threatening to ruin it all."

"Willow, Lauren wants to love Zach, but he's making it so difficult. Her heart is his, but she is losing patience and trust in him. The first beat is love and friendship, than it changes to frustration. The next beat is anger, and the dance grows aggressive. Finally, Lauren gives up and surrenders to him, but she has mixed feelings about their future." Tyson's voice grew soft and his eyes worried for the characters he had created.

"Try to think of a time in your life where you've felt these types of emotions. It can be a different experience for each beat."

Fear is the only thing I could think of. Fear of falling. Fear of Twinkie's seizures getting worse. Fear of singing in front of people.

And regret. I had plenty of that too! Regret that I hurt Eli three years ago. Regret that I was too gutless to try to crack through his steely defenses and talk about it. Regret that I hurt Jilly's feelings.

Pretty sad state to be in. Not much romantic love for me to draw from. Just fear and regret.

"What if I can't think of any?" I asked risking embarrassment.

"If nothing comes to mind, make something up that you can relate to," Tyson said. "For example, let's pretend the dance is about a juice box."

I raised an eyebrow at Eli. "Okay, we're dancing juice boxes."

"No," Tyson laughed. "Think of it this way. First beat. You are thirsty. So desperately thirsty that you can barely breathe."

Eli looked at him like he'd lost his mind. I had to agree.

"Second beat. You want a juice box. More than anything in the world, you need a juice box! Nothing else matters. If you don't find a juice box you might die. It's all-out panic." Tyson swung his hands as he spoke wide eyed. I almost believed he wanted a juice box. If only I had one to offer.

"Third beat. There's a juice box! You are saved! You will live! How do you feel? Elated? Ecstatic? I would think so. You drink the juice box. It is the most wonderful thing you've ever tasted; like nector of the gods. Show it. Final beat. You are satisfied; your thirst is quenched. Are you spent? Happy? Maybe even euphoric? If you believe it, the audience will too," he said.

"Do you follow me?"

"Sort of." But I wasn't sure that I really did. I studied Eli and thought about what Tyson said.

"She's looking at me like I'm a juice box," Eli said. "Not sure if I really care for that motivation."

Tyson gave us his megawatt smile. "You can use any situation that speaks to you to deliver this technique. It could be studying for a big exam. Panic about the exam. Taking the exam. Relief that it's over. Or maybe it's defeat because you know you failed."

"I can relate to that." I thought about my pathetic grades in History and Foods.

Frustration and anger are pretty obvious. All I have to do is think about last week when Chloe and half the cast were such assholes, and I stormed out of rehearsal. That's probably the most intense I've felt in my life.

"That's good," Tyson said. "The more real and honest the topic is for you, the more it will be true as you deliver your song or dance. Your audience will be captivated and compelled. When you dig in deep like this, you will elicit an authentic reaction from your partner."

He turned to Eli. "For Zach, the first beat is his complete and all-consuming love for Lauren."

Eli glanced my direction and huffed. It would take a Tony-winning performance for Eli to sell that one.

"Then Zach becomes over protective, obsessed with Lauren's safety," Tyson explained.

Eli shifted on his feet, and I knew how much he hated that he had to act this way with me.

"As Lauren grows frustrated, Zach deflects her anger and sidesteps her attacks with a steely determination to protect his true love. The final beat is his overwhelming relief that he has kept her safe. Got that?" Tyson said.

"Yeah, I think so." Eli nodded.

"Great, let's start this dance from the top, and I want you each to think of an experience where you've loved something more than anything. More than life itself. Something that brought you so much joy you could barely contain yourself."

I thought about a turtle sundae, and Breezy as a baby with cute chubby cheeks and huge blue eyes. Then I remembered when I first got Twinkie, Twyla back then, and took her for a walk down our street. I loved her so much, and I couldn't believe she was all mine. I could think of nothing else.

"Okay? You ready?" Tyson looked from me and back to Eli.

We nodded, and I wondered if Eli was thinking

about the time he won a first place trophy at a major dance competition with his jazz solo, or if it was the summer his parents finally gave in and let him go to a month-long summer dance workshop in Chicago.

Tyson stepped back and started the lyrical melody. The notes started dreamy and romantic. My body loved the music and moved to it perfectly, but I couldn't focus on Eli and think loving thoughts, even if the loving thoughts were about my dog.

Eli did better, except he focused over my shoulder and never actually settled his eyes on me, which was par for the course.

"Cut!" Tyson snapped off the music. "This is not going to work if you two refuse to engage with each other. This has been going on long enough." He stomped over. "Would you two stop being so damned polite to each other? You're either going at each other's throats or you're tiptoeing around. Come here."

I stepped closer, as did Eli, but he did it with a huff. Tyson took us by the arm to center stage and made us face each other standing only four feet apart.

"Look at each other," Tyson said.

Eli crossed his arms and looked away.

"Eli! Look at her!"

He reluctantly turned to face me.

"You are both gorgeous. Don't you see it? Eli, she's got the face of an angel, she smells good and has all those nice girl parts."

Eli rolled his eyes. I stuck my tongue out at him. Tyson frowned.

"Willow, look at him. He's buff, he's got that cool hair thing going on, he's got movie star good looks.

What's not to love?"

Tyson was right. I snuck a quick look and had to agree. Eli was damned hot. We just had so much baggage it was hard to see.

"You two should be in an ad for Abercrombie for Christ sake! I happen to know you guys used to spend every minute together. And now you act like you've just met. Well, jig's up. The two of you have so much chemistry, it's oozing out."

I looked at Eli in confusion. What the hell was he talking about?

"You guys can keep denying it, but it's there. You have a couple other kisses in the show, but this is the money kiss, the one that makes the ladies in the audience weep with joy, and this won't work until you two get past your crap. You need to get together and get comfortable with each other's bodies. You're dancers for pete's sake, and your bodies are instruments to perform emotion at the highest level. You touch in a lot of your dances, but it's like you don't feel. You're just going through the motions and that's gotta end." Tyson paced as he lectured us.

"A true artist will put his ego aside and see the beauty of another human being Artists take those moments, trust their partner, and show their vulnerability. You need to get together and relax with each other. Spend some time and check each other out."

I peeked at Eli. Tyson stopped pacing and faced us.

"I want you to get to know the contours of each other. Eli, get familiar with the small of her back, the curve of her neck, look at the elegance of her hands. Willow, touch his shoulders, his arms. They are the power that lift you. Look into his eyes. They hold so much untapped emotion. Meet him half way. Open up and really look at each other. Learn to find the trust in each other."

My eyes met Eli's. Tyson was right. Eli and I both knew it.

"You're right," Eli said.

"I'm sorry," I said. "We've been stuck in the past."

"We'll figure this out," Eli told Tyson.

And we would. I didn't know how we'd get past the barrier, but I knew Eli was as much of a perfectionist, as am I. We would not fail.

An hour later, as I walked down the Ex hall on my way out, Eli called out. "Willow, wait up."

I turned, a little shocked to see him approach. He looked different with his coat on and duffle over his shoulder. I'd grown used to rehearsal Eli, who only spoke to me when he had to. Now here he was out in public.

"What's up?" I pretended this was normal.

He fell in step with me. "So we've gotta fix that, you know, stuff that Tyson's freaking over."

"You mean our vulnerability and untapped emotions?"

"Yeah." He smiled sheepishly. It reminded me of the Eli I used to know.

"What did you have in mind?" I asked as we reached the doors.

"Tomorrow night. Messerschmidt Road." He pushed the door open for me.

"Huh?" I passed through, digesting his words. "Oh. OH!" I spun around.

He searched my eyes to see if I was on board. "I'll pick you up at nine."

Dumbfounded, I nodded. Messerschmidt Road. The make-out spot.

Chapter 21

Saturday night. Talk about awkward. I knew we both want to get to that magic place Tyson keeps lecturing about. It's just really hard to let your guard down when so much hurt has been passed back and forth. But we bit the bullet, and here we were in his mom's spacious Cadillac.

"Okay, so this is insane, right?" I tucked my hands between my legs for warmth.

"Yup." Eli drummed his fingers on the steering wheel and looked out over the landing strip before us.

I followed his gaze. Eli had driven us to Messerschmidt Road. I'd never been here before, but I knew a bunch of kids who had. It was a pretty spot on a hill that overlooked the airport. The runways were lit up with yellow, blue and green lights. Their reflection on the icy snow gave a festive air to the night. I shivered despite the fact I wore my wool peacoat, a thick scarf, and warm gloves.

"You cold? I can turn up the heat."

He adjusted the controls and turned on the radio, but I doubted it would help. I'd been a wreck since he set up this date. Okay, not a real date, a make-out date. No dinner, no movie, just a lip-locking, body-groping romp. Eli was determined we make our performance perfect, and we had to figure out how to sell it on stage.

I couldn't agree more. I hate to do anything halfway

when other people are involved. I don't like to let them down. I'd grown to trust and admire Tyson and I wanted to do everything in my power to make sure it was a success.

But that's easier in concept than reality. I looked out the windows. Somehow the confines of the car made sitting near Eli more intimidating. At rehearsal, a huge stage and auditorium gave us space, and even though we danced close and touched, it wasn't so dang personal.

Silence hung over us like a the lowering of a casket at a burial.

Eli gripped the steering wheel with both hands as if bracing for a root canal. "This is insane," he said. "It's not that big a deal, we can do this."

"Yeah, totally." I wished I had his confidence.

"It would help if you didn't look so scared."

"I'm not scared, I'm just nervous," I said. 'This whole 'perform on command' is a little warped. I'm just trying to get my head around it.

"Actors do it all the time. We can too."

"I know, and we will. We just have to figure out how."

"Okay, enough talking. Let's get this thing started." He turned off the engine but left the heat and the radio on. "I don't want us to asphyxiate ourselves." Eli unbuckled his seatbelt and pushed his seat back.

Oh boy! So this was it. My palms turned sweaty. Relax, I told myself. Deep breath, let the tensions go. Find your Zen place.

Eli turned toward me so serious and determined. I couldn't help but look at his mouth. His very sexy mouth. But this was Eli, and my feelings about him were so jumbled. The last time he kissed me was before freshman year outside of Miss Ginny's while waiting for my dad.

It had been a warm fall night and we'd finished a full schedule of classes. I still remembered the full moon and the fireflies floating in the air. We'd been totally relaxed, sharing a bag of cheetos.

Suddenly, he'd leaned over, wiped some crumbs from my cheek, and kissed me. I'd been so shocked, especially when our eyes met and his were filled with so much more than friendship. I'd panicked. There was no other way to say it. My best friend for practically my whole life had suddenly changed the rules.

Thank God my dad chose that moment to arrive, so I had a quick getaway. Now, more than three years later, here we were again, only this time locked in his mom's car, watching planes land, and getting ready for a repeat kiss. This time there was no running away. I chose to be here.

"All right," I answered and licked my lips. Oh, was that wrong? I shouldn't kiss him with a wet mouth. I swiped my mitten across my mouth.

We leaned forward and touched lips. It felt strange.

So this was me kissing Eli. His mouth was firm and warm. It was sort of an out-of-body experience. He leaned forward, and our noses bumped. We repositioned, and I ended up kissing the side of his mouth in a tight closed-mouth kiss. Eli reached for me, but grabbed only my thick coat and scarf. We pulled apart.

"This isn't working." He pushed at his hair, which

made it tousled in a cute sort of way.

"Nope. Felt like kissing a brother, if I had one, or a best friend." Deep down I thought his kisses would be great. I guess it was better this way.

"Well, I thought we were friends again," he said with an honesty I hadn't seen in a while.

"Are we?" It sure was hard to tell with his standoffish behavior.

"Yeah, I think so." He appeared to have just made that decision.

"Good," I said. Maybe we were finally making progress. It would be a lot easier to try to kiss now that I knew he wasn't mad.

"I think I know the problem. You've got too many clothes on. I can't even get to you."

I raised an eyebrow.

"You're wrapped up like an Eskimo. Could you lose the coat and scarf?"

"Sure." I removed my outer layer and stuffed it on the floor.

We faced each other over the front seat console and leaned in.

"Wait a minute, this thing is screwing us up." He slapped the console.

"Back seat?" I offered, not believing I actually spoke the words out loud. I sounded like such a *ho*.

"Yeah."

We both turned to crawl over. I realized my shoes might scratch the leather seats. "Shoes off?"

"Good idea," he agreed, kicking his shoes off.

At least we were working together. I slipped my shoes off and crawled over the top of the seats. I'm sure it didn't look too graceful with my butt up in the air. Eli didn't comment, he just followed me over, fell onto the back seat, and we rolled around trying to get situated. I laughed nervously. It felt cooler in the back seat, and we had a lot more space.

With one foot tucked under me I turned sideways so I could face him. He did the same. A few seconds ticked by.

"I think we need to go to Plan B. We need a little help," Eli said.

"What's that?"

Eli reached down, rifled around in a bag and pulled out a couple of bottles. "Liquid courage," he said with a grin, holding up brandy and Grape Power Aid. "It's not the greatest combination, but it's the best I could find."

I chewed the side of my lip, embarrassed at my relief. "Good idea." Drinking wasn't usually my thing, but we needed all the help we could get.

"Here, hold these." He handed over the bottles, dug through the bag and pulled out a couple of plastic tumblers with melting ice. Together we mixed our concoction like two co-conspirators. I poured the purple stuff, and he poured the brandy.

"More?" he asked holding the bottle ready.

"More," I answered.

He poured a couple more glugs of the amber liquid.

"A little more." I grinned and crinkled up my nose. "No inhibitions. If we're gonna do this, let's do it right."

Eli winked in response, and my heart did a little flip. He added more to each cup, then capped the bottle and put it away. We swirled our cups.

"Here's to going for it." Eli raised his glass.

I bumped my tumbler to his, and we drank. I shivered as the strong liquid burned. I took a breath and began to cough. I exhaled as much air as possible to cool my throat then tried to take smaller breaths so I wouldn't choke on the fumes.

"I think it needs to be mixed up a little more," I coughed.

Eli cleared his throat. "I'd say." He stuck his finger in his cup, stirred and took another sip. "Much better."

I did the same and raised my cup for another toast. "Here's to living life on the wild side."

"Here's to taking chances." We drank.

"Here's to what happens in the back seat, stays in the back seat," I said.

"I'll drink to that."

And we did.

"And no judging," I added.

"What?"

"No judging. I mean, I don't want you to judge my kissing skills. I haven't had a lot of experience in this department."

He arched an eyebrow. "You are bent, you know that?"

"I'm just saying."

"I thought you and that Rick guy were a thing."

"Yeah, but it hasn't been for very long." What a total liar I am! Girls always loved Eli. He had girls trailing after him all the time. I just couldn't admit my love life was less than awesome.

"So, are you two going out?"

"Ah, yeah. We go out with the squad all the time. Or I guess I should say we used to."

I got quiet knowing how pathetic that sounded.

"That must be really hard, having them all pissed off at you. Especially after all you did for them."

We sipped again.

"What'd I do for them?" It was more like what I did *to* them.

"You are clueless sometimes, you know that?" he said with a laugh. "They never would have gotten to Nationals last year without you, let alone won it." He leaned back and took another drink.

"How do you know about Nationals?" I asked.

"I know things," he said with a sly glance. I chose to ignore his comment.

"I would hardly say that. I'm just one cog in the wheel of that team. We worked our asses off to get there."

"Yeah, and who worked the hardest? Who did the hardest tricks and the highest flips? Who was always first to practice and last to leave? Hmm?" He knew me so well.

"How did you know I did the hardest tricks?" Eli had been pushed so far out of my life, I hadn't even thought about him much during that time, or at least I tried not to think about him. Yet he knew all about me.

"How could I not know? You guys were plastered all over the news. You performed at every possible sports event. I saw you perform during halftime of the Wisconsin Ohio college football game last fall. Your flips in the air were insane. You must have been twenty-five feet high. Plus, I spent most of my life dancing with you. You don't do anything halfway. Look at this show. You've had to catch up on weeks of missed rehearsals with almost no help. I know a lot of the girls have been giving you a hard time." His voice softened with that comment.

"That's an understatement. They hate me."

"True." He grinned.

"Thanks!"

"Well, it is true. You walked in and got the lead. They don't think you deserve it, but they're wrong."

"How's that?"

"You're better. You always were. It doesn't matter that you stopped dancing for a while. You have more talent in your little finger than they'll ever have, and you keep getting better."

What was he talking about, and why was he saying such nice things? He was wrong. I didn't have that much talent. That's why I kept working so hard. But I wouldn't turn away a rare compliment from Eli. "Thanks."

"You're welcome," he said matter of fact. "I can't imagine having to walk around with all your old friends mad at you and the cast, who should be your new friends, mad you too."

"It sucks, but I'll live." I hadn't realized how much the girls' animosity hurt. I tried to let it roll off, but after a while they had really gotten under my skin.

Silence filled the car as I took another sip and contemplated his words.

"So what happened with us?" he asked, his eyes filled with the pain of what I'd done.

I'd hurt him bad and he wanted to know why. I didn't blame him. I took a gulp from the tumbler, then gripped it like a lifeline in a turbulent sea.

"I got scared," I said softly and looked him in the

eye. All my memories of fear and regret flooded back.

"Of what?" he asked, confused.

"Of losing your friendship. That day you kissed me was so out of left field. You were my best friend in the world. I didn't want to lose that. I'd never thought of you in any other way."

I saw the hurt in his eyes and why shouldn't he be? What was wrong with me? He was totally gorgeous and the nicest guy on the planet. Girls always wanted him, but he and I had been glued at the hip, which I guess affected my perception. I just didn't see him the way they did. "Sorry, I just didn't. I trusted you. You were my everything, and then you changed the rules."

"You were afraid of losing our friendship, so you shut me out, and ended it yourself? Doesn't make a lot of sense." He looked so vulnerable and tortured.

"No it doesn't, but who says I ever made much sense?" My words slurred a bit and my head started to fuzz from the booze.

"This is true." He held up his cup in toast.

A plane roared overhead and came into view as it approached the airport. Its lights filled the windshield. We watched it land and make its way to the other end of the runway.

"So now you're in a car with me, back at square one."

"Pretty much. How did I let that happen?" We laughed at the irony.

"Only this time you have to let me kiss you." He flashed his eyes at me.

"Lucky me." I drank, my throat now numb from the booze. "So what's with Tyson and all the making out in the show?"

"He does seem a bit obsessed with it."

"Do you think he's gay? Cause why would a gay guy want all the kissing?" I asked.

"He's not gay," Eli said with certainty.

"How do you know? He's totally hot, he dresses great, and he's a dancer."

"I'm totally hot, I'm a dancer and I'm not gay." He said.

"Are you sure?" I giggled.

"Want me to prove it?" His eyes sparkled in the dim light.

"Yeah, I do." My heart began to pound.

Enjoying my buzz, I sank into the buttery soft leather seat, and lolled my head to the side. I watched Eli. I'd forgotten how good looking he was. He must be the nicest guy on the planet; and he had the greatest smile.

Eli leaned forward; his warm breath caressed my cheek. He placed his parted lips on mine. I thought maybe he forgot why we were here, but apparently not. This time it didn't feel like kissing a brother. It was all Eli. He took my face in his hands and kissed me, his moves slow and gentle. He tasted like citrus and booze. I turned my body to him. I couldn't believe I'd been so nervous.

We parted and gazed at each other. We'd figured it out. The alcohol took our inhibitions away. He took me in his arms and kissed me again. His fingers trailed up my back and into my hair, mussing it to his liking. I sighed. His other hand moved down over my hips to my lower back. I couldn't believe this was happening. I let his hands roam and had never been so turned on in my life.

"We're pretty good at this," I murmured.

"Yeah, I'd say. Still think I'm gay?" His breath tickled my neck.

"Not so much."

I played with his sun-touched hair. I'd wanted to know how it felt since we started dancing together again, but never had the nerve. Its rumpled perfection created a golden halo. With alcohol-induced bravery, I combed my fingers through the thick strands. They were silky soft.

I looked into his eyes, and he smiled with a sexy twist at the side of his mouth. Never had anything felt so perfect. I leaned down and met his lips again. I ran my hand over his shirt, feeling his solid chest. He felt firm and strong. No wonder he could lift me with such ease.

"Do you think Tyson would approve of this for a stage kiss?" he murmured in my ear, sending tingles down my back.

"Yeah, pretty sure," I breathed.

"I think we can do better."

"You think?" I turned my head to expose my neck.

"Only if you're game," he whispered and nuzzled. Warm trills danced upon my skin.

"You jump, I jump," I said and moved my hand from his lean hip, to his waist and the bend of his back.

Without another word, he leaned back on the seat and pulled me with. My body rested on top of him, connecting our bodies from hip to breast. I sighed. His right leg rested against the back seat. His other foot stayed on the floor. Between the angle of the seat and our position, my body nestled close to his.

My body flexed against him, revealing a hunger I'd never known before.

I looked at his face in the moonlit backseat. Deep pools of desire met mine. I leaned forward and kissed him; my tongue peeked out and he welcomed it.

His hands roamed my back and traveled low over my hips. I couldn't get enough of him. His touch, his taste. I felt like I'd been living in a cocoon and was now transforming and finally coming out of my chrysalis to a brand new world. Heaven, better than heaven.

Eli's hands caressed my bottom, my thighs and everywhere. I was afraid to breathe and ruin the moment. We lost ourselves in hot hungry kisses that explored our new connection. His kisses tasted so good I didn't want it to end. I never knew making out could be so addictive. So we kept going.

Chapter 22

I woke up warm and a little sweaty on my front side, but really cold on my back and legs. When I tried to sit up I couldn't and realized I was draped on top of Eli. The car felt very cold and quiet. I didn't know how long we'd been asleep. The car windows had frosted over on the inside and it was eerily quiet. Eli's arm wrapped over my back. I strained to peek at the clock on the dash; the clock was dark. I fumbled to grab the strap of my bag and pulled it into the back seat. I dug through to the bottom as I still lay on Eli, he moved and grumbled. I pulled out my phone.

3:12 am!

"Eli! Wake up, we fell asleep!"

He blinked his eyes open. "What?"

"We fell asleep! It's after three!" I tried to scramble off of him, but gravity and the angle made it difficult.

"Oh, shit!" He helped push me off and sat up. "We've gotta go! My dad will kill me if he finds out I was out this late."

Eli clambered over the seat, plopped into the driver's seat, and slipped his shoes on.

"We are in so much trouble." I crawled over after him and slid into my coat. I had never stayed out past one before, and that was with my parents' blessing.

"Maybe he won't hear me come in." Eli rubbed his face with both hands to shake the sleep out. He grabbed the keys, still in the ignition, and turned.

The engine turned over slowly once, ert.

Then slower the second time, errt.

And ground to a stop.

"No, no, no!" He looked at me in panic and tried again. One slow errrt, not even a complete turn of the engine and it stopped.

Dead.

He pounded the steering wheel. "My dad is gonna go ballistic."

I bit at my lower lip. Eli's dad had a temper. He'd always seemed to be barking orders at Eli whenever I'd been at his house. It'd always made me appreciate my own dad more. "What do we do?"

"We've gotta get a jump. The battery's dead."

I could see his thoughts darting around trying to figure out who to call.

He studied me for a moment. "Can we call your dad?"

"What?" I did not want my dad knowing about this night. What was I supposed to say we were doing? Messerschmidt Road? That was pretty self-explanatory.

"Your dad's cool, he won't get mad." Eli looked hopeful.

I have the most laid-back parents on the planet, but making them aware I'd been drinking and rolling around the backseat with Eli was the last thing I wanted to share. "I guess." God I did not want to make that call. "Can't we call someone from the cast? Maybe Jason?"

"We'd be asking him to sneak out of the house and hope he didn't get caught. I really don't want to get anyone else in trouble.

"You're right. I'll call." I picked up my phone and began to press the numbers. "Oh no," I stopped. "The car is in the shop. He can't come get us, he has no car."

"I am a dead man." He pushed his hands through his hair.

"There's gotta be someone." We had to figure out a solution and fast. The car was freezing. I could carve our names in the ice crystals on the inside of the windshield, but I doubt his mom would appreciate it.

"Well, there might be one person," Eli said.

"Who?"

"Tyson."

I considered it and giggled, apparently still a little drunk. "You're right. It's because of him we're here in the first place."

Eli smiled in agreement.

"Do you think he'll be mad? Would he kick us out of the show?" I really wanted to do the show.

"Yeah, he'll probably be mad, but how can he kick us out? Without two leads, he's screwed."

"I don't know, he kicked Jessica out for getting him high on pot brownies."

"That was the school's policy. I don't know if Tyson would have kicked her out. I don't really see any other option. Should I make the call?" Eli waited for my decision.

"What the heck." I held my fist up, and he bumped it.

Eli reached for his phone and brought up the number, but before pressing send he laughed. "I can't believe we're doing this. I'm gonna put it on speaker." He pressed send.

With my heart in my throat, I covered my mouth with my hands. Tyson was going to kill us. It rang three times. We shared a worried look. What if he didn't answer?

"Hello?" Tyson's groggy voice answered.

We looked at each other in panic.

"Hello?" Tyson sounded irritated.

I motioned at Eli to speak.

"Ah, Tyson?" Eli stuttered.

"Who is this?" Tyson paused. "Eli? Is that you?"

"Yeah, sorry to wake you." He looked at me. I held back a giggle.

"What time is it? Hang on a minute."

We heard fumbling on his end.

"Christ, Eli, its after three a.m., why are you calling? What's wrong?"

"Nothing's wrong. I need a favor. Actually, Willow and I need a favor."

I glared at him. Great, he had to drag me into it.

"Fine, anything you want, but tomorrow. Go to bed Eli, I'll talk to you tomorrow, we've got a big day. Good night."

"Wait!" Eli said.

"What?"

"Willow and I are stranded. The car battery is dead and we need a jump. Willow's dad doesn't have a car right now and my dad, well, you haven't met him, but if he finds out about this, I'll be grounded 'til graduation."

We huddled over the phone and waited. I could picture Tyson coming fully conscious.

"Fine. I'm up. Where are you?"

Eli looked at me. I pinched my lips shut to keep

from laughing.

"Messerschmidt Road."

"What are you doing on Messerschmidt...never mind. I'm on my way."

Tyson clicked off. Eli leaned his head back against the seat, and we burst into laughter.

A while later, the flash of headlights illuminated the parking lot as Tyson pulled in next to us. We looked at each other for a brace of courage then got out of the car into the frigid night. Tyson stepped out of a black SUV wearing jeans, a heavy black leather coat and a cool scarf tucked around his neck. He even looked great in the middle of the night.

Tyson aimed a stern glare at us. I guess it was supposed to scare us. Instead, we just grinned.

Tyson shook his head. "Messerschmidt Road? I thought they closed this place down."

"Hey, you told us to go out and...figure it out," Eli said.

Tyson sighed, since he couldn't argue with Eli's logic.

"Alright, let's get this over with." He walked past Eli to open the back of the SUV. "I've got cables right here."

Tyson paused then turned back. He leaned close and sniffed. "Have you two been drinking?"

Suddenly it was all very funny. I tried to stifle a giggle, but failed. Eli nodded with a shit-eating grin.

Tyson threw his hands in the air. "You two are killing me." He opened the front door of the car looking through the darkness. "Where is it?"

"What?" Eli said.

"The booze."

"Oh. It's in the back, driver's side floor."

Eli and I huddled close in the freezing air. Tyson opened the back door, pulled out the bottles of brandy and purple stuff.

"This is what you're drinking?"

We nodded.

"Kids today. Don't even know how to drink." He grabbed the bag and shoved the mostly empty bottles in and then rifled around and found the tumblers. Before he closed the door, he paused and looked at the large backseat then back at us, taking in our messed up hair. He shook his head. "You're killing me."

Tyson opened the back door of the SUV. "Get in," he said, defeated.

"We've gotta jump the car. I can't leave it here," Eli said.

"You're not driving intoxicated. That would go over real well with the school board. I can't believe I've brought in the biggest thing to happen in Madison theatre history; and what happens? My first leading lady makes pot brownies. Then my dream team goes out drinking and almost ends up wrapped around a telephone pole. Not going to happen. Get in."

I scrambled in first, thankful for the warm interior. Eli climbed in after me.

"Don't even think about vomiting." Tyson swung the door closed behind us.

"Did you notice how his hair looks like he styled it before he came? I told you, he's gay!" I said.

"No way. I have perfect gay-dar. The dude is straight. He just looks gay."

"Oh my god!" Tyson said climbing into the front seat. "That's the burning topic on your minds? Not, gee, will my parents find out, will the school suspend me, or will my director cut me from the show!"

"You can't cut us man, no one could learn our parts in time," Eli said.

"You got me there, but I have the power to put you in some very ugly costumes. A certain piñata costume comes to mind."

"Uh oh!" I said. "I'm sorry Tyson. We didn't mean to hurt your feelings."

"My feelings are fine. It's my blood pressure that you two are screwing with. Now listen up," he said as he backed out and left our magical make out scene behind.

"First I'll drop Willow off, then you Eli. Next I will rudely call and drag a buddy of mine out of bed so he and I can get your parent's car and leave it in your driveway. I'll put the keys in the mailbox. You can come up with a story for your parents about why it's in the driveway and not the garage." He looked at us in the rearview mirror. "Any questions?"

"Nope," we answered.

"Good. I recommend you drink two glasses of water when you get home and take some aspirin before you pass out in bed."

Tyson shook his head.

"And because you've disrupted my sleep, we will start rehearsal at ten instead of eight." He turned to look at us. "You're killing me, did I mention that?"

Chapter 23

The next morning, or I guess about six hours later, I stood on stage about to pass out when Eli walked in twenty minutes late.

"Nice of you to join us Eli, what happened? Car trouble?" Tyson needled in a none-too-friendly way.

"Yeah, something like that," Eli groaned.

"You missed warm ups, but you're just in time for the chase scene."

I knew right then I was gonna die. The chase scene is the hardest, most tiring number in the show. It's super physical, and we're always exhausted when we're done with it, and that's when I'm NOT hung over.

Eli trudged on stage to his place a few feet from me. "Hey," he said.

"Hey," I moaned back. Under normal circumstances I would have felt some emotion about seeing the guy I spent last night groping and making out with, but between my head throbbing and trying to fight off the need to hurl, embarrassment didn't exist.

"Anytime you're ready Eli," Tyson called loudly from down front.

Eli said his first line and the scene took off from there. Tyson never stopped us to correct anything, though I really wished he would have, so that we could have stopped to catch our breath. By the time the scene ended, Eli looked grey, and my weak body felt like a rubber chicken. I could barely breathe through the Sahara Desert of my throat.

"Willow, Eli, I'd like to see you. The rest of you get ready for the night club scene."

Thank God we didn't have to run the chase scene again. Once just about killed me. We dragged our pathetic carcasses down to Tyson.

"You know he made us do that number to get back at us," Eli said, wiping sweat from his brow.

"Yeah, it worked too," I said.

We approached Tyson who looked showered and refreshed. No sign of any effects from our middle-of-the night rendezvous. He looked at us with disappointment.

"That sucked." He stated the obvious.

"Sorry," I muttered.

Eli grunted.

"Here." He handed each of us a bottle of water. "Drink this. All of it! And have either one of you eaten anything yet today?"

I shook my head no, which made me a little dizzy.

"No," Eli muttered.

He tossed a bag of pretzels at Eli, who missed the catch and had to pick them up off the floor.

"Aspirin?" he asked.

"Yes please," I said. He handed me the bottle.

"Now go run lines in the back," he said, which was code for, "get your shit together." "You have twenty minutes and then I expect hard work and concentration for the rest of the day."

We nodded and slunk into the back corner of the aud to recover and try to create a miracle.

I slid down the wall to the floor. "I want to die."

"I'm pretty sure I already did, and today is my hell," Eli said with his head in his hands.

"Did your parents find out? Did you get the car back in the garage?"

"I got it put away in time, but they found out anyway."

"What happened?" I unscrewed the top of my water bottle.

"When I threw up in the bathroom, I wasn't too good at hitting the toilet. My mom threw a fit about the grape colored stains on her white carpeting. Who the hell puts carpet in a bathroom?"

"Oh no, are they gonna make you pay for it?"

"You can bet I'll pay, but not with cash. I'll pay and pay and pay."

"That sucks." I took a long drink of water.

We spent the rest of the day running dance numbers and hydrating. I swear Tyson brought a case of water bottles to rehearsal. Thank god. After our lunch break my headache and gut pains lessened just enough so that I felt human again.

Finally, at four o'clock, Tyson dismissed the cast. Eli collapsed on the floor; I joined him.

"I have to give you two credit. You delivered today. It was nice to see you gut it out. Now go home and rest up," Tyson said lounging in a cushioned auditorium seat.

Eli turned his head my direction. "You know, I think this confirms Tyson's straight."

"What does?" I asked. Tyson shook his head and laughed.

"A gay guy wouldn't punish us like this. He'd bring

us breakfast and have us put our feet up."

"I gave you pretzels. That's got to be good for something."

"I wish I could go home and relax, but I've got a lesson with Gloria in an hour on the other side of town," I groaned.

"I didn't realize you had voice today. I would have lightened up a little." He laughed, but did look a little sorry.

"*Now* you tell me," I said. "I don't like you very much right now."

"That's okay. I didn't like you very much last night." Tyson laughed. "At least Eli gets a reprieve."

"Hardly. Hillary and the Donald are making me go to some uptight fundraiser for the Republican Party." He lay with his arm over his face.

Tyson looked confused. "Who are Hillary and the Donald?"

"Eli's parents. They're clones of the real deal."

"Really? Lucky you." Tyson stood up, stretched his arms and yawned. "Well, I guess you better get moving. I think I'll go home, lie on the couch, and watch some hoops."

"I hate you," Eli groaned.

"I know. Isn't it great?" Tyson grinned.

And to add insult to injury, when I got to Gloria's, she said I needed an audience. So eight of her daughter's little friends sat on a blanket waiting for me to perform.

You can't imagine how stupid I felt trying to belt out songs to a bunch of first graders. But the thing is, it helped. They sat there all wide eyed as if I was the next

Selena Gomez or whoever the kids idolize these days. Obviously, they didn't know jack about a quality voice, but their cute little applause and bouncy enthusiasm boosted my confidence. Maybe I'd conquer this singing thing yet...

Chapter 24

The next night, I had a little free time after rehearsal. Since Mom had the whole week off, we finally got a chance to hang out and catch up. Mom loves scented candles and had them lit all over the living room and had turned off the lights. It felt like Christmas.

"So how are things going with Jilly?" Mom asked, as she worked on her latest hobby, crocheting. She started making a dish cloth, and when she didn't stop, it became a baby blanket. Now she had an odd-shaped afghan.

"Bad. She still won't talk to me."

"I'm sorry."

"I wish she would hurry up and get over it. That girl knows how to hold a grudge."

"Jilly is a very loyal friend. Right now, I'd guess she feels you broke that loyalty, and she's licking her wounds. Give her time; I'm sure she'll come around."

"I hope so." But I wasn't so sure. I had a track record of hurting my friends and they didn't just shake it off and come knocking on my door to hang out.

"You haven't told me much about the show. Do I get to know, or is it supposed to be a surprise?" Mom asked.

"No, it's not a secret. It's actually really cool. It's basically about a guy whose dreams become reality."

"Oh, like that show about the guy with the newspaper that printed the future news?"

"No, it's..."

"The guy in that show was so cute. Who was he?" She looked off into space trying to figure it out.

"I don't know, Mom."

"Darn, I wish I could remember."

I snapped my finger to bring her back to reality. "Mom! Focus!" Twinkie heard the snap and jumped up on the couch between us. I pulled the afghan over her, and she snuggled in.

"Sorry hon'."

"It's okay. Let me tell you about the show. It's kind of complicated. The show is about this guy, Zach."

"Who is played by Eli," she said.

"Right. Well, Zach has all these dreams about this girl, Lauren."

"You," she confirmed

"Yup. He first sees her in a dream and then meets her in person, but then he has a dream where she almost dies."

"So you get to die?"

"Maybe. But that's not the point. Zach…"

"Eli," she interrupted

"Right."

Mom's face turned tender. "So how is Eli?"

"Mom, not now."

"Sorry."

"So Zach has these dreams, which are really cool, because, face it, dreams are always so bizarre. Anyway, each dream is in a different era or style, so we get do dances and wear costumes from that time."

"But you die each time he dreams."

"No, I never said that. But Lauren's ex boyfriend, Victor, is a stalker. So when Zach is awake, he's trying to save Lauren from Victor. So early on, she falls in love with Zach, hence the dance of love."

"Sexy dress?" she asked.

"Don't know yet, but probably. Stop interrupting." My mom is the greatest, but I think she's a little A.D.D.

"Sorry."

"No problem. Later, Zach starts to drive Lauren crazy, because he's always trying to protect her. Eventually she gets really mad, because she thinks Zach's paranoid about Victor. They have a huge fight. Very fun. I get to be vicious. I jump on Zach's back and attack him." It's one of my favorite scenes. How often does a girl get to beat on a guy?

"I always liked Eli. How is he?" She set her crocheting down for a second. Mom loved Eli and could never understand why our friendship ended. I really didn't want to tackle the whole Eli subject. My feelings about him were a huge jumble.

"He's fine. Now back to our story. So we fight, and he throws me off, and it's very dramatic." I talked with my hands.

"You like this scene?"

"Yup, one of my favorites."

"Is this scene why you're covered with bruises?"

"It's one of them. Hip hop is worse. We do tons of flipping around and lifts."

"I don't know if I like Hip Hop."

"You'll like this. It's awesome."

"Why will I like it?"

"Because Tyson Scott choreographed it and he is a genius. Wait until you meet him."

"Is he cute?" She leaned forward and smiled.

"Oh my god! You are going to die, Mom. He is so hot!"

"Your dad used to be hot," she said with longing in her eyes.

"Eww, stop it."

"Sounds like you're crushing on your director," she teased.

"No. Of course, not! But he's so incredibly fun and nice and he says I remind him of his younger sister. Plus, he might be gay." What a shame.

"What do you mean he might be? Either he is or he isn't." She started to crochet again, stretching her yarn out across her lap.

"That's just it, he won't tell!"

"You asked him!? Does it matter to you?" Mom raised an eyebrow.

"No, I didn't ask, and of course it doesn't matter. It would just be more fun to know he's an eligible straight guy."

"All right. I guess I get that."

"So do you want to know how the show ends?"

"Absolutely!"

"Zach has a final dream. He rushes to find Lauren just as stalker Victor is about to kill her."

"Gee, that's fun," she said with sarcasm.

"Then, Zach is so upset, because he can't imagine life without her, that he kills himself too!"

"That is horrible." She set her project down. "What a depressing show! They both die. I don't think I want to go see it."

"Mom, you have to. I'm in it! And it's really not depressing. Les Mis is depressing, everyone dies. This is only a little bit depressing. BUT..." I paused for effect and spoke with a mysterious voice. "...do they really die?"

"They don't die?" She sat forward.

"I didn't say that." I tilted my head to the side.

"So what happens?"

I shrugged.

"You have to tell me. They live because it was a dream? Or they escape? Or it was all a figment of Freud's imagination? What?" She tickled my side.

"I'm not telling. You'll have to come and see the show."

"You're cruel." She poked my side with her crochet hook.

"I know. I can finally get back at you for feeding me soymilk and wheat germ all these years. Now you have to come see it."

"I still don't know if I want to. I heard the girl who plays Lauren is really mean."

"No, the girl who plays Lauren is really exhausted." I laid my head against the couch back. "Mom, it's so much fun. I can't believe how lucky I am. Other than the kids who don't want me there, it's perfect, and that's getting better too."

"I'm sorry we're leaving for Grandma's right as you're going into the last couple of rehearsal weeks. I wish Breezy's school break matched up with yours, so you could join us."

"That's okay. It's been planned forever and you need to go. She's been looking forward to it all winter. Plus, I'll be gone most of the time anyway. I'm just worried about Twinkie being alone so much." I reached under the blanket to pet her.

"She's doing much better with her new meds. She sleeps all the time these days. I don't think it'll be a problem. Plus, Mr. Walters said he can let her out a couple of times during the day. That way you don't have to come home early. Are you sure you're okay staying alone?"

"Are you kidding? I'm seventeen. I can handle it. So you gonna stock the cupboards with junk food for me? I'm a growing girl. Pleeease." I said with a cheesy smile and batted my eyelashes.

"Yeah, you'll be a growing girl if you eat all that garbage. I've got some frozen meals put together for you. There's a Tofurkey bean casserole, curried pesto zucchini and some roasted eggplant."

"You're mean."

"I love it when you say that." She leaned over and hugged me. "I'll leave you extra money for take-out, but make good choices!"

"You're the best. I love you."

"You're easy."

"Don't I know it," I said under my breath. I couldn't help but remember having my body draped on top of Eli as we made out last night.

Chapter 25

On Thursday, Tyson decided to push our buttons a bit and make us do the dreaded love scene dream sequence.

"You two are looking well today," Tyson said in his chipper voice. "Glad to see you've recovered from your hangover hell."

I gave him an annoyed smirk and lifted my chin. "Gee, thanks."

"Let's see if the fruits of your inebriated parking party paid off." Tyson's devilish eyes bounced from me to Eli and back again. My face warmed. I glanced sideways at Eli and met his eyes. We both looked away.

"You've gotta put it out there sometime. Might as well be today." He grinned.

"Fine. We'll do it." Eli nodded.

"Great. Let's get this show started!" Tyson rubbed his hands together and then left the stage to start the music.

Eli and I moved to our starting positions. "You ready to do this thing?" he asked so sincerely I almost forgot we'd ever been estranged. After all these weeks of strain, I finally felt kind of normal around him.

"You jump, I jump." I took a deep calming breath and focused on his eyes.

"I want to see some passion. No shortcuts. If you're not convincing in this scene, the audience won't believe the rest of it," Tyson hollered from below. "Oh, don't forget the kiss at the end."

I refused to look at Tyson. He loved to watch us squirm, and I refused to give him the pleasure.

The music began. The number was set to a beautiful ballad and the dance was incredibly romantic. If we did it right.

And we did.

I let the rest of the world go and pretended Eli was the sexiest guy on the planet, and I wanted him. He met me at every step. He held my face and gave a steamy gaze. We spun away. Each lift was slow, sultry, and seamless. As natural as water flowing over rocks. Thoughts of Saturday night fueled the energy. It was as if we were in the backseat discovering each other all over again as he trailed his fingers down my face then from my shoulder to finger tips. My hand cupped his chin, and he lifted me smooth as silk into another lift.

As the music ended, Eli took me in his arms, gazed into my eyes and the depths of my soul. His lips parted, and we kissed. My skin tingled as his warm breath swirled across my cheek. He caressed my jaw with his thumb. I kissed him back, my palm against his chest. His heart pounded so hard I nearly heard it.

When we pulled away and faced Tyson, I wanted to touch my mouth, but instead pressed my lips together to somehow savor the memory. My skin turned cool when Eli let go of me.

Tyson's jaw dropped open. Surprise and awe covered his face. He closed his mouth and swallowed.

"Well?" Eli's voice sounded completely void of the passion we'd just shared.

"That'll work." Tyson nodded, his eyes still wide.

Eli smiled and held out his fist. I bumped it, still recovering from the passionate dance and kiss. Eli didn't seem too affected. I had to remind myself that we were, after all, just acting.

Before heading home I decided to try to call Jilly again. I really wanted to wish her luck at sectionals and tell her about Eli and rehearsal and how confused things were getting. Under normal circumstances I knew she'd love to hear about it and tell me what to do, but we were still on the outs and I didn't know how to fix it. I resorted to texting her, since she didn't seem to want to hear my voice.

"Hey Jilly, good luck at Sectionals. I know you'll be awesome. With you flying they can't go wrong. Call me. I have tons to tell you."

* * *

A few days later, as I pulled up in front of Gloria's house, I saw her waving from her car. I parked, and then hopped in with her.

Gloria and I had developed a love/hate relationship. She loved to insist my voice would be ready by opening night and that I'd be able to match Eli in our duet, and I hated to hear about, think about it or talk about it.

We were fighting a stubborn battle of wills. I clung to my lack of natural talent, and she insisted all I lacked was self confidence and proper breath support.

Bullshit.

"Where we going?" I asked naively. I should have known better than to underestimate her.

"Did you warm up to the tape I gave you on your drive here?"

"Yeah." I buckled my seatbelt.

"Great. We're on our way to the Middleton Nursing Home for your first official vocal performance." My evil master had the gall to smile as she pulled away from the safety of my getaway car.

"What? We can't do that!" My stomach clenched into a tight ball.

"Why not?"

"First off, you didn't tell me!" She couldn't be serious, could she?

"I just did," Gloria said.

"But I'm not prepared. I'm not ready!"

"You're not ready to perform center stage at the Overture Center, but you are perfectly prepared for the senior residents at a nursing home."

My palms began to sweat and my eyes searched the car for an eject button.

Gloria placed her hand on my arm. "You'll be just fine. These people are very old and most are hard of hearing. They'll either ignore you or be tickled silly to see a young person."

It turned out she was right. The nursing home residents were lined up in their wheelchairs or seated with their walkers nearby. Many dozed or didn't seem with-it enough to know what was going on. A few others smiled at me with cute old wrinkled faces.

The director of the home introduced me. "This evening we are excited to have Willow Thomas here to sing a couple songs for you. She will be performing in a new musical at the Overture Center in a couple weeks."

The director clapped her hands and a few residents joined in. An old man snored loudly.

I grimaced and looked to Gloria who sat behind the piano and began the intro. I locked eyes with her to gain every ounce of strength I could. She mouthed the word "breathe." I took a last fortifying breath and sang. It wasn't great, but it wasn't horrible. Most of the patients looked bored, but some nodded their heads to the beat. One little old lady clapped offbeat the whole time.

Afterward, I thanked them, grabbed my coat and high-tailed it out before Gloria could make me sing any more.

"You did a nice job in there," she said.

"You think so?" I didn't, but her support meant the world to me.

"Absolutely. You see how nervous you were at the start, and by the end your knee knocking was barely visible."

"You're right. I guess that was a good exercise." Despite my nerves, a glimmer of hope eked through.

"However, you need to concentrate on your breath support. You'll feel stronger and it will help you hit the high notes with more confidence and power."

Of course, she couldn't let me have that small glimmer of joy.

Chapter 26

My drive home from Gloria's was slow. All day a steady fall of snow came down and the cars on the highway crawled along. A thick blanket of snow turned the neighborhood into an old-fashioned Christmas card. At least three inches of snow had accumulated on the streets and sidewalks. The forecast predicted more overnight. Mom, Dad and Breezy left for Vermont yesterday to see Grandma, so that meant I'd be the one shoveling tomorrow morning.

As soon as I stepped out of the car, a swirl of snow surrounded me. My shoes and the bottom of my jeans were immediately coated. Another bad day to wear flats.

Anxious to check on Twinkie I rushed up the slippery porch steps. Once inside, I noticed the coat rack lay on the floor. In the hall, a tall floor vase lay toppled with the dried curly willow stems splayed across the floor.

At first I thought someone had broken in, but then I noticed the money Mom and Dad left for me on the coffee table next to my iPod. A burglar wouldn't ignore eighty dollars. Just in case, I grabbed an umbrella for self defense. I figured I was safe, but you never know. Better safe than attacked by a criminal hiding in the closet.

"Twinkie?" I called out in my loudest whisper.
Nothing.
I walked through the living room with my spoked

weapon.

No dog.

I checked the dining room and kitchen.

No dog.

Now I was getting more worried about Twinkie than an attacker. Was she okay? Was I going to find her dead?

"Here girl...Where are you?" I called, but no sound of paws padded my way. I checked the pantry and was about to go upstairs when I heard a muffled sound coming from the bathroom. Inside the small dark room I found Twinkie wedged between the toilet and the wall with her tail tucked down and her whole body shivering like she had a bad fever.

I flipped on the light and crouched next to her. "Hey girl, what are you doing in here?" She didn't come out. I pet her and she seemed to calm down, but stayed crammed into the tight space. The wastebasket lay dumped on its side, but Twinkie hadn't shredded the tissues like she normally does.

"What's the matter? You don't want to be stuck in here." I pulled her out, which she seemed happy about. We walked into the living room with her pressed against my leg the whole time. I put a couple logs in the wood burner and plopped down. Twinkie crept to me on her belly and tucked herself between my legs.

"It's okay, I'm right here." And then her body locked up. "Oh no!" I scrambled away to give her space. Twinkie began to seize. I'd never seen it look so painful. Her neck had been curled toward me and now it froze in an awkward position as her body convulsed.

It was so horrible, like watching a car crash. You

saw it coming and there's nothing you can do, but stand back, watch and hope everyone's okay. So I perched on my knees and waited, knowing she wouldn't be able to take a breath until it was over. Her contorted neck jerked with each spasm, and I had to look away as her body beat against the braided area rug.

I chewed on my lip and waited and waited. It wouldn't end. This was a long one, a couple of minutes, and she hadn't taken a breath. Would it kill her? Had she been doing this while I was gone today? God, I hoped not.

The thump of her body against the floor slowed, and I looked over to see her body had relaxed. Now she lay seemingly lifeless, her eyes fixed and staring. "Oh girl, it's done now. It's okay." I stroked her head. Finally she heaved a breath. I dropped my head into the long fur of her neck. What was I going to do?

After a couple minutes of rapid breathing, she became alert again and her tail wagged. It broke my heart.

"Hey girl, you want a treat? You must be hungry after all that scary stuff." I ruffled her ears and then went to the kitchen to get her medicine. A note lay next to the pill bottle from the neighbor, Mr. Walters. Twinkie had two seizures when he came over at lunch to check her. He gave her a valium before he left. It obviously wasn't working.

A loud crash came from the dining room. I rushed in. Twinkie walked on the open display shelves, knocking off Dad's sculptures and vases.

"Twinkie, what are you doing?" I called her, but she stayed pressed to the wall and knocked over anything in her path. Mom's dried flower arrangement, crashed over, the magazine rack, down. I rushed over and saved the wine rack filled with Dad's home brews as Twinkie pushed between it and the wall.

"Come here girl." I grabbed her collar and led her into the kitchen where I pushed her meds into a blob of peanut butter. "Eat this. It's nummy, and you'll feel better." She licked it off my finger in a second. "Good girl," I said. "Let's see if that will stop those crummy seizures."

Before my dad had left, he'd reminded me to use the valium if her seizures worsened. I'm so glad he did. Just as I turned to get the valium bottle, I heard a thump. There she was again, frozen on the floor as the seizure gained momentum and took over her body like a possessed demon.

"Oh no!" Her body began its violent attack, and her head kept hitting the hard wood floor. I rushed to the living room and grabbed Mom's afghan, returned and tucked it under her head.

This was getting out of hand. I watched her for a while, but then had to turn my back I couldn't stand it anymore. This one lasted even longer. After she came back around I gave her another valium in hopes it would act faster.

I checked the clock. It was after ten, which meant in Vermont it was after eleven. I grabbed the wall phone.

Thud. Another seizure. Only a couple minutes had passed since her last one. Why wasn't the valium working? I covered my face with my hands and cried. I didn't want to look away, but watching hurt so bad.

I dialed Dad's cell. They were staying at Grandma's

mountain cabin. The phone rang and went to voice mail.

"Dad, it's me. Twinkie keeps having seizures, and they won't stop." My voice sounded high and tight. "I gave her the meds, but it's getting worse. Please call me right away." I stepped around Twinkie as her body whacked itself against the floor again. I couldn't stand there and watch; I had to get away from it. The helplessness ate at me.

I didn't want to be alone for this. Dad was supposed to handle it, not me. I went in the living room and looked out the picture window. A blizzard of snow whipped through the air like a churned up snow globe. I grabbed the pill bottle from the kitchen and dialed the number of the vet.

"Emergency Pet Clinic," a woman answered.

"Hi, You guys saw my dog over a couple weeks ago for seizures. Well, I came home a while ago, and she was hovering in a corner and has been knocking things over in the house. Now she keeps having really long seizures one after another. She's had three in the last twenty minutes." I turned my back on poor Twinkie. I couldn't bear to watch it any more. I was such a coward.

"What's your dogs name?" the voice asked.

"Twinkie. Twinkie Thomas." I answered, embarrassed such a beautiful dog had such a stupid name.

"Let me look up her record."

I peeked at Twinkie where she lay still locked in torment and shuddered. Would it never end?

"Got it. I see you have phenobarbital and valium."

"Yes. I've given her seizure meds on schedule, and I gave her a valium this morning, and she got one at lunch. I just gave her two more a little while ago, but it's not doing anything." My panicked voice cracked.

"All right, you can give her another one. If that doesn't do it, in fifteen minutes try one more."

"Why is this happening? Why is she knocking everything over?"

"I can't say for sure without having her examined, but most likely she's lost her sight. If she has a brain tumor, as the doctor suspected, it's a common progression along with loss of the use of her limbs."

I looked at Twinkie who now lay exhausted. "So what do I do?"

"It's up to you at this point. You can keep her comfortable through her last days or bring her in. We can monitor her or put her to sleep."

"Oh." I swallowed. Tears filled my eyes.

"I'm sorry I don't have a better prognosis for you."

I nodded, then realized she couldn't hear my gesture. "It's okay. Thank you." I sniffed.

"Give us a call back if you decide to bring her in."

"Okay, I will." I hung up before I started to bawl. I slumped down the side of the cupboard to the floor next to Twinkie and wove my fingers through her fur. She raised her head and tried to look at me through blinded eyes. "I'm right here, girl."

I reached up for the valium bottle and gave her another. She barely had it in her when another seizure came on. I covered my face. Thankfully, this one was less severe. Her body twitched a lot, but it wasn't like the violent attacks of earlier. The medicine must finally be working.

I pulled my cell out of my back pocket and dialed

Dad again. No answer, so either he was asleep or there was no reception in the mountains, which I knew happened a lot. I tried Mom's cell too. No luck.

I really needed to talk to someone, but who could I call so late? I tried Jilly, in the hopes she'd stopped hating me by now, but she didn't pick up. I didn't bother to leave a message.

So I dialed another number from memory. It's funny how you remember some things after years of not thinking about them. A couple rings and Eli's confident, friendly voice came on.

"It's Eli. Can't talk, so leave a message. Or not." Then a beep.

Caught off guard, I wasn't sure what to do. But the night we'd gone parking he'd said we were friends. While he's been decent to me ever since, he still acts guarded and keeps his distance. I couldn't afford to worry about that distance now. I needed a friend.

"Hey Eli, it's me. Willow." The second I spoke his name, all this emotion flooded out.

"My dog is really sick, and I'm pretty sure she's dying. My Mom and Dad are out of town, and I was just hoping to talk to… somebody." My voice came out shaky. "I guess you're already in bed, so, um, I'll see you at rehearsal." I gasped a breath, clicked off, and tossed the phone on the floor.

So it was me and Twinkie alone to weather the storm. Probably her final storm. After a while, she came around again and whimpered.

"I know girl, it sucks. I'm so sorry you have to go through this." I held her for a while then tried to give her food, but she wouldn't eat. I couldn't get her to go outside to the bathroom either. So I moved her into the living room by the wood stove. She wobbled on her feet, but seemed happy to stay by me.

I cuddled her on the big braided rug. A couple of seconds later, she whined and another seizure started. I must say, I was pissed. Enough already. I left her on the rug and grabbed the peanut butter jar and valium. As soon as she came to, I gave her another. These things were gonna stop. Now!

I lay on the floor and spoke quietly. She whined a couple times, but didn't have another seizure. She seemed to like the sound of my voice.

"Remember the first day I met you? You were a big golden ball of fluff. You were so cute and you used to chew on my shoelaces." I pet her beautiful soft coat. "And remember that time when I was eleven and I ran away? You followed me. You were the only one who understood me." I sniffled and wiped my nose on my sleeve. "I only got three blocks before I changed my mind and came back. But you were so sweet and loyal and you always comforted me. I'm not gonna leave you, girl."

Twinkie fell asleep to the sound of my voice. I stroked her and then moved her legs to get up and go fetch a tissue. Her legs hung limp, like wilted celery. I gasped.

"Oh my God." I moved each of her legs, and they hung lifeless in my hand. Was she dead? Did I kill her with so much valium? My eyes welled up. I gently took her head in my hands to lift it and it flopped as if she didn't have a neck. I set her head down, grossed out by the feeling.

I covered my mouth with my hand to hold back the horror of what I had done.

Then a knock on the picture window startled me.

I looked up and saw Eli. I heaved an anguished breath and scrambled to my feet and let him in. Cold air and snow pushed through the front door along with him. Snow dusted his hair and coat. I quickly shut the door.

I'd never been so glad to see someone in my life.

"Are you okay?" He searched my face, his beautiful blue eyes filled with concern.

"I think I killed her." I burst into tears.

Eli pulled me into his arms, folding them around me like ribbon on a gift. He held me close, his head nestled against mine. He made soothing sounds and kissed my hair. I felt like a frightened child who'd woken up from a bad dream and was being soothed by their mother. Except I wasn't a child, this wasn't a bad dream, and it was Eli who ran his hand over my head and rubbed my back.

I looked at him with watery eyes. "Why are you here? I thought you were asleep." Up close I was inches from his mouth, the one that kissed me last Saturday and at rehearsal. This time, he kissed my forehead.

"No, I was in the shower when you called. You sounded so upset. I didn't think you should be alone." He smoothed my hair.

"You drove through a snow storm," I said, still stunned to see Eli here, larger than life in my living room. Last time he'd been here, he'd been a gawky boy. Now he was tall and strong and here because he cared.

"Hey, it was fun. I rarely get to use my four-wheel

drive. So tell me what's going on with Twinkie?" He unzipped his coat and laid it on the floor next to the coat rack, toed off his snow-covered boots and took in the scene. "It's a disaster here. What happened?"

I told him the whole story, including all the Valium I'd given her. We crouched next to Twinkie, and I wiggled her limp legs. Eli leaned forward with one hand on her chest and listened at her mouth for breath.

"She's still breathing." He sat back on his legs. "She's stoned out of her mind. Not a bad place for her to be, all things considered."

"Thank God." I breathed a sign of relief and leaned against the couch.

Eli scooted next to me and stretched out his long legs. He wore an old pair of grey sweats, a faded blue t-shirt and no socks. He didn't waste much time getting here. Now that he was here, and Twinkie was out of immediate danger, I could relax a little. The seizures had stopped, and I didn't need to make any difficult decisions.

"So where are your mom and dad?"

"Visiting my Grandma in Vermont. They were going to her cabin up in the mountains. That's probably why my dad didn't get my call."

Eli gazed around the room. "You know this place has barely changed since I was last here." He took in the school art projects taped to the wall, the stacks of organic living magazines in the corner, and the jungle of plants near the window. "It's like a time warp, other than all the broken pottery in the other room."

"Yeah, things never change much around here."

He spied the black box in the other room. "That isn't

a…"

"Coffin? Yes. Breezy is going through a vampire stage, so Dad built her a mini coffin to play in."

"I love your Dad. How's he doing?"

"The same. Happy and content. His latest project is growing his own cultures for yogurt."

Eli raised his dark blond eyebrows.

"The fridge looks like a science experiment. Hungry?" I offered.

"Not for yogurt. Got any more brownies?"

"No, but I have leftover Chinese."

"Deal." He got up, held a hand out, and pulled me up. "She should be out for a while, so I don't think you need to worry too much."

We went into the kitchen where I pulled out the leftovers. We ate in the living room and watched Twinkie sleep. I breathed a huge sigh of relief knowing I didn't have to be alone because Eli, who I trusted, had come to help.

Chapter 27

An hour later, Twinkie whimpered. I crawled on the floor next to her. "It's okay, girl," I whispered and touched her long fur.

Eli stretched out on the floor next to me and put a comforting hand on her.

"Do you think I should give her more valium? I don't want her to have another seizure, they're horrible."

"I don't know. Let's give it a few minutes and see how she does. Maybe we should stagger the medicine, so she doesn't get totally wiped out again."

So we lay on the floor with one hand on Twinkie and our heads resting on throw pillows. We lay in comfortable silence and I had to say it seemed just like the old days.

Twinkie's whining got worse, and I could tell the seizures were trying to fight their way out. Eli got the pill while I scooped some peanut butter. She licked it down right away, which sort of broke my heart. I couldn't bear to see her suffer so much, but drugging her to oblivion didn't seem right either.

After a few minutes, she calmed down. This time she didn't turn into a limp dishrag. Exhausted from the stress of the day, I lay down next to her. The next thing I knew, a blanket covered me and another pillow appeared. I opened my eyes long enough to see Eli settle in beside me. I smiled and drifted to sleep.

Twinkie whined off and on all through the night.

Whenever it got really bad, we would give her a single pill, but never more than one at a time. When morning came, I woke nestled up against Eli with his arm draped over me. I liked it there. He smelled like sleep and warm blankets, and the weight of his arm reassured me that I wasn't alone. Just like when we danced, he always had my back. How could I have shut him out all that time? What an idiot I had been.

Morning light shone through the window. I listened to Eli snore softly, content to lay in his arms all day. Then Twinkie whined. I twisted to check her. Her front leg twitched, but at least it wasn't a grand mal seizure like before. The seizure twitches were gaining strength despite the meds. She'd had a rough night, and I knew what had to be done.

Eli woke, and peeked at me through sleepy eyes. His mouth turned into a smile. He realized how close we were and stretched out, moving his arm over his head. Underarm hair peeked out of the edge of his t-shirt.

"How's she doing?" His morning voice sounded low and gravely. He rubbed his hand over his face.

"I don't know. She's twitching, but that's it." I inched away, not sure he welcomed my body attached to his side like a refrigerator magnet. I looked at Twinkie; her tail gave a meager little wag. Then it stopped, and her body stiffened, but not too much. Tiny spasms shook her. Nothing big like last night, but a constant reminder of her torment.

"Hang in there girl, it'll all be over soon." Tears welled in my eyes, and I hugged her stiff little body. Thankfully it didn't last long, maybe a minute. The meds were still helping.

"We should give her another one," Eli said.

"Yeah, and let's see if she needs to go out. Twinkie, want to go outside!" I said in the chipper voice we always used. She responded by sitting up on her front paws, but her back end didn't move. She tried again, but couldn't get up.

"Here, let me help." Eli jumped up and gently lifted her hips to a standing position, but as soon as he tried to release her, her legs slid out from under her at awkward angles. Sadness filled his eyes. "I'll carry her."

So he pulled on his coat and slipped on his boots and carried Twinkie to the backyard. I followed to help. He set her in the newly fallen snow and her back end collapsed. We tried a couple times more, but there was no way she could walk or even hold her own weight.

Eli hefted her back into his arms and carried her inside by the wood stove. I brought her water dish and had to hold her head so she could drink, which seemed to make her happy. As we gave her another pill, the phone rang. I startled, and shared a look with Eli. "I hope that's my dad." Eli gave Twinkie a dollop of peanut butter as I went to answer.

"Hello."

"Hey kiddo, how's she doing?" Dad asked in a calm concerned voice.

"It's really bad." I couldn't help it; I started to cry. I turned my back so Eli wouldn't see. "The seizures won't stop, and now she can't walk."

I went into the pantry and talked to Dad for a few minutes. We agreed what needed to be done. I came out and hung up the phone, but my hand wouldn't let it go, I didn't want to lose the connection to Dad and face reality in the next room.

Eli's hand covered mine, the heat of his body warmed me. He removed my hand from the phone. I dropped my head and couldn't hold it back any longer. I turned toward him, and he nestled me in his arms as I bawled.

He stayed by my side as I called the pet clinic and arranged a time to bring Twinkie in. We opened a can of tuna to give her a special last meal. His phone rang. He pulled it out and frowned.

"It's my mom. I better take this before it turns into a national crisis." He stepped away. "Hello, Mother." He looked at me and frowned. "I'm at a friend's." He listened as his mother ranted so loud I could hear her across the room. He pushed a hand through his hair.

"I know. I'm sorry." He glanced at me and shook his head as the ranting continued. "I'm at Jason's. He had an emergency and needed a hand." He rolled his eyes.

"No, it won't happen again. It was late, and I didn't want you to worry." More yelling could be heard. "Oh shit, I totally forgot. Yeah, I'm on my way." He ended the call.

"I'm so sorry, but I've got to go. I've got an exam in AP Lit at eight. I can't blow it, or my life will be a living hell. And if I don't get a 4.0, my dad threatened to cut off my college money, and I need to get the hell outta there."

"Okay, go." I grabbed his coat as he slipped on his boots. "I'm sorry they put so much pressure on you."

"I'm a McAvoy. This is how we live. I don't get a choice." He pulled his coat on. "Are you sure you're going to be okay taking Twinkie in? I can come back after my exam."

"I'll be fine. Thanks for offering." I gave him a half smile, because we both knew I wouldn't be fine. In a way, it would be better if it was just me.

He nodded, then went over to Twinkie and talked to her softly. When he got up, his watery eyes met mine. "Hang in there. Call me anytime."

I nodded.

"I'll see you at rehearsal. Okay?"

"I'll be there."

Awkwardness sprang up between us, reminding me how distant we'd been up until a few days ago. Last night was a huge step in repairing our friendship, but we still didn't know what to do with it. Was it possible to get back what we once had? I hoped so.

"Go! You're going to be late."

"All right." He paused at the door. "Good luck today."

"Thanks."

He disappeared out the door, leaving me alone, my dying dog at my feet.

* * *

Saying goodbye to Twinkie and putting her to sleep was the most horrible thing I've ever been through. I couldn't bear the idea of going to school.

Back at home, I took Twinkie's collar and gathered up the rest of her stuff and put it in a box. I couldn't look at it. I stuffed the box in a closet for Mom and Dad to figure out what to do with.

Mom called and we talked for a long time. She said taking the day off school was perfectly fine. I didn't mention I would miss a history exam. She offered to come home to be with me, but I told her not to. They just got to Grandma's, plus I'd be busy with school and rehearsals the whole time anyway. I cleaned up the broken pottery and put the house back together. I folded up the afghan and hugged it close. The hint of Eli's scent gave me a little comfort.

* * *

That night after rehearsal, I tried Jilly again. If my friendship with Eli could start to heal, maybe Jilly would be ready too.

"Hey Jilly, I heard you guys rocked it. I'm so glad. I knew you could do it."

Actually, I heard they didn't rock it. A guy from the show said his sister cheered for Memorial, and he heard the Capital Flyers barely made the finals. Anna fell out of her sit pose, which is the easiest position ever. And Brittany blew her Scorpion move. Ms. Klahn went ballistic and made them run laps around the school before she'd let them on the bus to come home.

After that call, I finally understood how Eli must have felt when I abandoned him all those years ago. I didn't like it. It sucked not having anyone to talk to. I had been such a jerk.

Chapter 28

By rehearsal the next day, I'd cried myself out. A long shower and careful makeup erased the outward signs of my grief. It seemed like a week since she'd died, not one day. The distraction of the show helped me push my sadness over Twinkie to the back of my mind. Life moved on and I rode the fast train with the show. The good news, things were looking up.

I sat in the front row with the other principals. It's the position of power. Position is a funny thing. When I started the show, I always stayed in the back of the crowd, mostly because I didn't have a clue what I was supposed to be doing, but partly because I hadn't earned it.

Now, I knew my stuff inside and out, and I wasn't ashamed to be seen in front. If they criticized me now, it's because I screwed up and deserved it.

The tables were turned. Now they were screwing up, not me. Probably because they weren't working 24/7 like I was. They might be keeping their GPAs up, but I knew every line of dialogue and every song and every dance step.

Eli and I sat in the front row with Jason and the other principals watching Tyson walk back in forth. Anyone with a brain could see how stressed out Tyson was. He kept pushing his fingers through his hair and chewing on his fingernails. But did the other kids shut up and listen? No, of course not.

"We are ten days from opening. It's time you stepped your game up." He paced in front of us. The cast filled the first four rows of the house.

Eli pressed his knee against mine. We felt terrible for Tyson. This was his dream, and half the cast wasn't taking it seriously.

"Everyone should be off book and for pete's sake, learn the words to the songs! I know you have school and homework, but at some point, you have to make a choice. Are you going to pull together and put on a kick ass show, or go home and play video games?"

Behind me, I heard kids grumbling.

"And how many more times must I talk to you about emotion? I want to see emotion in everything you do up there. Every song. Every dance. I don't care if you're front row or back! No more breaking character." Tyson faced us with weary eyes. His own conviction kept him going. "When you step on that stage I want to see passion and enthusiasm, not the lackluster indifference you've been delivering. You're tired and I'm tired, but we're heading into the final week, and it's going to be a ball buster. You have no idea what's about to hit, and you better be ready." He looked from one cast member to the next hoping they heard and understood his message.

He shook his head. "Okay, enough lecturing, I see you've tuned me out anyway. Time for a little show and tell. Maybe that will motivate you." He looked straight at the front row. "Eli, Willow. Take the stage. They haven't seen your fight number."

We looked at each other. *Crap.*

When we'd done run-throughs the past few days, we'd always skipped Eli and my numbers because the group numbers needed so much work. It's easy to blend in when you're in a group, but front and center with the cast watching? Yikes.

Eli tapped my foot with his toe and winked.

So we hoisted ourselves out of our seats and took position on stage while Tyson cued up the music on his sound system. He looked at us, mouthed, "Don't fuck it up!" and hit play.

Gee, thanks Boss.

Eli and I shared one last fortifying glance. The music came on, and we focused on the dance and each other. We let the rest of the world fall away. This particular dance was filled with lifts. We'd practiced it until we were black and blue and knew it so well we could do it in our sleep. Almost.

The music is this awesome wild rock music with electric guitars. It's a physical dance with anger and rage. Lauren tries to hit and attack Zach and he has to deflect it. I leap at Eli like a storm and he catches me midair, whips me over his head and sets me down. It comes off looking like a funnel cloud. The music is so awesome and builds through the number. At one point I jump on his back like a cat on a tree, he spins and flips me off. It's really hard to do, but a ton of fun. And when we do it right, it looks effortless.

I get to take all my fury out in this dance. I motivate by pretending Zach's the one responsible for all the shit in my life. He's the reason I got hurt in cheer, he's the reason everyone in the show was so mean to me. He's the reason Twinkie died and he's the reason I can't sing better.

And to give Eli credit, he fends off each attack with finesse. While I let loose my wrath, Zach is filled with angst as he tries to save Lauren from evil Victor.

It's a violent number that leaves me emotionally spent. Connecting with Eli like this fills my soul and yet drains me. Like so many other times in our lives, he takes my abuse, lets it roll off and keeps coming back for more. His eyes are filled with misery and pain as he gently averts each of Lauren's strikes.

We show every emotion and thought on our faces and in our eyes and in the way we move. I get to be this other person and that is something I've always loved about dance. Acting each song as if it's a story is like a drug.

By the end of the number we are exhausted. Emotionally and physically. Lauren continues to fight his protection but Zach won't give up. Lauren makes one final attempt to fight him, but he lifts her from her feet and locks his arms around her. Lauren surrenders.

We finished the dance a sweaty mess, Eli's arms protectively around me, my soul bared open. I liked the sensation of being in his arms. The music ended. We held the moment, and then he released me.

The cast watched, a couple with dropped jaws. They jumped to their feet and rewarded us with catcalls and applause.

"Now that's what I'm talking about!" Tyson yelled with pride.

Eli and I stepped apart and caught our breath.

That was the day I knew for sure I deserved the lead role of Lauren.

Chapter 29

"What exactly are you trying to make?" Eli asked from his perch on the counter.

I invited him to come over for my Foods class make-up assignment.

"Chicken Cacciatore. I think."

"Looks more like Chicken Catcha Disaster. You're making a huge mess."

"Yeah, it's part of the creative process, what can I say." I dumped out the bag of carrots on the cluttered counter.

"Why are you wearing sunglasses?"

"For the onions. I figured if I block the onion fumes with sunglasses and burn a couple candles, I won't cry. I'm so done with crying. It's overrated." I lowered the shades and peeked at him over the top to prove I'm *all that*!

"I don't think wearing sunglasses is going to make any difference."

I aimed my butcher knife at him. "Do you really want to hassle the girl with the knife?"

"You're right. It's brilliant." He held up his hands to fend me off.

"Thank you." I returned my attention to the onions.

"So, how's that working out for you?"

"Not sure, I can't really see what I'm cutting."

"Is it too late to order a pizza?" He said with a lazy

smile and relaxed tilt of his head. The little grey flecks in his eyes caught the light.

"You're damaging my delicate ego?"

"I'm just trying to protect us from food poisoning."

"There. That's all the vegetables." I dumped the onions into a large bowl with the other veggies. "On to the chicken!" I raised my knife in the air.

I owed the Foods teacher two more meals, for the days I missed school after my big fall. Next week, I'd miss one more cooking day because of the show, so this was my warm-up meal.

I lifted a slimy chicken breast from the package. "This is disgusting. What's all that white stringy stuff hanging off?"

"I believe it's fat." His eyes danced with humor.

"Gross." I crinkled my face and flopped the poultry on the cutting board, its slippery juice oozed around it. Disgusted, I stuck my tongue out and tried not to gag.

Eli cracked up. I wasn't trying to be funny.

I placed the knife on the chicken and tried to cut it into strips, but the whole gloppy piece moved with the motion of the knife. I pushed harder and broke through the skin. "Come on you pathetic piece of poultry, cut!" I concentrated and pushed harder. Finally I had to hold the chicken in place with my hand so it wouldn't slide back and forth as I sawed.

"I am never eating chicken again." I finished up the rest and dumped the slop in with the veggies.

"Are you sure that should be touching the vegetables?"

"Why not? It's all getting cooked together anyway."

"I'm just saying. And you need to wash everything

that touched the raw chicken with hot soapy water. Including your hands."

"What? These hands?" I came at him with my slimified hands.

"Get those away from me, you sicko." He jumped off the counter then turned on the tap to hot.

"You're such a germaphobe." I stuck my hands under the warming water.

"No, I just want to live to do the show. I'd be really pissed to miss it because you didn't clean the raw chicken off your hands. There's going to be a casting agent there who I need to impress and meet with."

"Okay, Doctor Oz. I'm washing."

"Don't forget the knife and cutting board too." He pointed.

"Fine." I plugged the sink and filled it with hot soapy water.

After detoxing my hands, I sloshed oil in the pan, dumped in the bowl of ingredients and turned the stove on high to get it going. I grabbed the measuring spoons and poured out the salt and dumped it in too.

"Isn't that a lot of salt?" Eli jumped up and sat on the counter next to the stove while I worked. He looked all tall and cute, and I kept pretending to accidentally bump his arm.

"You are such a critic."

"You just poured in a heaping tablespoon of salt. That seems like a lot."

"Look genius, it says one t of salt." I shoved the print out of the recipe at him.

"Excuse me? Small t means teaspoon, capital T means tablespoon, and it doesn't say heaping. You just put in about five times too much."

"Oh."

I reached in with my fingers and grabbed a few pinches out and dumped it on the counter. "There. That should be better." I wiped my hands on my jeans.

Eli shook his head.

I nudged his knee. "I've gotta get the lid." Eli stretched his knees apart. I opened the cupboard door and reached past his legs for the thick glass lid. I set it on the pot.

"Ta da!" I said and took a bow.

"Alright Emeril. You're a rock star," he said. "You remember how many times we hung out in this kitchen while your mom made us cookies?"

"Yeah, a lot." I returned the olive oil and salt to the pantry.

"They were the weirdest cookies I ever ate, but I loved them. They were a lot better than the boxed kind my mom bought."

"How is Hillary?" His mom's name was really Ruth, but she was a lawyer for the most prestigious law firm in town, Schmidt, McAvoy and Allen. I grabbed the wastebasket and scooped the unused veggie remnants into the trash.

"She's obsessed with getting nominated to the State Senate." He grabbed an orange from a bowl on the counter and tossed it in the air. "Which is good for me, because she's gone all the time at some fundraiser or another."

"And The Donald?" I leaned against the counter across from him.

"The ole man is pissed his son isn't working to his

full potential," Eli mimicked and gripped the orange. "He's determined I follow in the McAvoy footsteps and go to Northwestern for my undergrad and Harvard for a MBA. *You know Elliott, four generations of McAvoys have attended Harvard."*

I cringed. "I'm sorry." I couldn't picture Eli in big business. It would suffocate his carefree personality, not to mention totally squash his creativity. "Ease up on the fruit, you're making orange juice."

"Sorry." He returned it to the bowl.

Eli's dad was a power hungry mergers and acquisition guru. One look at Eli, and I could see how the pressure from his parents weighed on his normal light-hearted attitude.

"Can you tell him you want something different? That you aren't like him?" I couldn't imagine my parents forcing me to do anything I didn't want to.

"He knows I'm not like him. Not in the slightest bit." Eli shook his head and I wanted to give him a hug to wash away the pain of his home life.

Then he got this screwy look on his face and said, "Speaking of wanting something different, do you really want to be with that guy Rick?"

He caught me off guard. Rick had been an excuse to show Eli I really did have a life and that someone cared about me. I grabbed the dishtowel and started twisting it. I looked at Eli who watched me with something more than casual curiosity.

"No. I don't want to be with Rick. Fact is I lied about that." Embarrassed to be caught in my own lie, I shifted from one foot to the other.

Confusion shaded Eli's eyes. "But you said you two

were going out."

"Yeah, that wasn't true. I made that up."

"Then why did you say that?"

"We were at Messerschmidt Road, and I didn't want you to think I was a total loser. Girls are always hanging around you, and you're probably going out all the time." The dishtowel stretched as I continued to strangle it. "I was nervous and didn't want to look pathetic. For all I know you have a girlfriend!"

I'd never even thought of that before! Shit. I wanted to slink away and never come back. Why hadn't I asked him?

Eli must have been able to read my thoughts. He lifted an eyebrow and tilted his head to the side in that special way of his.

"I don't have a girlfriend." He leaned back on his hands as his legs hung over the side of the counter.

My dishtowel twisting ceased. "You don't?"

"Nope." He smiled, showing off his pearly whites.

I stared, dumbfounded. I was relieved he didn't have a girlfriend, but confused at what to think or do about it.

"Ah, Willow?" he said glancing past me.

"Why not?"

"Ah, Willow, it's burning."

"What's burning?" I said.

"You're chicken cacci trouble."

Sure enough, the smell of charred chicken filled the air.

"Oh no!" I quick grabbed the lid to help it cool down. The scorching heat burned my fingers. "Shit!" I dropped the glass lid, it crashed against the stove, broke and fell to the floor. "Dammit, I burned my hand."

"Quick, get it under cold water." Eli hopped off the counter, grabbed me by the wrist, pulled my hand under the faucet and turned it on full blast cold. The water soothed it immediately.

"You know, maybe cooking isn't such a good idea." He turned the stove off, turned on the overhead fan and used the oven mitt to push the pot off the hot burner.

I examined my burned fingers and thumb. Eli's arms came around me, took my hand and pushed it back under the faucet.

"Keep it under the water," He said super close to my ear.

"It's freezing cold." I turned my head and looked up at him, his face was mere inches away.

My breath caught.

His eyes grazed mine. "It'll feel better," he whispered and held my hand captive under the water, numbing my fingers. His body brushed against me, putting my nerve endings on high alert.

Suddenly, any thoughts of my burned hand evaporated with the scorching awareness of Eli's arms wrapped around me like a blanket. I didn't move a muscle, afraid of the sensations coursing through me. Then I relaxed and leaned against him just enough that I could feel the strength of his body on mine, and he wouldn't notice. I released a sigh.

His arms hugged closer, locking me in the glory of his touch. I leaned my head against his neck and sighed. The beat of his heart pulsed against my back. Cold tap water rushed over our hands, his breath warmed my cheek.

"Thanks, it feels better," I whispered.

"Are you sure?" He tilted his head to look at me and let our hands drift away from the water.

"Yeah," I angled to see him but not disturb his gentle hold. Our eyes connected and gravity pulled us together.

Eli's lips parted and he kissed me. Long and slow.

"Was that practice for the show?" I murmured.

"No. That was for me." His eyes searched mine to see if I'd run. "Is that okay?"

I nodded. I wasn't running anywhere.

"Good." His mouth settled on mine. I leaned against him. He tilted my chin closer. His fingers caressed my neck. I'm pretty sure I had died and gone to heaven.

I turned and wrapped my arms around him. I couldn't believe this was happening. I gazed into the depths of Eli's eyes, aware of him for the first time.

"Where have you been hiding?" I whispered.

"Right here. Waiting for you." He smiled, his dark eyes all dreamy. He reached past me to turn off the water and then wrapped his arms around my waist and looped his thumbs in the top of my jeans.

If I wasn't so stunned to realize how much I really liked Eli, I might have felt embarrassed. All those years together and I never saw him this way. I guess the attraction had been fighting to come out ever since my audition. Why had I been so stupid and blind? I caressed his back.

"You're hands are freezing," he said.

"That's your fault."

"As I recall, you're the one that burned your hand."

"This is true. I'm glad I did, or I'd never have seen

you clearly."

His smile lit the whole room. "It's about damned time."

Eli took my hands and linked his warm fingers with my cold ones being careful not to touch my burn, then wrapped our arms around my back. Holding me captive, he took my mouth with his. We went from zero to sixty in mere seconds.

After long minutes of exploring the contours of Eli's lips and mouth. He sighed and leaned his forehead against mine. "I think this would be a good time to order that pizza."

Leave it to Eli to be the responsible one. "You don't want charred chicken caccatore?"

"No, I definitely don't want that."

I pulled him in for a slow kiss. "You'd rather have pizza than this?" I breathed.

"Hell no! But we'll need energy to make it through the night."

*   *   *

After eating a little pizza, we turned on the stereo and picked up where we left off, this time on the comfort of the couch.

Eli held me in his arms; my world had never been better. He brushed a wisp of hair off my cheek and behind my ear than wove his fingers deep through my hair. His mouth moved over mine with gentle kisses. Like an engine, my heart started at a slow idle and now revved out of control. I disappeared into this new world we'd discovered.

I lifted my head and discovered a deep hunger in his eyes. I felt a passion I didn't know possible. He held my face, his gorgeous eyes pulled me in like a fish on a line.

With our legs tangled together, his hands roamed my every curve sending tingles to new places. He ran his hands over my jeans, and caressed my bottom. The sensations coursing through me awakened every nerve ending. He pulled me closer, our bodies intimate. Hungry. Without realizing, I squirmed for more, and Eli groaned with desire.

And that's how Mom, Dad and Breezy found us when they barged in, carry-on bags in hand.

I don't think Eli'd ever moved so fast in his life. Unfortunately, our legs were linked and as he tried to leap off me, we ended up on the floor.

"Hi Eli, whatcha doing?" Breezy asked as if it was an everyday occurrence to find him wrapped around me like a pretzel.

I pulled my shirt down as we struggled off the floor.

"Uh, yeah. Hi Squirt." Eli floundered for words. "Willow asked me to come over and help her make out, I mean make up one of her cooking assignments."

"And how's that going?" Dad tipped his head toward the barely touched pizza on the coffee table. I couldn't think of a single word to say.

"Oh that, oh, well, sir. It burned. The dinner that is."

"It seems really hot in here. Ralph, did you notice?" Mom fanned herself.

"Sure is. I'd say steamy," he answered with a straight face.

"You're right. Maybe we should open a window to cool it down in here."

"Good idea. These poor kids look overheated." Mom bit back a smile.

I rolled my eyes. There was no stopping them now.

"It's a good thing Willow doesn't cook more often."

"True. They could burn the house down." Dad acted concerned.

"That, or we might be grandparents soon," Mom said matter-of-factly.

"Mom! Dad! Stop it!" I interrupted.

They grinned, so proud of themselves. I wanted to throw some of Breezy's paints at them.

"You're gonna be a grandma?" Breezy asked. "Who's having a baby?"

"Oh. My. God!" I said.

Eli's cheeks turned pink, a sight rarely seen.

"And to think we were worried she'd be lonely." Mom shook her head.

"I don't think she's lonely. Breezy, does your sister look lonely to you?" Dad said.

"Not so much." She shook her head, finally catching up to the conversation and joining their evil game.

"Enough already!" I stood up, Eli followed.

"Sir, I'm really sorry..."

"Eli, it's nice to see you again. How've you been, son?" Dad held out his hand.

"He looks pretty happy to me," Mom answered, fighting back a grin. I gave her the evil eye.

"Hello, sir. I mean Mr. Thomas." A confused Eli shook his hand.

It was strange to see Dad and Eli, now the same height, standing eye to eye. Last time I saw them together, my dad took him fishing down at Bowman

Park years ago.

"I think you're old enough to call me Ralph," Dad said.

"Thank you. I will."

Poor Eli. I wanted to hug him and smooth down his hair where it stuck out funny from all our, uh, fun.

"You got big," Breezy said.

"Hey Squirt, so have you. Last time I saw you, you were only this tall." He held his hand out to show how small Breezy once stood.

She giggled. "Wanna see my tattoo?"

Eli looked at Mom and Dad as if they'd actually let an eight year old get a tattoo.

"It's a spider." Breezy dropped her coat and held out her forearm to reveal a lick and stick tattoo.

He bent over to examine it. "Wow, that's really scary."

"Thanks. Wanna see my coffin?"

"Breezy, leave him alone," I said.

"I should really be going." Eli took his first opportunity to escape. I wished I could escape with him!

"Are you sure you don't want to stay?" Dad asked.

"You can have more pizza or maybe take a cold shower?" Mom offered as she choked back laughter.

Man, I mention I hate my family sometimes.

Chapter 30

A few days later, right before I left for my voice lesson torture with Gloria, Mom gave me an address and directions to some place in Fitchburg.

"What's this?" I knew immediately I wouldn't like it.

"I don't know. Your voice teacher called a few minutes ago and said you needed to meet her at this address." Mom feigned ignorance.

"That is evil and cruel and mean."

"You shouldn't talk about her that way. She's working very hard to help you."

"I'm not talking about Gloria. I'm talking about you!" Mom knew exactly what Gloria was up to and I knew she wouldn't spill it.

"Oh, in that case, thank you!" She kissed my cheek. "You better hurry. Don't want to be late."

I slammed the door on my way out. Why, when things were finally going so well, did I have to still be tortured? The last few days, things with Eli were better than ever. We'd grown closer and closer since the night I tried to cook him dinner. I still can't believe how blind I was. I guess it was fear. This super hot guy with more talent than anyone I know—except Tyson, of course—wanted me! I get to spend time with him every single day. God, life is good.

I pulled out of the drive and called him. We now

spent every spare second together and talked on the phone the rest of the time.

He answered on the first ring.

"Hey you." His voice sounded like cool magic.

"Whatcha doing?" I asked.

"Other than thinking about you?"

"You are such a suck up!" I laughed

"I thought for sure you'd fall for it." The low rumble of his laugh made me smile.

"Nice try. You are not going to believe what Gloria is doing now."

"You mean besides turning you into a great singer?"

"She gave my mom some mysterious address with directions, and they won't tell me what it's about. I know she's going to make me sing in front of people again."

"You realize that's a good thing, don't you?"

"No, it's not! I hate singing in public. You know that!"

"Well in another couple weeks, you're gonna have to whether you're ready or not. And I'd appreciate you not sounding like a squeaky mouse."

"Ouch! Whose side are you on?"

"Mine! Tyson's. Gloria's. Listen, I know you can do this. You've just always been too self conscious to try before. Give me the address, and I'll look it up."

I read him the address. "So what are you really doing, watching Next Top Model?"

"Cute. You're a riot. I'm working on a paper for AP Lit that's due next week."

"Wow, you work ahead." I thought of my history paper that was due last week. Oops.

"It's fifteen pages and twenty-five percent of my

grade. Oh, here we go, she's sending you to..."

"Where is it? Tell me it's a vacant lot or a cemetery."

"Oh. Interesting," he said.

"What? Where am I going?"

"I think it's better if you see when you get there, but you're on the right track."

"What, a cemetery?"

"I'm not gonna tell you, so you can stop asking."

"You are a total shit! You're supposed to defend my...I don't know. My whatever!"

"Sorry, you need this. You'll do great. Just relax and have fun."

"You know this is grounds for a break up."

"You'd never do that. You want me too much." I could practically see the grin on his face.

"You are in so much trouble. I'm deleting you off my phone!"

"Hang up now, and do your warm ups. You'll be glad you did."

"You are so bossy, but right. I'm hanging up. Bye."

"Bye, break a..."

I clicked him off. The jerk.

As I turned onto the road listed in the directions, I discovered my final destination; The Hospice Care Center.

"Oh boy." I knew what this meant. I had to sing in front of sick people.

Correction.

Dying people.

I did not want to walk into that building, let alone force these dying people to listen to my ineptness. Not to mention, sick people gave me the creeps. I know it's wrong, but it's true. What do you say to someone who is terminally ill? Hi, how's it going? What did you do today? Anything fun coming up? Oh yeah, death!

Singing at the nursing home was bad. The people were old and dying, but these people wouldn't be that old. I walked past the pristine landscaping to the front entrance. Each step filled my stomach with dread. Gloria came out.

"Please don't make me do this," I pleaded.

"Willow, you have a beautiful gift to share, and these people deserve as much joy as possible in their final days."

"But I'm no good. Let's call Eli. He'd be good at this." He probably wouldn't be creeped out, either. His heart was better than mine.

"Willow, the nurses and staff have brought these patients together to hear you. They're waiting. Would you deny them whatever entertainment you can provide?" She gave me one of those looks that said stop being a selfish little twit, it's not about you.

"No. It's just that they deserve so much better. They shouldn't be forced to listen to a breathy, nervous teenager."

"So don't be breathy, and don't be nervous," Gloria said, as if it was easy as pressing a button on the TV remote.

I chewed my lower lip.

"Come on in. You're third in the line-up. Watch the ones before you to get your bearings." She took my arm and led me inside.

I followed her into a beautiful entryway with

stained glass windows. We walked down a long hallway with dozens of quilts displayed. Each quilt was made up of large squares with names and dates of people who died. Some included a picture of the person. Their smiling faces followed me as I passed.

We rounded a corner to a large carpeted gathering place. In front, a man played guitar. Rows of people in upholstered chairs lined the room. Loveseats and sofas created the side of the performance area. Next were a row of people in wheelchairs, many with a loved one at their side. At the back, five hospital beds occupied by patients overlooked the performance.

The patients were in varying degrees of illness. At least it looked that way. A woman wore a scarf wrapped around her bald head. A man had oxygen tubes around his ears and under his nose. A young-looking guy was attached to an IV drip.

My throat tightened when I noticed two little kids snuggled next to their mother in her hospital bed.

Gloria waved me to a seat in the back. The man playing guitar finished. Next a little boy about ten years old came up with a basket. He pulled a couple balls out and proceeded to juggle. He was really good too! That kid juggled behind his back, up high, under his leg and even spun between throwing a ball and catching it.

Every person there, including me, smiled. Then he pulled out juggling pins and made a huge fanfare. Then up they went one after the other, and he flipped those pins into the air and expertly caught each one again and again. When he almost missed a pin, he made a big deal of lunging for it and then quick wiped his brow with his arm between throws. He held the audience in the palm of his hand.

Next the little goober set the pins aside and spoke. "What is the most dangerous item to juggle?" he asked with a dramatic voice and serious face.

"Scissors!" yelled the girl cuddling with her mom.

"No, but that's a good guess," he answered.

"Broken bottles," said the older man with the oxygen tube.

"Yup, that's dangerous...but not the most dangerous."

I noticed an older woman wearing a bathrobe, sitting in a soft love seat, beaming at the little boy. A younger woman with the same color hair as the boy sat next to her. Her eyes twinkled with pride. It must be his grandmother and mother.

"Give up? The most dangerous item to juggle is..." He paused for effect, and I found myself leaning forward, eager to know.

"A sword!" He pulled a long plastic sword from his basket and held it high in the air.

"And what is more dangerous than a sword?" he asked.

"Two swords!" said a thin man dwarfed by his wheelchair.

"That's right!" The boy pulled another plastic sword out. "And even more dangerous?"

"Three swords!" called the little girl in the back.

"Yes!" He pulled the last sword out and held them all in the air.

We all cheered.

"Now ladies and gentlemen, I'm gonna have to ask you to move back, because I don't know how this is going to go. I'd hate to slice one of you open." His devilish eyes shone.

A couple scooted their chairs back to appease him.

"And now, may I have complete silence as I attempt this rarely successful challenge."

Every person in the room focused on this sweet, funny little kid. A few nurses gathered to watch.

He took a deep breath, focused as if he held lethal weapons and not toys. Suddenly he tossed one in the air, then another and then the last. He whipped those swords around, the blades spun in precise control. Then for his finale, he flung them one by one high overhead nearly hitting the ceiling lights of the great room. He eyed them closely as each one fell and he caught them smooth as could be.

The audience of Hospice patients and their families applauded and cheered as the little imp grinned and bowed.

Now that was a performance!

"He's awesome!" I said to Gloria.

"And you will be too," she said dragging me back to reality. Her steely look promised there would be no backing out.

The juggling boy had distracted me so much I'd forgotten why I was there.

"How am I supposed to follow that?"

"You get up there and concentrate. You know what to do. You have the tools. It's time to face your fears and go for it. Stretch yourself."

I swallowed down the stage fright that tried to overtake me and looked at the little boy hugging his grandmother. If he could do it, I guess I could give it my best shot.

Gloria took a seat behind the piano and waited as the Hospice woman introduced me. I straightened my shirt and gave a nervous smile to the people who waited so patiently as if they had all the time in the world.

These people were so sick. They knew they were dying, and it was only a matter of time. Their family members sat at their side. One of their last memories together would be of this evening's odd assortment of entertainment.

The love in the room overwhelmed me. The support everyone gave each other created a beautiful energy.

Gloria began the intro to my first song, an upbeat snappy number. I took a deep breath and hit my opening note right on time and in key! I moved to the beat and smiled. The song bounced along in a fun, sunshiny way.

The onlookers didn't seem bored and no one fell asleep like they did at the nursing home. They appeared content and happy, which meant I didn't totally suck.

My other number was a ballad with a power ending. It's a song about love and letting go. My character, Lauren, sings it about Eli's character, Zach. She loves him but has to let him go. Suddenly I saw the parallel to these people who had to let each other go.

I focused my energy and blocked out everything except the meaning of this song. I sang with as much love and emotion as I knew how. I thought of Twinkie and how much I loved her. I sang soft where I was supposed to and put all my emotion and heart into it.

I sang to each of the patients and to each of their loved ones. Their eyes didn't leave me the entire time. I felt their energy tied with mine. More staff from the center came into the atrium area with awe on their faces. I let go of everything, and by the last verse I put all my strength behind it and let my voice soar into a crescendo of power that almost knocked me off my feet.

Tears rolled down the cheeks of the woman holding her children on her bed. Never had I felt or delivered such power when I sang. I belted that final note with my arms reaching skyward. When it ended, silence filled the room; then suddenly a huge applause filled the air. The little kids clapped. The adults beamed.

Gloria nodded and controlled her grin of approval. My heart floated above me because I knew I'd done well. Something inside me came alive. By focusing on the meaning of the song and forgetting about myself, I'd figured out how to dig deep and bring out my voice. Inside, I did my happy dance and back handspring. On the outside, I smiled my gratitude, took a quick little bow and made room for the next entertainer.

"What did I tell you?" Gloria said as we left the building.

"I can't believe I just did that!" I almost skipped.

"I can." She grinned, put an arm around my shoulder and hugged me.

Chapter 31

Friday afternoon during fourth block there was an all-school assembly. The principal talked about mid-term schedules, a mandatory locker check, and the Prom Planning Committee. The pep band played, and the cheer squad performed the routine they'd do when they competed for the state title this Saturday.

The assembly started halfway through fourth block, so I sat with my history class. I moved as close to the door as possible. My feelings about cheer and watching them perform were mixed with fear and apprehension. Would I miss cheer? Would it scare me to see the girls launched? Would they be better without me?

None of it should have mattered, because everything in my life was perfect. I was still flying high from my Hospice performance. Other than the horrible loss of Twinkie, I'd never been happier. Eli and I were together. I loved the show, Tyson, and most of the cast. I had an awesome family–whacked out, but still awesome–and spring was on the way.

My mind wandered throughout the student council president's prom update. Next, the basketball captain blabbed on rocking from one foot to the other. He really needed a public speaking class.

Finally, they announced the National Cheerleading Champion Capitol Flyers. The students went ballistic. My heart blocked my throat and threatened to cut off my air supply. I clapped a couple times and waited.

The squad bounded out in their short polyester skirts and tops, giving their one pump victory sign. They performed eagle jumps and single high kicks to work up the crowd.

It was familiar and yet foreign at the same time. I knew the music and the drill. It pulled me in and yet part of me pushed it all away to protect myself.

The competition music blared through the sound system, and their routine took off. I watched, frozen, as they did the tumbling runs, simple lifts, and jumps. I couldn't relax. My gut tightened, and I gripped my arms. Most of the routine remained the same as when I cheered with them five short weeks ago, but some of the more difficult stunts that I performed were replaced with easier, less daring tricks. As the music built to the climax, I noticed Jilly and Carly prep for the final trick. Rick and Kyle placed their arms out just like the last time I flew. I held my breath. Jilly stepped into load in position.

My heart pounded, and my forehead beaded with sweat. They tossed her, and I dug my fingernails into my arms. She performed a simple jack knife and basket catch. I released my breath and the terror it held.

Quitting cheer was the right move, no doubt about it. Even after five weeks, I practically hyperventilated just watching!

The students yelled, stomped, and applauded. As my pulse slowed, I realized they had performed a solid routine, but the daring, challenging elements that made it pop and pushed them to the highest competitive level had all been removed. They ran out of the gym smiling. Jilly high fived Anna.

It didn't even bother me. Much.

Chapter 32

The first two hours of the day were music rehearsals. Tyson said that because we'd spent so much time on dance, he wanted to nail down the music and make sure we had it committed to memory.

After my breakthough in singing at the Hospice Center, so much of my anxiety disappeared. Don't get me wrong, I was still really nervous about the solo and duet numbers, but now I knew I wouldn't totally suck.

The combined voices of the entire cast never fail to amaze me. Our choir at Capitol is pretty good, but nothing like this. Every voice in the cast was strong. Tyson certainly did take the very best of the best when he cast the show. The pressure of having to sing a solo when there were so many great singers was daunting, but Gloria continued to push me hard, and I practiced every extra moment I had.

With my newfound confidence, I relaxed and let my notes roll out like powerful waves. I sang with all the joy I'd been missing for the past few weeks. My voice blended with the others in volume and perfect pitch.

Next to me, Sophie sang soprano. She'd been doing summer stock shows on the East coast since she was thirteen. Little goose bumps danced on my arm from hearing our voices mix.

I noticed Tyson deep into his paperwork at the tech table as Ms. Klahn directed. We got to a part where I had a solo line. I belted it out, pure and clean. Tyson stopped what he was doing and looked up. He raised an eyebrow of approval and nodded with a grin as if to say *See, I knew you could do it!*

I smiled back, so relieved to know he liked my progress. The last thing I wanted was to let him down when he'd put so much faith in me. He returned to his paperwork, but wore a big smile.

At the end of the song, Sophie leaned over. "You sound really great!"

I heard respect in her voice, and I could have jumped up and punched the air in celebration. Eli caught my attention and winked.

Yes!

* * *

Saturday night, Eli and I faced a bit of a problem. Tyson invited us to join him after our full day of rehearsal. It started out harmless and fun, but now, the man had turned into a wreck.

"Tyson, are you okay?" Our awesome director, the guy who could make just about anything happen, held his hands over his face and mumbled incoherently from our booth at the Great Dane Brew Pub. The Saturday night crowd buzzed with energy.

"I think he finally broke from all the stress," I whispered as I sat next to Eli with our legs pressed close together.

"Tyson?" Eli leaned close to him.

We exchanged a worried look when he didn't respond right away.

"I need another beer," he muttered and raised his glass as the waitress came by. She scooped it up and promptly brought a fresh one.

Tyson had been here a while before we'd arrived, so who knows how much he'd already had to drink.

After fortifying himself with half the contents of his glass, he leaned his elbow on the table to hold his head up; a little beer foam glistened on his razor stubble.

"I've created a nightmare. This whole project has become a house of cards. If one more thing goes wrong, the whole thing will fall apart."

"What are you talking about? Everything is going great," Eli said.

"No, I bit off more than I can chew this time. Dreamers beware!" He raised his glass in the air for a mock toast. "You just might get what you want!"

"Nothing's going to go wrong," I said. "The run-through today went great. We're ready for move-in tomorrow."

"I'm playing, director, producer, fundraiser. I'm trying to coordinate set design, lighting, union workers, sound mixing, publicity, interviews..." He raised his glass and took a long swig.

"And you're doing a great—" Eli started to say.

Tyson held up his hand to stop him. "I'm not done. I've got to handle the stage manager, staff, orchestra, plus bring in and impress the New York producers, agents, investors." He shook his head. "And that doesn't include trying to control my underage cast of drunk, horny students."

"Come on, the cast isn't that bad," Eli said.

"I'm talking about the two of you!" He focused his

droopy, intoxicated eyes on us.

"We're doing great. You said so yourself," I added, and Eli squeezed my hand.

"Yeah, well it's all a big ticking time bomb waiting to go off." He stared at his glass as the beer bubbles slid to the bottom.

"Tyson," I said to distract him and maybe lighten things up. "I promise, I won't let you down. It will all be okay."

He drained his beer and raised his hand for another. Eli and I cringed.

"Are you just really thirsty or are you trying to get drunk?" Eli asked.

"No, actually, I wasn't; but it's a great idea." He held his glass outside the booth for the waitress, but thankfully she was waiting on another table.

"Why don't you let us drive you home? It's getting late, and we have an early call tomorrow," I said.

"Seriously? You want to drive me home? How apropos." He gazed at the bottom of his empty glass. "You guys go on. I'll hang out for a while and sober up."

Eli shook his head. "No, I think it's time to go. Tomorrow's another big day, and we need our fearless leader." Eli and I stood up.

"Ha, that's pretty good kid." Tyson followed our lead and got to his feet. He reached for his wallet, fished out some bills and tossed them on the table.

We walked to the parking lot. Tyson staggered. Even drunk he still looked good.

"Hand me your keys, man." Eli held his hand out expectantly. Tyson dug around in his pocket for a while, swaying on his feet. "Got 'em." He tossed them to Eli.

I tried to hide my grin. Who would believe we'd be driving our director home drunk? Too funny. Eli handed me his keys while keeping a close watch on Tyson.

"Careful now, it's leased." Tyson fell into the car. Eli waited for him to pull his legs in, then shut the door and got in the drivers' seat.

I hopped in Eli's car and followed as he pulled out and headed toward the highway to a newer condo development. When we arrived, we had to wake Tyson up to get him in his building and up the elevator to his door. While I tried to find the key on his jumbled key chain, Tyson kicked the door repeatedly and yelled.

"Hey John, open the door!"

"Shh, you're going to wake up all the neighbors," I said.

"Shh," Tyson mocked me. Then he leaned forward to talk to us. "I love you guys. Did you know that?" he whispered.

"Yeah, back at ya," Eli laughed.

"No. I really mean it. Forget the drunk shit. You two have made this thing so much fun. You're such sweet kids and so cute together." He patted my cheek. "I really love you guys."

"Thanks, we love you too," I said. He probably wouldn't remember in the morning, but it still was nice to hear.

"Hey John!" Tyson yelled and pounded the door again.

"Shh," I giggled. "You have to be quiet."

"But I gotta take a leak," he whispered.

We burst into laughter.

Suddenly the door opened and Oh! My! God! A guy

wearing boxers, and I mean only boxers, squinted in the bright hall light and rubbed his face.

If Tyson was the GQ cover model, John was the swimsuit guy. His muscular arms and flat abs stared back at us. I quick turned my head away and looked wide-eyed at Eli. *Oh my god!* A half naked man stood in the hallway! Eli choked back laughter.

"John!" Tyson cheered.

John nodded acknowledgement and yawned. "I'll take him from here."

We stood back so Tyson could stumble forward.

"Come on, party boy. Let's get you to bed." He took Tyson's arm and led him in.

"I love you, John," Tyson swayed and spoke in a sappy puppy dog way.

"Yeah, I know."

"Here are his keys." I handed them over with my body angled away and eyes averted.

"Thanks for bringing him. You kids should get home now, too."

"We're on our way," Eli said.

"See you opening night." John closed the door.

Eli and I stared at each other. "You thinking what I'm thinking?"

"Yup, I think so," I giggled. "He loves John."

Eli put his arm around me as we walked out. "Yes, he does."

Chapter 33

The next morning I flashed a grin at Eli and climbed into his jeep. "Hey."

His smile flipped on an electrical current that hummed through me. Can you die from overwhelming joy? God, I hoped not. Please don't let me die and miss one second of time with Eli. It's like when you worry about some random tragedy striking you dead and making you miss something. I felt that way about the Harry Potter movies. I prayed at night that I wouldn't die of some freak accident and miss the next movie. This was a lot like that.

Eli leaned over and kissed me. Oh heaven, thank you. He smelled so damn good, a combination of soap and aftershave. Why did we have to go to rehearsal when all I wanted to do was make out?

"Good morning," he said, his voice low and breathy.

"Morning." I gazed into his beautiful blue eyes. Eli could have anyone, but he wanted me. How did I get so lucky?

He pulled out and took off downtown for the Overture Center, our new home for the next week. He parked in the ramp behind the theatre, a quick half block away. He slid his arm around my waist and held me close as we walked to the stage door, where we signed in and were given passes for the duration of the show.

I've danced on a lot of stages over the years, but

never anything like the Capital Theatre. It's a block from the actual Wisconsin State Capitol and almost as old. It's been refurbished a couple of times and has fancy ornate decorations, antique chandeliers and an old historic pipe organ.

We were directed straight to the house to wait for the others. In the theatre, a tech table was set up midway back over the top of the seats. Tyson spoke to a couple of people I didn't recognize. Stretch lights and a microphone were attached to the table. Binders lay open near crumpled papers, several coffee containers and a walkie talkie, among other things, lay strewn across the table. Looks like he'd been here for a while.

Ten minutes later, with most of the cast assembled, Tyson joined us, switching from his usual intense gaze to an animated one.

"Welcome to the Capitol Theatre. What do you think?" He lit up as he spread his arms wide to show off the historic venue. "Not bad, eh?"

We all nodded, giddy to be there. Chloe, McKenna, and Alex walked in.

"You're late," he said in a stern tone. "You're excused this time, but don't let it happen again." We could tell he was serious.

"We've had a lot of fun the past couple of months, and you guys have worked your tails off. Today everything switches gears. We have a team of professionals who have come in to get this show up. When one of them asks or tells you to do something, I expect you will listen and obey. I want you to give them every ounce of respect and make me proud. I am no longer the only person you report to. In a minute you will meet Jerry, the stage manager. What Jerry says is law. He has a team of assistants, and their word is law too. You've met your costume director and will meet the lighting director and all the others as the day goes on."

The tone of the production was definitely changing. Everyone sat up and paid attention.

"The good news is that you're in great hands. The bad news is that all the horsing around and goofing off has to end. You are now a small cog in the machine of this show. If you don't have the right cues for lighting, set changes and music cues, there is no show." Tyson grabbed a clipboard and glanced down at his notes.

"Today you're going to start with a tour of the theatre, including back stage, stairs, entrances, lines of death. You will receive every possible safety note you may need. Pay attention. You'll be getting your dressing rooms and learning about the make up room, trap room, backstage sound systems and more. After that we're going to start our tech rehearsal, so be patient and ready to do a lot of standing around."

I looked at Eli and some of the others. *We weren't in Kansas anymore.*

"Ah, here he is." Tyson pointed. "This is Jerry Block, your stage manager. Please listen up and make me proud. Jerry, they're all yours."

"Welcome! I've been looking forward to working with all of you. We've got a great show to put on, so let's get down to business."

Jerry split us in two groups, and we toured the whole place meeting different theatre veterans along the way. Each one had their own area of expertise.

"Are you half as intimidated as I am?" I whispered

to Eli.

"Oh yeah. Now I understand why Tyson was freaking out last night. If we screw this up, there's an army of people we'll bring down with us."

"I'm glad I'm not you, lead of the whole shebang!"

"I thought I was ready for this, but now I think I need another month."

"You'll be great." I squeezed his hand.

"At least you'll be with me half the time I'm on stage."

After Jerry's talk, we spent hours working on light checks. For each scene, we had to stand and block each spot on stage for lighting cues. It was tedious waiting while they adjusted the lights for color and intensity over and over. Suddenly there were far more important things we needed to do. Like practice!

Finally, at the intermission point of the blocking, the lighting director called a half hour break for lunch. The house lights came up, and Tyson walked out to the aisle with Jerry.

A tall woman with a mane of honey blonde hair, skinny jeans tucked into knee high boots and a designer bag entered through the back doors and sauntered up behind Tyson.

Those of us still on stage watched, transfixed by this new arrival.

"Who's that?" I asked Eli.

"I don't know, but looks like she's here to see Tyson."

"Maybe it's his sister," Alex said eyeing the leggy beauty.

The woman stood with a devilish smirk, just out of Tyson's view. Jerry took one look at her and forgot what he was saying.

Tyson turned and his face lit up like the night sky on the Fourth of July. She stepped into his arms and he held her in a way that suggested much more than a polite acquaintance. When he released her, he kissed her quick on the mouth and then introduced her to Jerry who appreciated the display as much as we did. He smiled wide, shook her hand, and then stepped away.

"I don't think she's his sister," said Sophie.

Tyson pulled the woman close and brushed a lock of long silky hair behind her ear. His gaze devoured her. He flashed an eyebrow then kissed her again.

"Definitely not his sister," said Troy.

"I feel like we shouldn't be watching," I said, but couldn't look away.

"I don't think he loves John, the way he obviously loves her, " Eli said to me.

"Yeah, they should get a room," said McKenna.

"Woo hoo!" Jason cheered. We applauded, and Eli whistled.

Tyson turned to us and laughed. Nothing could wipe the smile off his face. He wrapped his arm around her narrow waist and walked down to us. "So does this end the speculation?" he asked.

"Damn, I was so sure you were gay," said Jason.

"Pay up," Troy said with his hand out to Jason.

The beautiful woman laughed easily; the guys couldn't take their eyes off her. By now the word spread and the whole cast gathered at the edge of the stage like preschoolers waiting for morning snack.

"Everyone, I'd like you to meet Samantha. Samantha, this is everyone."

"Hi, great to meet you." She had a mega watt smile. Despite the fact she looked better than a runway model, she seemed instantly nice and totally down to earth.

"Samantha will be helping direct traffic this week. So if you have a problem or question and I'm unavailable, Sam's your girl."

"I'm good with that," Jason said.

Tyson ignored his comment. "Now go grab lunch before you're due back on stage." The cast dispersed. "And don't be late!" he hollered.

Eli and I started to leave with the others.

"Willow, could you join us for a sec. Eli, you too." Tyson called.

"Sure." We took the temporary steps set up to the stage.

"Samantha, this is Willow and Eli, my stars." Pride shone in his eyes.

"I don't know about stars, but we're doing our best," said Eli.

"Hi." I shook her slender hand.

"It's great to meet you both. Tyce has told me so much about you. Something about Messer something Road."

My head snapped to Tyson and Eli's jaw dropped.

"Don't worry. Your secrets are safe with me." She winked.

"Samantha has been lead in many shows and knows all the ins and outs of what you're about to face. Willow, she's going to help you out during the show and serve as your dresser."

"Oh. Thanks." I didn't know what to say. Tyson's girlfriend was going to dress me?

"What about me?" Eli said. "I have a ton of costume changes too."

Samantha laughed.

"Don't worry. I have a guy for you. He's about five foot two, tops the scale at about two hundred fifty and sweats a lot."

"Gee thanks. It's good to know you have my back," Eli said.

"Always." Tyson grinned.

Chapter 34

The next days were hectic with piano tech, mic checks, and media interviews. We were now working with the orchestra, who blew me away! The professional musicians transported the show to another level. The cast was so excited, because now we knew the show would be a hit. All pistons were running smoothly. Before I knew it, it was Wednesday and our final dress rehearsal was the next night.

"Eli, Willow, can I have a minute?" Tyson called to us where we did our dance warm up with the rest of the cast.

"Sure." I stood up from my spot, nudged Eli's foot, and held out my hand. "No rest for the weary." Eli popped up. As we joined Tyson at the production table, he still held my hand. The connection felt so natural now.

"I need to talk to you both about a change in the final scene."

Just then a trumpet player in the orchestra began blasting notes. An electric guitar riffed up and down the scale, and a keyboardist joined in the racket.

"Let's take a walk. I can't think with all this noise." He slipped off his headset, tossed it on the tech table, and we followed him to the side door.

"Much better!" Tyson said now that we were in the main marble and chrome corridor of the Overture

Center. He wore a rumpled shirt, and his jeans sagged like he'd worn them too many days in a row. Stress creased the corner of his eyes and dark shadows lay beneath.

"Listen, we've had a huge screw up with the lighting projector that creates the special effects we need for the death scene." He rubbed his hands over his weary face and through his hair. He walked us over to the rotunda that overlooked a lower level performance area.

"So what happens now?" Eli leaned against the marble ledge.

"We'll have to do it old school after all."

The hair on my neck stood at attention as dread crept up my back. "What exactly does old school mean?" My voice sounded eerily calm in my now buzzing ears.

"Does this mean we get to fall into the pit? Eli's eyes were wide with anticipation.

"That's exactly what it means." Tyson laughed and shook his head at Eli's boyish enthusiasm.

"Yes!" Eli punched his fist in the air. "How far do we fall? How's it going to work?"

"We're going to bring back the rooftop set from Scene Four. The fight will end on the rooftop. The floor trap will be opened below with a crash pad."

I felt the color drain from my face. This could not be happening. They couldn't possibly expect me to get pushed into thin air and hope I made it to the crash mat below.

"When do we get to try it?" Eli bounced on his feet like a giddy little boy.

"Tonight, after the run-through. We can't take any

time while the orchestra's here. They are contracted for exactly three hours. We can't go over."

I put my hand on the wide marble ledge to keep from swaying. The cold stone matched my emotions.

"I need you both ready immediately after the general cast dismissal so we can get this blocked before the union crew kicks us out of the building."

I barely heard his words through the white noise of my mind as my inner voice kept chanting, "No! No! No! No! No! No!"

"Willow, are you okay?" Tyson asked, his brow furrowed.

Eli smiled. His joy kept him from seeing the panic in my eyes.

"Yeah, fine." I covered. What the hell was I supposed to say? No flippin' way am I jumping off a set fifteen feet above the mat.

"Willow, I wondered if this change would be a problem for you, but this fall will be much simpler than the stunts you did in cheerleading. All you do is free fall. No spins or flips. Piece of cake." Tyson actually believed his words and looked so positive.

Fool.

"Right," I mumbled. It would be a goddamned terror-inducing, skull-crushing fear fest. Tyson might believe it was a piece of cake, but I couldn't do it.

Oh god, I couldn't tell him. It'll ruin everything. Perspiration broke out across my forehead.

"Tyson, can't someone fix the projector or get a new one?" I asked.

"Not in time. The closest replacement would have to be shipped here from New York, and the soonest we can get it is Saturday. Repair isn't possible, the damage is too severe." He looked at my face. A crease of concern crossed his forehead. "Willow, are you worried about the fall?"

"Oh no, it's just that we won't have much time to practice, and tomorrow is the final dress rehearsal, and the school will be here." My school, Capital High. As a thank you to the school for the use of rehearsal space, the entire student body gets to see the final dress. Oh shit, oh shit, oh shit!

One of the techs popped out of a door. "Tyson, we're all set here."

"Thanks, we'll be right there." We walked back to the theatre. Tyson put his arm around my shoulder and gave me quick squeeze. "You'll be fine. You are as much of a professional as I've ever met. I've seen you grow and care so much about this show. You'll be great. How fortunate for me that I cast a former cheerleader who knows how to free fall."

I forced a smile that came out more as a grimace and had to restrain myself from turning and running away as I walked with Tyson on one side and Eli on the other; ushering me back to the fears I'd run away from.

* * *

The terrifying view from the second story rooftop set paralyzed me, and watching Eli jump off with such boyish pleasure made me want to hurl.

"Eli, perfect! I couldn't have done it better myself. Come on back up." Tyson called, learning over the precipice. I wanted to pull him back, but that would mean moving toward the edge.

"Woo hoo! That was awesome!" Eli bounced up from the mat far below.

"See, Willow, easy as pie. Do you know where your mark is?"

I nodded.

"Do you know the timing set up?"

I nodded.

"And you know where to aim your fall on the mat?"

"Yes." I understood all these things. I'd spent hours on end practicing falls, tricks and stunts during cheer camps and with Jilly at her uncle's gymnastics school. It didn't mean I could pull it off.

I bit my lip and pressed myself as far from the edge as I could. Hot panic consumed me like a blast of heat in a sauna.

Tyson started to chew at his fingernails when, for the fifth time, I didn't budge. "Willow, just relax, take a deep breath, and let gravity do the work."

But gravity was the problem. Gravity would pull me down. I wouldn't be in control. Despite the fact that the trap opening in the stage floor was ten feet wide. I could still miss it. Anything could happen. I could hit my leg and snap it in two or smack my head on the edge and bleed to death of a brain hemorrhage. I shivered at the thought.

"Tyson." I mustered all the courage I could and prayed he'd understand. "Is there any way I can not do this?" I know he saw pure terror on my face.

Eli joined us from his last thrilling fall to the mat.

Tyson blew out a huge breath of patient frustration and put his hands on his head. "Oh boy." He contemplated me and this dire situation.

"What's going on?" Eli looked at Tyson and then me. "Why haven't you gone?"

I averted my eyes so neither one could pin me with disappointment. Tyson didn't speak a word. He must be screaming inside.

"Willow, what's wrong?" Eli asked, still oblivious. How could he not see the problem?

He stepped next to me. "You're trembling. Are you okay?" He held my shoulders and leaned down to see my face. "Willow, talk to me."

"I can't do it." I whispered, because I didn't have the guts to admit it any louder.

Eli's face screwed up, and he looked at Tyson who raised his eyebrows in a sign of defeat.

"You're kidding? Right?" He asked and then dawning struck. "Oh my god, are you scared?" Disbelief shown on his face. "Oh, Willow. It's okay." He hugged me and chuckled at the irony of the situation. My body was rigid like a telephone pole.

"It's gonna be okay. You can do this. I'll help you." He smiled up close, so confident and trustworthy.

I stared back like a little kid afraid to go in the pool. There was no way to make them swim or get in the water, short of lifting them and throwing them in. He better not even consider that. A new wave of horror shook through me.

With his handsome, innocent face close to mine, he spoke calm and quiet. "First, take a couple of deep breaths. You've got yourself all worked up over nothing."

I looked into his wide dark eyes and focused on his

words. Tyson watched and I'm sure prayed Eli could turn this situation around. I took the breaths and exhaled. It helped in the teensiest way.

"You've done tons scarier and more difficult stuff than this as a cheerleader. You can do this one simple fall. Just think of it as a cheerleading trick."

Which was the worst thing he could say, but I couldn't tell him that.

"Eli," I whispered again. "I don't think this is going to work."

"Sure it will. Here, take my hand." He stepped toward the edge and held his hand out to me. I clenched my jaw and focused on him. I wanted to take his hand, I really did, but he stood so close to the edge. I worried he'd slip and take me with him to my doom.

I took another deep gulp of air, moved a tiny step and gripped his warm hand with my clammy one.

"See, that's great." The encouragement in his voice began to sooth my erratic nerves. "Now another step. We're just going to look over the side."

Tyson observed in steely silence but didn't interfere.

I took the step, my legs shaking like a paint can in a mixing machine.

"Good," Eli's voice soothed.

"Nice job," Tyson said.

Being treated like a child by these two confident guys was humiliating, to say the least. I let out a sigh. Maybe I could do this. I leaned forward just enough to see part of the trap far below. My head spun. It looked like a frickin' postage stamp on the enormous stage floor.

No way could I make that! I whipped my hand away and ran to press myself against the safety of the back wall.

Eli huffed, his patience running out. Tyson turned to Jason, who had stayed in the shadows off to the side this whole time. "Why don't you head out," he said in a quiet tone. Jason gave me an encouraging smile and left.

"That's okay. Come back over here," Eli said his words a little clipped.

I stared at him, unwilling to budge.

"Come on, let's try it again." He waved me over, patience growing thin.

I didn't move. My heart pounded in my chest. They both kept staring at me like I was some freakazoid.

"You have to try," Eli implored.

I shook my head, no. "I can't do it."

I prayed the clock would move faster so we'd have to leave. I locked my frightened eyes with Eli's frustrated ones.

Eli huffed, turned to Tyson and threw his hands in the air.

"Let's take a break," Tyson said.

"No! This is unacceptable!" Eli erupted. "Willow, it's time to put your big girl pants on and get this done. We're running out of time."

"Eli, I can not do this! Back off!" Tears threatened. *I would not cry. I would not cry.*

"Of course you can, you just need a little tough love." He took my upper arm with gentle hands and began to pull me away from the wall.

"No! Don't touch me!" I screamed.

He and Tyson stared at me as if I'd lost it, which I pretty much had. Eli released my arm, but didn't let up. "Willow, you have to do this."

"No, I don't!" I snapped.

"Eli," Tyson interrupted. "That's enough."

"Do you have any idea how many people are counting on you? Including me? You have to do it so you don't screw up the show. There's going to be a casting agent here. What's he and the other New York people going to think?" Eli said, all pissed off, with his hands planted on his hips.

"I don't give a flip what other people think. I'm not going to do...it!" I couldn't even say "jump off". *What a coward.*

"Why?" he demanded. "You'll do every possible cheerleading trick, no matter how dangerous, but you won't try one puny fall!?" Eli yelled.

"No. I won't!" I yelled.

"So what's the deal? You scared?"

"Eli." Tyson tried to warn him off; Eli ignored him. We'd passed the point of no return.

"Fine! I'm scared. Now you know, I'm afraid, so I guess that makes me a failure. I'm out of here."

I glared at Eli, he shoved his stubborn chin out and glared back. I tried to move past him, but he blocked my way. I'd have to walk near the edge, and he knew I wouldn't go there.

"You know that every time you get scared you run away. Did you know that?" he spat.

Out of the corner of my eye, I saw Tyson shake his head in useless frustration.

"You did it three years ago with me, you did it with cheerleading, and you're doing it now," he said with open disgust. "I'm so sick and tired of you jerking me around."

I gulped. Everything he said was true, but he had me cornered, and all I cared about was escaping that rooftop set.

"This time your spoiled little girl act is affecting more than just me. If you don't do this fall, you're screwing it up for everyone! It's time to fucking grow up!" he screamed.

"You're an asshole! I hate you!" I lashed out.

"I'm not the one switching directions like a ping pong ball. One minute you're freezing me out, the next you want to hook up, and now you hate my guts. Make up your mind!"

"Go to hell!" I screamed and shoved him out of my way and didn't care if he fell off or not.

"Right back at you!" Eli retaliated.

Chapter 35

I caught Tyson's look of helpless defeat as I stormed past. Nothing I could do about it now. I ran down the steps, bolted past the stage manager to my dressing room, grabbed my bag and jacket and flew out the stage door.

Afraid Eli or Tyson would try to catch up to me, I ran the first few blocks up State Street. I needed as much distance between me and the gaping hole in the stage floor. Once I got past the State Capitol, lit up in all its glory, my adrenaline began to slow and left me shaking like a leaf. I pulled out my phone and called home.

"Dad." My teeth chattered with emotion. "Can you come get me?"

"Willow, are you okay? Where's Eli?" His normally laid back voice slipped into protective dad mode.

"I'm fine. I just need a ride home. I'm on Willy Street." I rushed along. My gait was long and quick.

"On my way." He clicked off without another word. I pictured him bolting out the door to the car without a coat. He was my hero.

Five minutes later, the crooked headlights of our car came around the corner, and I waved Dad down.

I climbed in and leaned my head back on the headrest, thankful to be safely away from the threats at the theatre.

"You and Eli have a fight?" Dad asked, while I

buckled up.

I took one look at him. "Oh, Daddy." And started to cry.

He leaned over and hugged me. I felt five years old again, and that was fine with me. Those were good years.

"Tell me what's going on," he said as he pulled away from the curb.

And so I did. I told him the whole story, from why I really quit cheer to how hard it had been with everyone so mad at me and how terrified I am to do that fall. Dad drove around aimlessly while I spilled my guts. Then I realized we were at the McDonalds drive through. I never noticed him pull in; I was so busy blabbing.

He handed me a chocolate shake.

"What about Mom?" I asked, knowing how freaked out she'd be that Dad went out of his way to give me refined sugars.

"We don't need to tell her. It'll be our secret, and I'll hide the evidence."

I took a couple huge mouthfuls and consoled myself with creamy cold chocolate heaven. As I drowned my troubles with ice cream, I contemplated my mess.

"Dad, I can't do it."

"What do you want to do? " he asked as he pulled out and continued our wandering drive.

"What do you mean?"

"It's up to you. It's a free world. You can do anything you want. So what do you want to do?"

"I don't want to do that fall." My hand became cold from gripping my shake. "I really want to do the show, but I seriously don't want to do the fall."

"Okay, so don't do it. So what?"

Easy for him to say. It wasn't his butt on the line.

"But it will ruin the show! And Tyson has been so great. I don't want to do anything to hurt him. He's done so much for me."

"Maybe it will hurt the show and maybe not. This Tyson sounds like a pretty smart guy."

"But it's such a terrible thing to do to him."

"Then don't do it."

"You are so aggravating. You make it sound like it's not a big deal, but it is!"

He smiled in that *I'm so wise and you're so young and naïve* way. "Can I offer some advice?"

"Sure, but I might not take it." I cocked my head sideways and smirked.

"That's your choice. You need to give yourself a chance to succeed. If you don't play the game of life, you'll never win. If you turn your back on every challenge that comes along, you'll be missing out on some awesome stuff."

I hate it when parents make sense, and what he said did. Plus, Dad knew me well enough to know I'm not a quitter. I slurped down more of my shake, the sugar did a good job of raising my spirits.

Dad turned onto a side street and drove slower. "Do you remember when you were little and I worked at the Ad Agency? He glanced over at me.

"You were never home."

"That's right. I wanted to make a living by creating ceramic art, but I was afraid to quit my job. I didn't want to let your mom or you and Breezy down. I didn't know how we'd pay our bills. Finally, I realized life is too

precious to spend ignoring the things you care about."
He looked over at me.

"It's the best thing you ever did," I said.

"Let's look at when you quit dance because Eli
wanted to lock lips with you."

"Dad!" I nearly spewed my shake across the
dashboard.

"Why were you afraid?"

"I was afraid I'd get hurt, and we wouldn't be
friends anymore."

"And what happened?"

"I ran and was hurt and lost his friendship anyway."

"And what about cheer? Why were you afraid?"

"Because I didn't want to die!"

"Good reason." He smiled. "So you quit and didn't
give yourself a chance to see how it might go? What was
the result?" He slowly drove past the parked cars.

"I lost my best friend and the squad hates me."

"And they didn't make it to nationals either. Hmm.
My point is that each time you turned your back when
you got scared, you got hurt and hurt others. However,
you also found some new amazing things. That's how
you found cheer and Jilly, and then it's how you found
Dream Chaser and hooked up with Eli and met the
amazing Tyson Scott!" Dad said it like a game show
announcer. "I can't wait to meet this guy and see if he's
half as wonderful as you say."

I grinned slow and sly. "Oh yeah, he is."

"Back to the point. Whatever decision you make is
okay. Running away from your fears will be painful, and
you will probably end up hurting some people, but
something new will evolve from it. The world isn't static.

Energy is always moving and changing. You and your decisions are just part of that energy. As you decide what to do, be true to your authentic self."

"Yes, Oprah."

"That was Dr. Phil." He smiled and pulled into the driveway. "Does that help?"

"Kind of."

As we walked to the front door, I noticed a familiar SUV at the curb. My chest tightened.

"Looks like we have company," Dad said and eyed me knowingly.

"Uh oh." I dropped behind Dad.

The lights inside shone bright despite the late hour. Dad glanced back at me. "I wonder who this could be?"

I let him walk in first. My human shield.

"Hi Honey! I'm so glad you two are back. We have company." Mom nearly oozed with joy as Tyson stood up from our afghan-draped couch with a half dozen of Breezy's fake vampire teeth scattered on the coffee table before him. His leather coat was unzipped with a designer scarf thrown carelessly around his neck and those jeans that made all the girls salivate. His eyes sparkled with calm warmth even though inside he must have been freaking out.

"Joe, honey, meet Tyson Scott." Mom introduced them, biting back a smile.

Tyson reached out and there in my screwy house my hippy dad and the suave New York hottie shook hands.

Weird.

"Nice to finally meet you," Dad said. "We've heard so much about you."

"My pleasure. I hope what you've heard isn't too bad. I've been pushing the kids pretty hard. Let me say you have an extraordinarily talented daughter."

"Thank you. We think she's pretty special." Dad put his arm around my shoulder for a squeeze. He barely concealed his smirk when he glanced at me. I could read his mind. *Ha ha! You're back in the hot seat. No running now!*

"Tyson has been telling me about the show." Mom said in a sing-song way. "Sounds like it's going to be wonderful. I had no idea all the detail that goes into it."

OMG, Mom was flirting with my director. Gag.

While they chatted like BFF's, I tried to sink into the braided rug.

"It's getting late, and we have another big day tomorrow. If it's alright, I'd like to talk with Willow for a couple of minutes," Tyson said.

"Of course, you go right ahead." Mom said and nearly pushed dad out of the room. She didn't miss the opportunity to mouth the words. "He is so cute!"

I gave her the *get out before I hurt you* look. She grinned and fanned herself. I almost asked if her menopause was acting up again. Dad pulled her away.

Once we were alone, Tyson indicated the couch, and we both sat. "Your parents seem like great people."

"Oh yeah, they're just terrific," I said loud enough I knew they would hear.

"Thanks, honey," Mom called back.

Tyson fought back a laugh. "I see where you get your personality."

I rolled my eyes.

Tyson focused on me for a couple seconds and

finally said. "So that was quite a mess tonight."

"Yeah." I nodded and stared at Breezy's plastic fangs.

"I apologize for that. It's my fault. I should have never let it get out of hand. I didn't realize the situation."

My head snapped up in surprise. It wasn't his fault; it was all me. I shook my head. "No!"

"Don't be surprised. Asking you to do such a dramatic stunt with literally no time to process the idea or prep was unacceptable, and I'm sorry."

I'm pretty sure my jaw lay on the floor.

"I forget that you guys are so young. Making changes this close to opening night is something even professionals would freak out about."

He stood up and paced in front of the coffee table. He pushed a hand through his hair. "With all your cheerleading background and all your stunt work, I assumed the fall would be simple for you. I had forgotten about your serious fall in cheerleading. Now that I have all the information, it makes total sense. I just wish you would have confided in me right away."

"But it won't make any difference. If I don't do the fall, it'll ruin the show."

He stopped in his tracks. "Don't worry, I'll figure something out."

I couldn't let him do that. I didn't want to compromise the show. If I dug deep enough, I knew I could do it, and I wanted to make things up to Eli. I'd acted like such a bitch.

"I've been thinking a lot about it while I rode home with my dad. You're right. The news of the stunt surprised me, but I've had time to think about it, and I'd really like to do it."

Tyson looked at me with skepticism.

"I know it's hard to believe that after my behavior tonight. But I know I can." I swallowed not wanting to even begin to think about how much I had screwed things up with him. "I've done much harder and scarier things a million times. I know exactly how to do that…" I cleared my throat. "…fall."

Tyson considered me. "Are you sure that's a good idea? It's obvious you still have a lot of fear related to your accident. I don't want to put you in a situation that's uncomfortable or unsafe."

"I'm absolutely sure. If you want, we can go downtown right now, and I'll show you."

His mood seemed to brighten. "The place is locked up, but we can run it before show time tomorrow."

"Sounds great." I said with a confidence that wasn't as strong as it sounded.

"You're positive about this?" he asked, offering me an out.

"Absolutely."

"Well then, I'll get out of here and let you get some rest."

I walked him to the door. "I'm really sorry about tonight and that I acted like a total lunatic."

"Don't worry about it. We all need to let off some steam once in a while. But do me a favor will ya?"

"Sure."

"Go light on Eli. He's under a lot of pressure too." He smiled.

"I will."

"Goodnight."

I let him out, and no sooner had I locked the door than Mom and Dad came around the corner.

"Your dad filled me in on what's happening." Mom said with concern.

"Well? What did he have to say? Did you decide anything?" Dad asked.

I leaned against the door. "He was really nice and we talked it all out. And...I'm going to perform the stunt. I know I can do it."

"You're sure?" Dad asked.

"Positive." I lied. I didn't want to let anyone down and I wouldn't. I just didn't know how to get myself off that edge.

"I'm glad it all worked out," Mom said. "Your director seemed like a very nice man, and, oh! You did not do that man justice!"

"I told you!"

"Ralph, do you mind if I put Tyson Scott at the top of my list?"

"Eww, Mom."

"What? I can have anyone I want on my list." She raised her eyes suggestively at my dad.

I shook my head. "I'm going to bed." The exhaustion from all the drama had caught up with me.

"Hey Willow?" Dad asked as I climbed the steps. "You sure you're okay?"

"Yeah, I'm fine."

And I kept telling myself that through a fitful night of sleep and all through school on Thursday.

Chapter 36

Dress rehearsal sucked. The whole day sucked. The whole day my adrenaline was revved up high. I couldn't stop fidgeting, and any time someone spoke to me, I jumped.

The closer it came to my call time, the worse it got. Mom forced me to eat a little dinner, but after a few bites my stomach started to roll.

Eli didn't call, and I didn't try to call him either. There was just too much to say and not enough time to figure anything out.

After I drove around the parking ramp ten times, not ready to face the music, I walked into the theatre twenty minutes late. I wanted to throw up. Instead, I swallowed my sense of doom.

I could do this. I would not run. I would not quit.

The makeup room streamed with activity. The company applied most of their makeup on their own and then the make up director Mary Gorman, or one of her assistants finished them off with dramatic eyes, including false eye lashes for the girls and contouring shades on the guys.

Mary applied my make up. I wasn't even allowed to touch a brush. "Are you ready for tonight?" she asked, unaware of the drama churning inside me.

"As ready as I'll ever be." I tried to block out all thoughts of that stupid fall. I knew I had to do it, but each time I tried to picture myself falling off that set piece, I shuddered in revulsion as an image of me splatting to my death took over.

"Five minutes to full cast run of the Party Scene," Jerry's voice boomed over the backstage sound system. "Ten minute call for Jason, Eli and Willow to run the final scene."

"Shit." My adrenaline pumped up another notch as I made my way to the stage with the others who laughed and joked with nervous excitement. Everyone was present; orchestra, lights, sound. No breaking character or stopping for anything.

"Places everyone," Tyson called. He looked even more ragged than last night.

We all shuffled to our starting spots. Eli and I began at opposite sides of the stage. I caught his eye, and he looked back with a stubborn set to his chin, but a softness in his eyes. He nodded, but didn't smile or give me any sign of forgiveness or reconciliation. I nodded back and hoped things would improve.

"Heads in the game people!" Tyson called out. "Let's get this down the first time. We don't have time to rerun it."

The Party Scene has been one of our biggest challenges. It's a big band scene. It's crowded and busy, with a lot happening. The conductor signaled the orchestra and the intro began. I tried to concentrate on the steps and not my next task: falling through the trap.

"Much better," Tyson said when we finished. "Clear the stage for a set change, and then I need Willow, Eli, and Jason."

Here we go. I snuck a look at Eli. He looked at me,

but said nothing. I'm sure he was biting his tongue to see if I'd do the fall or not. He could wait all day, cause I was about to deliver the goods.

My body shuddered.

"Somebody help!" Sophie yelled.

A commotion started behind me.

"Give her room." Alex sounded really serious.

"Tyson, you better get up here, something is wrong with Sophie."

A small crowed blocked my view. I edged by and there on the floor, center stage, lay Sophie having a grand mal seizure.

Chapter 37

I had to look away, but could still hear the sound of Sophie's body as it seized against the hardwood stage floor. The sound transported me back to Twinkie's suffering only a couple weeks before.

Eli's eye caught mine. He let down his anger for just a second. We knew better than most the horror that was attacking poor Sophie. Please, oh please, God, don't let her have a brain tumor.

Tyson appeared in an instant and pushed through the cluster of onlookers. He took one look and yelled, "Jerry, call 911!"

McKenna started to cry. I wanted to join her.

"And call Sophie's parents too!" Tyson pulled off his sweatshirt, knelt down beside her and slid it under her head. "Give her some space. In fact, why don't you all finish getting ready back in your dressing rooms."

"Are we still going to do the show?" McKenna asked.

"Yes, the show is on. Unless terrorists attack the State Capitol, the curtain rises at eight p.m. sharp."

Eli and I shared a charged look as we went our separate ways. The sound of sirens could be heard as I entered my dressing room. It reminded me how fragile life can be.

* * *

But I couldn't stay away. I had to know she would be okay, so I watched from the darkened wings as a team of paramedics surrounded her. They spread out their medical equipment on the stage and tended to her. A gurney waited nearby. My heart clenched as I peeked glimpses of Sophie looking so vulnerable. I prayed she didn't have a brain tumor. The only positive aspect of the scary scene was that it prevented me from practicing the fall. After what felt like an eternity, the ambulance whisked Sophie away.

Tyson spoke to us backstage minutes before curtain. "The excitement is over. Sophie is in good hands, and we'll get an update from her parents as soon as possible. Now I want you all to clear your heads and focus on the show. We have a full house out there thanks to Capital High School.

He pulled me aside. "Willow, we're not going to have a chance to practice the fall." His brows lowered over his intense eyes. "Tell me now if you are up for it or not."

There was an out?

"How do we end the show if she won't take the fall?" Eli barely masked the angry frustration in his voice.

"I don't know. We'll turn it into a stabbing or gunshot or something." Tyson said.

"But we don't have time to choreograph something new. Plus that'll be lame. How will I die then? It needs a dramatic tragic ending."

"Eli, stop worrying about it. You need to concentrate on leading this show. Get your head in the game." Tyson patted Eli's shoulder then returned his attention to me.

I did not want to ruin the show. I agreed with Eli that we needed a dramatic surprise ending. I knew how to take that fall. It wasn't difficult. Physically. I just needed to get my head to cooperate, but thoughts of Sophie's seizure and the sound of ambulance sirens brought back my greatest fears.

My body was rigid with determination. "I'm good. I can do it," I said.

Eli raised an eyebrow of doubt.

"I got it!" I huffed.

"You're sure?" Tyson asked.

"I'm positive," I repeated, truly believing my words.

"Great." He smiled in relief. "Let's get this show up." He queued the stage manager.

"Places!" Jerry called.

And the show began; fifteen minutes late.

* * *

Unfortunately, after the scare with Sophie, the disasters kept coming.

Eli's mic kept going out during the first scene. Damian's shoe flew across the stage in a big dance number, and Jason forgot his lines. Twice.

And then, during the love scene my spacing was off and I elbowed Eli in the jaw so hard he fell back and tripped me as he tried to catch his balance. I hit the floor in the most ungraceful fashion. All in all. It sucked.

I didn't hear myself sing. It was all remote control and probably not very good. I kept thinking about Jilly and the cheer squad watching and judging my every move. I'm sure they wanted me to fail, since they didn't make nationals. I didn't blame them.

The disastrous excuse for a show was winding down, and the final scene loomed. All night I'd forced it out of my mind as best I could, but as Samantha helped me change into my next costume, I knew there was no more hiding.

"You ready?" she asked as she pulled the dress from the last scene over my head.

"Sure," I answered, kicking off my shoes and pretending the next scene didn't terrify me. I couldn't let anyone know how hard this was.

"Need a pep talk or a shot of whiskey?" She grinned and I could see why Tyson adored her so much.

"Tyson would love that!" I laughed and held my arms up as she pulled the new costume on.

"If there is anything I can do to help you through this, you let me know." She spoke direct at me as she adjusted the dress. "I've faced my own share of 'issues' over the years, and I don't want you to feel alone in figuring this out."

"Thanks. I think the best plan is to avoid thinking about it until the last second and just do it." I lifted a foot and she slid on a shoe and buckled it.

"Alright." She nodded, but said nothing more. I wished she would've said, *Great plan! You'll be great! Don't worry.*

But I was worried. Very worried. I kept trying to block it out of my mind. I wanted to cover my ears and say "la la la la la la la," like I do when Mom lectures me about the dangers of processed foods.

"You're all set. Go knock 'em dead."

As I left the dressing room, my heart pounded heavy exploding beats.

Shit, oh shit, oh shit, oh shit.

No, I could do this. I would do this. I have to do this.

With only a few seconds before our scene, Jason approached, his forehead creased. "You okay? You going to be able to take the fall?"

"I'm fine," I snapped and immediately regretted it. He flinched, but said nothing. Jason had always been nice to me. I wanted to apologize, but was too wrapped up in "Willow's World" to think about anything but my own problems.

The lights came up, and Jerry cued our entrance.

No looking back now.

The scene was a blur.

I went through the motions, but inside my mind battled my gut. Suddenly Eli, Jason and I were on the rooftop with the fight about to hit its climax.

The bright lights glared. The sound of the orchestra was drowned out by the eerie pounding of blood through my panicked brain.

I saw shadowy images of the audience through my haze.

The music built.

I saw the edge.

I saw the open trap in the stage floor below.

My pulse raced.

Jason rushed at me. Eli watched, his character reacting in horror.

This is when I teeter on the edge and then fall to my death.

I moved to the edge.

It was too far. Too dangerous. I stepped away from the edge.

Panicked, I turned to Jason and then Eli, whose eyes were wide in a different kind of panic.

"Go!" He seethed between clenched teeth.

I gave the slightest shake of my head.

No.

The music vamped on, the director probably flipping out because we passed the crescendo of where I'm supposed to fall.

I looked back and forth from Jason and Eli again, each of them not knowing what to do.

So I collapsed.

On the rooftop set. I fell close to the back wall where I couldn't fall off and get hurt.

Not off the side through the trap to the mat.

I just collapsed in place up on the rooftop right in front of them. What the hell else could I do? I knew I had to die. So I lay there like a dead fish collecting flies.

Confused, Jason stared like I'd lost my mind.

"Stab her," Eli whispered to Jason.

"What?" he looked at him in disbelief.

"Pretend to stab her!"

Jason came at me. He raised his arm high and with an invisible knife and stabbed me in the heart.

Eli came up behind Jason. Jason turned and fake stabbed him too.

Eli fell on the rooftop floor next to me. Jason eyed us both and then ran off stage. The music hit its high note, finished the dramatic last couple notes, and the stage went black.

"Oh my fucking lord! What the hell was that!" Eli

seethed in the dark.

"I'm sorry," I said filled with so much regret.

"Sorry? You made a fool out of Jason and me, not to mention you ruined what was supposed to be the climax of the show!"

We got up in the dark to move off stage for the mega mix, which was supposed to happy and joyous.

"I know. I didn't mean to. I really didn't," I cried.

"Tyson asked if you could do this, and you said yes. You could have been honest. You could have 'fessed up and given him a chance to figure something else out." He took the steps at the back of the set.

"I said I'm sorry. What more do you want?" Tears streaked my face as I followed, stepping on the glow-in-the-dark tape as I went.

Eli stopped and faced me. "Be honest with people for once in your life and stop running or cowering from everything that scares you."

I couldn't agree more. I didn't know what to say, so I said nothing. He huffed and stormed off to change for the Mega Mix.

Back in my dressing room, I fought the tears, put myself on automatic and went through the motions like a robot. Samantha gave me a hug and a little smile that was supposed to make me feel better, but instead told me what a failure I was.

"I'm sorry. I didn't mean to ruin the show." I choked back a sob.

"Shh." She gave me a big hug. "What's done is done." She proceeded to help me into my angelic white finale costume. I gulped air, trying to calm myself down.

"I've ruined it for everyone. Tyson's going to hate

me."

"All set," she said a minute later. "Tyson won't hate you. He's a much better man than that. Now chin up. Go finish the show."

"Right."

I pasted on a fake smile and left. I didn't look at Eli or anyone else for that matter. My bow was a pathetic half-hearted leap that barely got off the ground.

The student filled audience applauded. I didn't know why, as we, no I, sucked! The curtain came down, and the cast reacted with a mix of relief it was over and frustration at all the screw-ups.

I approached Eli to test the waters of his mood. I noticed his swollen cheekbone from where I had smacked him during a number. He backed away

"I'm so mad! I can't even talk to you right now! I have no idea what to say." He shook his head in a combination of disbelief and frustration. "I gotta get out of here." Eli stormed off stage left.

I went stage right back to my dressing room. Jason grimaced as I trudged by. I let him down and made him look like a fool. "I'm sorry," I said as I passed.

How many more times did I need to apologize? As I walked past more of the cast, I received silent stares. It felt like the first week of rehearsals all over again.

Thankfully, Samantha wasn't in my dressing room. She probably went to calm Tyson down after the train wreck he'd just witnessed. I changed and hung up my sweaty costume. Tyson's voice came over the intercom. "No notes tonight. We all have a lot to think about. Let's hope everyone got the jitters out of their systems. Go home and get a good night sleep; we have a big day tomorrow."

I stared at my made-up face in the dressing room mirror. I looked amazing. I almost didn't recognize myself. The make up lady knew her stuff, but behind the artful cosmetics were sad, lonely eyes. I grabbed some wet wipes and washed the fake beauty away. Finally, my normal, scared self looked back.

That girl I knew well.

With nothing left to do, I decided to face the music and go find Tyson. The backstage area was quiet except for Jerry and a couple of stagehands finishing up.

"Hey Jerry, have you seen Tyson?"

"Yeah, he left a few minutes ago for the hospital to check on Sophie."

"Thanks." Tyson had more worries than just me, but I'm sure I must be one of his bigger headaches.

Outside, the mild night air reminded me spring was almost here. I decided to walk for a while instead of calling home for a ride. Only occasional piles of snow remained from our stormy winter. They'd become dirty grey piles of ice on the street corners. Walking helped clear my head.

I knew why I couldn't fall off that ledge, but why did I have to lie and promise I could? Why couldn't I be honest and admit I couldn't do it. This was not the girl I wanted to be. I hated being afraid, and lately it seemed I was always afraid of something. Cheerleading, singing, falling, what next?

I reached a large intersection and had to wait for the walk signal. A car pulled up with a bunch of the cheer kids. They must have been cruising around downtown after the show. One of the guys noticed me and pointed and laughed. I tried to look away, but my eyes locked onto Jilly in the back seat. She didn't laugh. She looked back and gave a small grimace. It's the most communication I'd had with her in over a month. She saw my misery. She knew me well. The light changed, and the car squealed away.

I didn't blame them for laughing. Tonight, I embarrassed myself in the show. They witnessed my screw-ups. Plus, they were still ticked off that I quit cheer and they didn't win State let alone get a shot at Nationals again.

The walk sign changed, and I crossed the street. What a fine pickle I was in this time. Block after block I walked as the night grew late and the moon came up. What was it my dad said? I could do whatever I wanted, and it would all work out one way or another. True. Life goes on. It's our choice how we deal with challenges.

By the time my feet hit our front porch, I knew what I wanted to do. The porch light glowed, and Mom and Dad waited in the candlelit living room.

"Hey hon', how'd it go?" Mom asked the moment I walked in. They were terrible at hiding their concern.

"Horrible. Anything and everything went wrong."

"Oh no. Like what?" Mom asked.

"Let's just say between faulty mics, missed cues, and my pearl necklace in the nightclub scene breaking and beads rolling all over the stage; it was less than mediocre."

"Ouch." She cringed.

"And?" Dad asked, waiting for the inevitable.

"And I didn't do the fall," I sighed. "I'm a failure."

"You are not a failure. Never have been and never

will be," he said.

"Your dad is right," Mom said. "You work harder to succeed than anyone I know."

"That's not true. I failed when I quit cheer, and if I don't get my shit together I'm going to fail Foods and History."

Dad raised an eyebrow. "How do you fail Foods?"

"Haven't you seen her cook?" Mom said under her breath.

"Oh, got it. But that's beside the point." He refocused. "So what happens next? Is Tyson going to change the ending?"

"Not if I can help it. I think I might have figured out how I can do the fall, but I need to borrow the car. Is that okay?"

"Of course, but it's after eleven. Where are you going?"

"I'd rather not say until I know it'll work."

Mom and Dad shared a concerned glance. "All right, but promise to call if you need anything!"

"I will." I scooped the keys off the side table in the entryway and left. I knew what I was going to do, but I couldn't do it alone. I fished my phone out of my pocket, called Jilly and held my breath that she'd answer.

Chapter 38

Twenty minutes later, Jilly unlocked the front door of her uncle's gymnastics studio.

"Thanks for meeting me," I said.

She flipped on the lights and locked the door behind us. "I figured I couldn't let you crash and burn like that. After the cheer squad blew it at State, we need something for the school to be proud of." She grinned her dazzling smile.

"Before we start, I just want to say again how sorry I am I bailed on you by quitting cheer. I never meant to hurt you."

"I know, and I was a total bitch too," she said.

"Yeah, you pretty much were." I grinned and she hugged me. Her embrace took a little of the weight off my shoulders.

"Good. Now that we got that mushy stuff out of the way, where do you want to begin?"

"The pit," I said.

"All right. Let's get this party started." She flipped on lights as we made our way into the huge padded floor gymnasium complete with balance beams, parallel bars, giant mats and, at the far end, a large open pit filled with giant foam squares.

This used to be one of our favorite spots to goof off. Plus it was great for learning cheer stunts. You could do all the twists and rotations and fall into the safe, deep cushioned comfort of the pit.

"Jump in anytime, " she teased as I stood and stared at the pit. "We haven't got all night. Okay, actually we do have all night, but it would be nice to a get a little sleep."

I sized up my nemesis and knew this was going to take a while. I looked square at Jilly. "That is the problem. I can't just jump in." I bit my lip and raised my brows.

"Seriously?" She finally realized the depth of my problem. "That bad?"

"Oh yeah." I nodded, contemplating the mound of spongy foam and knowing I would sink once in it. That was scary.

"How about if I hold your hand, and we jump in together?"

I considered it, then shook my head. "Nope. I don't think so." Finally I could speak honestly about my fears. It felt good.

"You could sit on the side of the pit and jump from there?" she offered.

I cringed. It wasn't far, but still. That sensation of not being stable just freaked me out. "Could we get a rope so I can climb in from the side? At least until I get used to it? That way I'm always holding on to something."

"Sure. Good idea." She looked around the gym for a rope. "While I do that, why don't you get on the trampoline and bounce a little. Remember what it feels like to feel a little air under your feet."

"Do I have to?" I scrunched my nose up.

"Yes! You have to!"

This was the kind of tough love I needed. Soft and gentle. So I climbed onto the trampoline where Jilly and I used to practice triple flips. My heart raced as I worked to keep my feet solid on the pad. I lightly walked toward the center and took little mini bounces that kept me touching at all times.

"I don't see any air over there," she hollered from the side of the pit where she tied a rope off to a large vault.

I stuck my tongue out at her, but then did bounce a little bigger. My feet left the mat for at least a split instant, and I didn't die. That was progress, so I kept at it for a while and worked my way up to a small bounce. My feet left the trampoline, and I had at least a foot of air. I just about had a coronary. But again, I didn't die. I stopped to catch my breath.

"Nice one. Keep it up," Jilly yelled.

"I think that's good for now. Let's try the rope now," I yelled back.

"Stop being a weenie. No rope until you get a good three feet of air."

"I hate you," I yelled as I bounced, but inside I loved having Jilly back.

"I hate you too," she countered.

Fine. So I bounced and bounced and allowed myself to leave the mat a little more and a little more. It no longer terrified me; I had the rhythm down. I did it over and over again.

"Can you believe how high we used to launch off this thing?" I marveled.

"Some of the best times of my life," she said. "You can still do it if you want."

"Whoa, slow down your horses, honey. Remember, baby steps!"

"Looks good. I now officially graduate you to use a rope to climb down into the pit."

"Oh goody!" I mocked, climbing down from the trampoline and not jumping off with an eagle jump like I used to.

We spent the next fifteen minutes with me lowering myself with the rope into the unstable foam squares. I bounced a little in the pit and would climb back out and do it again. We worked up to me sitting on the ledge to jump in, and eventually to Jilly holding my hand and jumping in together. Of course, I was tentative and had my hand out to catch myself.

"See, you're doing great!" she said.

"Yeah, if you're with me on stage tomorrow night I can jump two feet into a pit of foam."

"Stop being so hard on yourself. Look how far you've come in, what? An hour and a half."

It was one in the morning already! "We need to speed this thing up. At this rate, I'll be here until after curtain tomorrow night. What's next boss?"

"You need elevation. We're going to work you up little by little so you're jumping in from higher levels. First we'll bring a couple of aerobic steps and stack them for you. After that we'll use a chair, and then we'll slide the vault over, then higher and higher 'til we reach...how high?"

"Fifteen feet." I cringed.

"We'll have to haul over the giant utility ladder."

And that's how it went. I started from those damned aerobic steps. It terrified me to be elevated another two feet off the floor. But I did it again and again. Each time using the rope to help pull myself out of the pit. It didn't take long before the exertion of climbing through the foam to the side exhausted me. I graduated to the vault and then the ladder. Jumping from each step over and over until I didn't feel like throwing up before I did it.

"So tell me about Eli," Jilly said as I climbed the ladder for the umpteenth time.

"Huh? What do you mean?" I wasn't sure if I had ever mentioned Eli to her or not.

"Come on! He is totally hot, and holy cripes, the way you two dance together is criminal. I mean geez, get a room."

I bit back my smile and felt myself blush.

"See! I know you! You are so into him, aren't you?"

"Yes, actually we're going out, but it's complicated." I sat on the edge of the pit to take a break.

"A show romance! That is so cute. Seriously. You are so lucky. I would die to date a guy that cute."

"Right now, he pretty much hates me." I kicked at a huge piece of foam.

"Why?"

I gestured to the pit.

"Oh! You messed up the show, and he's mad."

"It's bigger than that. A lot of important people are going to be at the opening tomorrow night, and his dream is a career on stage. If I mess up, he looks bad to them, and there's supposed to be a casting guy there." I stood up and climbed the ladder again. Each rung took me higher. The air seemed to grow thinner and choke off my breath. My fear had returned, but I was determined to overcome it.

"No, if you mess up, you look bad. No offense." She pointed out.

"None taken." I stopped a step higher than my last fall.

"Sounds like he's a little arrogant, but heck, good looks trump asshole."

"No, he's not an asshole at all. He's sweet and funny and the way he kisses! Oh my!" I reached into the air and fell from the ladder into the pit with only a little scream of fright.

"Look at you," Jilly laughed.

"What can I say," I spit a piece of foam from my mouth. "I've fallen for him."

Jilly grabbed a hunk of the spongy stuff and threw it at me. "Well, won't he be happy when he sees your fall tomorrow night!"

"I hope so."

We spent another hour and a half working. The higher we moved, the easier it became. It seemed once I got used to the falling sensation, the height wasn't as terrifying as before. Don't get me wrong, my stomach still lurched every time, and I screamed, but Tyson had told me to scream, so it was all good.

I finally got home around 4:30 in the morning. Mom slept on the couch.

"I'm home," I whispered softly.

"How'd it go?" She sat up and blinked the sleep away.

"Fine. I can do it. Now go back to sleep."

"That's great, hon! I love you."

"I love you too, Mom."

"Now get to bed and don't set your alarm. No use

making things worse by showing up exhausted," she said pulling the blanket back over her.

"Thank you." I trudged up the stairs, exhausted and covered with foam bits from the pit. My arms ached from pulling myself out of the pit so many times.

Once in my room, I pulled out my cell phone. Seven missed calls and a text. The calls were all from Tyson. Even though it was the middle of the night, I had a hunch he'd be awake. I called. Two rings and he answered.

"Willow." His voice sounded exhausted, but wide awake.

"Hi. Listen, I'm so sorry about the dress rehearsal. I totally blew it. But I can do the fall and I don't want you to worry anymore."

"No, it's okay. I've figured a way we can redo the ending without too much hassle. We just need to find an hour sometime to get in there and work it out."

I pushed a few buttons and hit send. "Tyson, I just sent you video of me doing the fall. I did it from eighteen feet more than twenty-five times."

"Willow, I can't take any more chances."

"If you want me to come down to the theatre right now and show you I will, but I have a witness who can vouch for me."

"Really? Are you positive?"

"Please, just look at the video."

"Hang on."

I heard him fumbling with his phone. While I waited, I plopped down on my bed and kicked off my shoes.

"Willow?" he came back on the line. "You are

awesome!" His voice lit up like I hadn't heard in a while.

"Hardly, but I promised I wouldn't let you down and I won't."

"Thank you. Now get some sleep."

"No argument there."

"I'll see you tonight," he said and clicked off.

After that I read the text from Eli.

'I'm sorry for being a jerk.'

I texted him back, *'it was your turn.'* And sent him the video. Then I turned my phone off, closed the curtain and climbed under the covers.

Chapter 39

Dad pulled up outside the stage door. "Have a great show tonight!" His warm eyes wrinkled at the corners.

"You're supposed to say 'break a leg'," I said, gathering my bag off the floor. "Anything else is bad luck."

"I just can't get past the break part. I thought our goal was not to break anything."

"The big party is right afterwards, and please don't wear sandals. It's supposed to be dressy. And don't let Breezy wear a cape or vampire teeth."

Dad grinned. "Don't worry, we'll show up in proper form."

I reached for the door handle. Dad touched my arm. "Willow, I am so proud of you."

"You're not going to cry or anything are you?"

"No, but remember, whatever happens tonight, have fun."

I leaned over and gave him a big hug. "Thanks Dad."

As I checked in, a definite buzz lit the air. My body revved into high idle. I walked through the energy filled theatre. People milled around everywhere, going from make up to wardrobe, talking in small groups.

I needed to be close to the action and get the feel of everything. I wanted to make sure I'd done everything humanly possible to be ready. A couple stage hands mopped the stage with a bucket of cola so it would dry and be tacky in time for the show.

I went to Eli's dressing room to make sure he and I were okay. He wasn't there, but his wardrobe rack stood ready, loaded with his various costumes from tuxedo to jeans to his all-white costume for the finale. I smoothed my hand along the clothes and could almost feel his presence. In a couple hours, we'd be under the lights and hopefully delivering Tyson his dream show on a silver platter.

Checking the time, I realized I better get to hair and make up, and I still needed to find Tyson to see if he wanted to run the fall scene before we opened. A little shiver threatened, but I stomped it down. No doubts this time. Just action.

I dug in my bag but couldn't find a pen to write a note. But I found an eyebrow pencil, so I fished it out. Make-up pencil poised, I hesitated. I wanted to apologize and tell Eli how much I loved him and that I wouldn't run away from him ever again. But that was too long and probably too much to fit on his dressing room mirror.

So instead, I wrote:
You jump, I jump!
Love, W

And for good measure I kissed the mirror next to my W, which left a rather nice watermelon glossed lip print.

As I crossed the stage to my dressing room, I saw Sophie

"Sophie! How are you?" I rushed over and hugged her, relieved to see her out of the hospital.

"I'm fine. I have mild epilepsy, and it flares up sometimes. I just can't believe it happened in front of everyone," she said, dipping her head.

"Don't even worry about it. I'm so glad you're okay. Can you do the show tonight?"

"Yeah, my doctor said I should be fine with my new medicine, and Tyson said that if I feel up to doing the show, he's good with it."

"I'm so glad you're back! Last night we totally bombed. With you back we'll be on track again."

McKenna and Chelsea spotted Sophie. "Sophie!" They hurried to join us. "Are you okay?"

Sophie glanced at me and smiled. "Yeah."

"I've gotta get to my make up call, but I'm so glad you're okay." I hugged her again and left her to talk with the others.

I swung by my dressing room to drop off my bag and my breath caught as I discovered a big bouquet of pink roses on my dressing room table. I reached through the baby's breath for the card and pulled it out.

You jump, I jump!
And if you don't, I still love you!
Eli.

I held the card to my heart.

"I take it the flowers are from Eli." Samantha smiled from the doorway dressed in designer jeans and a cute navy bazaar. "All is good between you two?"

"Yeah!" I grinned

"You made up." She entered with a dress bag over her shoulder.

"I haven't seen him yet, but, yeah, I think so."

"I'm glad. Now are you ready for tonight?" She raised an eyebrow. "Tyson showed me the video you sent him last night. I must say I think you're pretty amazing. I'm so proud of you."

"Thanks. I knew I had to figure something out and it was the only thing I could come up with.

"You must be exhausted," she said and hung up her bag.

"No, my mom let me skip school, so I slept in really late. I think adrenaline will keep me going now." An image of me singing center stage shot a fresh jolt through me.

"Good. Now you better get down to make up before Mary comes looking for you. And be sure not to skimp on your warm up. Take your time. The last thing you need is an injury."

"I will. Thanks."

I didn't see Eli in the make up room, but finally found him warming up on stage with Alex and Damian. He jumped up as soon as he saw me, took my hand and pulled me backstage behind the third wing curtains.

"I'm so sorry I was a jerk." His concerned eyes gazed into mine, and I'd never felt so lucky in my life.

"You were fine. It was my fault. I'm sorry I made such a mess of everything."

"Are you okay?" He squeezed my hands.

"Yes, I'm fine. I'm just so sorry. I can't believe you put up with me. But don't worry, Jilly helped me work it out last night. I can do the jump. I promise!"

"Shhh." He pressed his finger to my lips. "I know. I saw your video. I'm so glad you figured it out, but even if you didn't, we'd make it okay. I don't ever want to let something dumb like a stupid fall come between us again. "

"I love you." I moved into his arms. He held me close and looked down.

"I love you too." He lowered his mouth to mine and gave me the sweetest, hottest kiss.

"Hey, save it for the show!" Tyson interrupted.

He wore a sharp black suit with a dark grey shirt open at the neck revealing a peak of chest hair.

"Sorry." Eli pulled away, but kept his arm tucked around me.

"Are you two ready?" Tyson asked.

"Oh yeah," Eli said. "I've been waiting all my life for this night." He pulled me close.

"And Willow, are you still up for the fall? I wanted to run it before the show to make sure you have your bearings, but the trap operator is late, and we won't have time before curtain."

"It's okay. I'll be fine," I said with confidence and mostly believed it. I knew I could do it. I refused to believe otherwise, but butterflies had taken over my stomach as the time grew closer to curtain. I figured it was normal pre-show jitters.

"We can always re-enact last night's fake stabbing," Eli teased.

"No!" Tyson and I blurted at the same time.

"Just kidding!" Eli said, and we all laughed.

"You two go warm up. Vocals are in twenty minutes," Tyson directed.

Dressed in our thirties era nightclub attire, the cast assembled in places behind the main curtain as the overture played. Another minute and the curtain would rise on the premiere of Tyson Scott's Dream Chaser.

The churning of my stomach helped distract me from the fact I really needed to pee. At the other side of the stage Eli, looking hot in his vintage tuxedo, bounced on his toes and shook out his hands to stay loose.

Our eyes met. Eli checked out my elegant form-fitting gown, raised his eyebrows suggestively and winked. Another few seconds and the show would open with a dream sequence set during the big band era, and our characters would meet.

Somewhere out in the audience sat my family, Jilly, and Miss Ginny, all waiting to see if I could pull this off. Tyson would likely be chewing his nails. I could barely handle my own jitters; I don't know how Tyson managed with so much pressure. Eli seemed to feed off the adrenaline.

The orchestra hit its crescendo. The lighting created a dreamlike mood. Energy crackled in the air, and the illuminated stage looked glorious with our period costumes and set. We all hit our marks, and the curtain rose.

The number went off perfectly without a missed step by anyone. The moment Eli smiled and took my hand for our elegant ballroom number, the last of my butterflies disappeared. We floated across the stage as the outside world fell away and we became Lauren and Zach.

After the opening, each scene went better than the last. Yesterday's mishaps became a distant memory. Samantha helped me through each of my costume changes. As soon as intermission began, Tyson joined us backstage.

"What did I tell you? Bad dress rehearsal, great show! I'm so proud of every one of you. Now don't let your energy drop. Keep the momentum flowing in the second act through to the end of the Mega Mix."

A buzz of relief went through the cast. Sophie was doing great, and Jason had nailed every line. Tyson came over to Eli and me.

"Great job. How are you guys holding up?"

Perspiration covered me and glued my costume to my sweaty back. "I'm good."

Lines of sweat ran down Eli's neck, but he looked great. "I can't wait for Act Two."

"Get down to make up for touchups and be sure to hydrate. If there's time, I'd like you to run the lifts from the fight scene too. Let's keep this show rolling smoothly."

"Willow, are you ready to do the fall?"

I knew he wanted to have faith in me, but needed to ask anyway. Eli waited for my answer but didn't say a word.

"Yes, I'm solid. I'm ready. I wish I could make it so you guys didn't have to worry, but I can't. You'll just have to trust me."

"And I do," Tyson said. "I've just gotta keep tabs on you. If anything changes, you let me know."

"I will." His confidence and support boggled my mind. After all the drama I'd put Tyson through, he treated me like a professional. I didn't deserve it.

"Now go get ready for the second act."

"On our way." Eli took my hand and pulled me away. He kissed my temple as we walked. Did life get any better?

The second act flew. The audience reaction and roar of applause blew me away. They loved the show, the orchestra was phenomenal, and we nailed every scene. During my solos I owned the stage. I belted out my songs and bared my soul. It never even occurred to me to be nervous. I don't know if it was because of Eli's constant focus, the voice lessons, or the thrill of the show, but somewhere along the way everything fit into place.

Suddenly the show was almost over and it was time for the death scene.

This was it.

I waited backstage for my cue, Jason at my side. I made the mistake of thinking about how horrible last night's show went and how petrified I felt when looking over the side of the elevated set. It must have shown on my face.

"Are you okay?" Jason whispered with more than worry in his eyes.

"Oh, yeah. I'm fine." I shook off the feeling of terror. I knew the entire cast was waiting to see what I'd do. Would I blow it again? I pictured Tyson holding his breath until the scene ended. Eli doubt me too? I'd let him down so many times before, and I didn't want to do it again. I prayed that my long night of work with Jilly would pay off. Hopefully my body would remember and not let my head take over.

The stage darkened and Jason and I took our places. During that three-second pause I saw Eli off stage right. With his raised eyebrows, he asked the question everyone wanted to know. Would I take the fall? In that quick instant I crossed my fingers for good luck, shrugged my shoulders and nodded.

The scene began and I put it on autopilot. I focused on Eli and Jason. I refused to go to my scary place. That is, until I stepped onto the rooftop set. Out of the corner of my eye I saw the giant sunroof trap slide open like a gaping abyss.

Don't look. Don't think. I chanted to myself.

I knew the audience couldn't see the opening or the approaching no-turning back moment.

The orchestra's sound filled the theatre, building the momentum to epic levels.

The scene moved on. Victor punched Zach, knocking him to the floor of the rooftop set.

I was next. Victor lunged, and I evaded him, moving closer to the edge. The audience gasped.

Don't look! Don't think!

Zach yelled to warn Lauren.

I focused on the image of Jilly encouraging me to fall from the tall ladder at the gym last night.

It was time. Fall or fail.

I made a split second choice and gave a slight nod to Jason that only he and Eli could see.

Jason rushed toward me. I took a step to the edge and planted my foot. My arms flailed like any sane person would do who didn't want to fall.

But this was a show, and a mat waited below to cushion me. The audience gasped again.

I leaned forward just enough to let gravity pull me over into a free fall.

Chapter 40

My scream could be heard in Canada, but luckily that part was in the script. As a former expert at free falling, I turned during the fall and safely landed on the mat with a huge whoosh. I wanted to get up and cheer!

A stagehand reached out to help me off the mat because Eli would fall in another couple seconds. His character Zach is devastated by the death of his true love and follows her to a tragic death.

Another gasp erupted from the audience. I looked up and watched Eli in a perfect dead man's fall. He dropped through the air and landed on the mat in front of me.

I climbed back on to the mat just as he popped up.

"You did it!" he said. "I'm so proud of you. You never even hesitated."

"You were awesome!" I hugged him. "And it was fun!"

Eli started kissing my face.

The stagehand shook his head.

"Eli, we have to change for the Mega Mix."

"Let a guy have his moment here, would ya?"

I kissed him back, and then we climbed off the mat.

"Can't you just see Tyson out there about to have a coronary."

"Poor guy."

The giant trap door closed above on the darkened

stage as sad mournful music played. We hurried to our dressing rooms.

"Way to go!" Samantha high fived me.

"Thanks!" I couldn't hide my grin as I kicked off my shoes.

"Ready for the finale?" She unfastened the belt of my costume.

The monitor on the wall showed live feed from the stage. Soft light appeared and grew brighter like the dawn of a new day. The set had been changed to a cheerful blue sky with huge puffy clouds. Fresh, light music began in a playful pace. A wisp of fog streamed across stage.

Heaven.

"Am I ever," I said as she stripped clothes off me and pulled new ones over my head.

* * *

Fully dressed in my all-white costume of snug low-rise pants adorned with a wide looped silver belt and a little midriff top. I headed back down under the stage to a smaller trap and waited for my entrance. Eli joined me, dressed in fitted white jeans and a tank that showed off his assets. Another monitor allowed the technician to know exactly when to raise or lower the trap.

Eli stood behind me, with his arms wrapped around me, as we watched the finale on the monitor. I leaned against him, more content than ever.

A change in music from the band and the lighting on stage softened. The music pumped through the place like the best rock concert ever. This was heaven.

First, a group of girls danced out to the catchy beat. I could feel the excitement in the theatre. Another group of girls joined the first, and then another, until their movements created an amazing crescendo of synchronized choreography. The music built, increasing the momentum of energy on stage.

The guys did the same, beginning with a small group and adding more until a mass of guys overtook the stage. Their power mesmerized me as I watched the monitor under the stage.

The music shifted again. Eli quick kissed me, and we took our places at opposite spots under the stage.

More heavenly clouds spilled onto the stage from the fog machine. A trap door in the floor opened on each side of the stage. I rose from one and Eli from the other like we were floating into heaven, which at this point I pretty much was. Eli and I locked eyes as the lift raised up to stage level. The audience roared their applause the moment they saw Zach and Lauren together in heaven, as the rest of the cast jammed in the background,

I ran across the floor to him, jumped with all my might, and Eli lifted me high in an overhead lift. We nailed it. The audience roared. Then he turned me, lowered his arms and flipped me onto my feet. I took his hand, and we shared a quick joyful smile. Then we began an upbeat version of our ballroom rumba, but in double time. The band played it total rock and roll as Eli's strong hold whipped us around the stage. The audience totally loved the "dancing in heaven" finale.

The best part was sharing this with Eli. We were back together again on stage and off, grinning, giving it every ounce of energy we had. The lights swirled and changed to the beat of the music, showing our rock version of heaven.

We finished our dance duet with synchronized pirouettes. It was my favorite part, and the audience loved it. One spin, then two spins, three, four. The audience applause filled my ears as I spotted each turn. Five, six, seven and eight! I heard catcalls as we finished with a double pirouette. The crowd partied on their feet as the band jammed on.

We all ran off stage, and then the bows began, with each cast member crossing the stage with a signature move. Sophie did a beautiful switch leap and pointed to Alex. He did a head spin onto his back then flipped onto his feet as Chloe crossed with her move. On and on it went, each dancer giving the stage to the next.

When my turn came up, I did a tumbling run across the stage ending with a double twist. I pointed and handed the stage over to Eli. The moment he appeared, the volume of applause increased a few more decibels as Eli executed a series of traveling Russian leaps so high he sailed effortlessly through the air. We broke into the final chorus of the theme song with the cast members standing in formation around the stage. Eli and I ran front and center to where the footlights shone strongest. Through the bright lights, I could see the audience still on their feet, as the band played in the pit below.

Eli stepped aside and held his hand out to me and I bowed, then gestured to him and he bowed. We joined hands and took one more together. Eli waved the rest of the cast forward and gave the cue. The crowd wouldn't quiet. We all bowed again then gestured the band and gave them one more bow.

Stepping back, Eli squeezed my hand. The heavy curtain closed in a whoosh but the applause didn't stop, so up the curtain went. The song ended and my pulse crashed through my body. Every ounce of myself, I gave; and in return I was filled with such euphoria I could barely stand it.

We bowed one more time, a united cast of laughter and joy. We waved at the audience and bopped to the music as a glimmer of hands waved back.

Eli caught my eye and winked. We grinned like idiots. The curtain lowered for good and the stage lights came up. I launched myself into Eli's waiting arms. He swung me around like a rag doll. I never wanted to let go!

"We did it! I can't believe we did it!" I yelled.

He held me so close I couldn't breathe, but I didn't care. Then we started hugging everyone else. Sophie cried with a group of girls, and a lot of others were high fiving it.

All the ugliness of the beginning was now long in the past; except Chloe, she kept her distance, which was fine with me.

Tyson appeared in a euphoric glow. We surrounded him like a swarm of bees to honey. The joy on his face said it all. His perfect white teeth grinned, erasing all the earlier stress and struggle we put him through.

"You did it! I knew you could." Tyson beamed like a proud father. The sparkle in his eye sent me over the moon. He gave me the biggest warmest hug ever.

"I'm so glad I didn't screw it up. I put you through a lot."

"You were awesome!"

Eli joined us.

"Eli, I'd give you a Tony Award right now if I could. You slam dunked it!" He pulled Eli into a hug and slapped him on the back a couple times. Eli couldn't stop smiling.

"You guys killed it out there! You didn't miss a thing from the lifts to the emotion and then you both did perfect free falls."

We soaked in his excitement, so thrilled to know he loved it. Tyson moved on as we celebrated our success.

Back in the dressing room, I rushed to get ready. Standing in my underwear, I washed the sweat off my body with about twenty baby wipes. A far cry from a real shower, but at least now I smelled powder fresh. I slipped into the little black dress and strappy heels my mom bought and applied normal make up.

By the time I left the cluttered dressing room behind, the rest of the cast had already left.

Except one.

Eli leaned against the back wall in that sexy adorable way of his. His hair was damp on the ends where he must have stuck it under a faucet to wash up. He was dressed in a silky black shirt, open at the neck, black dress pants and shoes. My stomach did a little flip.

"Hi!" He kicked away from the wall the moment he saw me. Appreciation lit his face. "You look amazing!"

"Thanks," I joined him and wrapped my arms around his neck. "You look pretty fantastic yourself."

"Yeah?" Eli lowered his head touching his nose with mine.

"Oh yeah?" I leaned up and kissed his soft lips. He slid his arms around my waist and pulled my body against his. We fit together so perfectly. He tilted his head and our kiss deepened waking up all my nerve endings.

When we parted I gazed into his eyes. "I love you so much!"

"I know." He grinned.

"You are such a shit." I lightly slapped his chest.

"Yes, and you still love me." He rested his forehead against mine. "And I love you."

Warm, happy joy filled me. "There's one thing I need to say."

"Oh, you getting serious on me when all I want to do is make out?"

"Only for a second." I took a moment to collect my thoughts. "I want to apologize for letting you down."

"Whoa! Oh no you don't. You have nothing to apologize for. I was a jerk too."

"No, please listen. Freshman year I walked away from you because I got scared. You were my best friend in the world. When things changed, I freaked out and ran away. I did that with cheer, and I did it this week with the show. I want you to know that I will never run away from you again, even when I'm scared. Thanks to you and my mom and dad, I've figured it out and I know what I want."

"And what's that?"

"Well, you for one thing." I leaned against his firm body and peeked up from under my eyelashes.

He wrapped his arms around me again. I snuggled in. He bent to kiss me.

"Save it for the back seat, you two!" Tyson came through the doorway looking smooth as James Bond.

"Sorry man." Eli stood straighter and loosened his hold on me. I stepped away, allowing air to cool our heated bodies.

"Shouldn't you be schmoozing with all the New York big wigs at the party?" I asked. "You can't let them get away."

"Samantha is holding them hostage with the dress she's barely wearing." He joined us. "Everyone's asking for the stars of the show, and I promised to bring you. Listen, I know we still have more shows this weekend, but I wanted to take the time before all the craziness of the party and the rest of the weekend to make sure you two know how proud I am of you."

Eli gave my waist a squeeze.

"This show wouldn't have gone off so well with anyone other than the two of you. In fact, when the school kicked Jessica out of the show, it's the best thing that could have happened. She wasn't right."

I wanted to point out all the headaches I gave him, but decided not to spoil the moment.

"This is my dream, my baby, and it happened tonight with the two of you leading the charge. I know how hard you both worked. I never asked you guys to devote your lives to this show, but you did, and I am eternally grateful. Thank you."

I couldn't believe our director, looking all Hollywood in his dark suit, was thanking us, when all I wanted to do was thank him for giving me this phenomenal life-changing opportunity.

"If either of you ever need anything, and I mean anything, from college reference letters to a place to crash in New York, promise you'll call. In fact, come out this summer. I know you have my number, since you called me at three a.m." He eyed Eli. "I will never look at a grape Power Aid again and not think of you two fools."

"Me either," I groaned recalling the experience.

"I'm serious about the call. Eli, I know you have your eyes set on Broadway. When the time comes, call me. I'll help set you up with some auditions."

"Thanks. I will." Eli shook his hand.

"Thank you," I said. "For everything. You'll never know how much working with you has meant. Thank you for giving me this chance and sticking with me when I went psycho." It started to get a little too touchy feely, like somebody might cry. "And I'd love to see New York!"

"Great! I'll talk to both your parents about it. Now let's get you to the party. Everyone's waiting."

"We'll be right behind you," Eli said, and Tyson returned to the party.

*　*　*

Eli and I stood outside the open doors to the swanky reception. The rest of the cast and crew partied inside along with parents, friends and orchestra members. A ton of people I didn't recognize held fancy drinks; by the way they dressed, I'm pretty sure they were the people from New York.

Give it up to Tyson, he knew how to throw a party. I spotted Mom and Dad with Breezy. "Look at my mom in a slinky black dress! And my dad is in a suit! I didn't know he owned one!"

"It looks like he shaved." Eli said.

"Who are those people? And what did they do with my parents?"

Eli's parents talked to some men in suits; his dad was probably trying to land a business deal. I spied a beaming Miss Ginny who looked the same as always visiting with Samantha who wore a gorgeous gold dress held up by teeny little straps. Tyson held a martini and laughed with a large group. He fit well in any situation.

Eli curled his finger around mine. "Part of me doesn't want to go in."

"We should go for a little while," I suggested.

He took my hand and cradled it in his. "Yeah, that would be okay."

"What do you want to do afterward?"

A devilish smile covered his face. His strong arm pulled me into a close embrace. "Take a drive over to Messerschmidt Road."

"Can you get your mom's car with the big backseat?" I gave him a sly smile.

"Any time. You say the word."

I arched an eyebrow and said, "You jump, I jump."

~ ~ ~

About the Author

Angie Stanton never planned on writing books, she wanted to be a Rockette. However, growing up in a rural setting with her brothers' 4-H pigs as pets, dance didn't work out. Instead she became an avid daydreamer. After years of perfecting stories in her head she began to write them down and the rest is history.

She loves dipping French fries in chocolate shakes, all natural disaster movies, and Broadway Musicals. When not writing, Angie is concocting ways to make more dreams come true, whether it be tickets to a Broadway show or convincing her family they should rent an RV and travel the country.

Angie is a proud double finalist of the 2011 National Readers Choice Awards for Love 'em or Leave 'em, as well as a finalist for the Golden Quill Awards.

Look for Angie's other books, Rock and a Hard Place, Snapshot, Under the Spotlight, Royally Lost, Snowed Over, Love 'em or Leave 'em and the highly acclaimed Waking in Time.

If you enjoyed this book, please leave a review at Amazon.

Acknowledgements

Special thanks go out to my fabulous critique partners, Linda Schmalz, Deb Barkelar and Rachel Michaels, your eye to detail is a godsend. My terrific Beta readers were Kate Grout, Kristi Tyler and Margo Zimmerman.

For all the research assistance I thank: Scott Bowne for his expertise with stage traps and theatre operations; Sheila Noone of Varsity Brands, Inc. for her assistance with cheerleading terminology; dance team member, Allison Martin, for her terrific input on hip-hop; David Kuelz and Donna Kuelz for their theatre insights and Kathleen Chesley Williams, a gifted dancer, teacher and choreographer for her generous time and knowledge of everything dance.

A special thank you goes to Virginia Davis, the fabulous woman who taught me how to tap so very long ago and has inspired thousands of young dancers at the Virginia Davis School of Dance.

Of course, I must thank my family, Ed, Kristi and Kevin, who listen to my crazy ideas and always nod and smile, even though deep down they think I'm nuts. They're right, but it's nice they know how to fake it. And my brother Pat who was always amazed I could write a story. Sorry I didn't get to yours in time.

And finally, to that boy in high school who took me to Messerschmidt Road on a cold winter night. I never guessed it would end up in a book!

~ ~ ~

More books by Angie Stanton

*Two college students share a boring ride home
until a blizzard changes everything.*

What others are saying about **Snowed Over**.

I loved this book! From the very beginning to the end I
loved it. It makes me want to go on a road trip with a
cute guy and get snowed in a cabin :)
~SugarAndSpice

I fell in love from the moment I started reading
everything else just faded away and I got lost within the
pages! Snowed Over is fun, charming, magical and
romantic!
~Booklover

I loved this book! I was completely sucked into the story
and didn't want to put it down.
~WickedWolvesandDreamingDragons

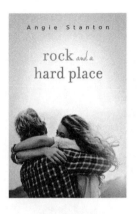

An average girl.
A rock star.
An impossible love.

What others are saying about **Rock and a Hard Place**.

Wow! **Rock and a Hard Place** took me places I didn't expect to go. I thought I had this book all figured out from the description, but it was so much more.
~ *Reading, Eating & Dreaming*

This book was so good! I would recommend this 1000%! GREAT, GREAT, GREAT read!
~ *lowshie*

This book was an absolute joy to read. I laughed and loved with Libby and Peter, but even more, I cried as if it were actually happening to me.
~*fasnfuurious*

I can't seem to get this one out of my head. I laughed, I cried, I got pissed, I cried some more.
~ *rookiegolf*

*A camera-shy girl accidentally ends up on a
reality dating show.*

What others are saying about **Love 'em or Leave 'em**.

I loved every minute of this book…a delightful look into
what happens when a woman is mistakenly cast on a
matchmaking reality show…entertainingly fun read.
~ *L Schmalz*

For all the fans of reality shows like "The Bachelor"
you're going to especially love this book!
~ *Meg Valentine*

I loved this book. It was like watching the Bachelor or
Bachelorette!
~ *Annie ~ Goodreads*

Waking in Time

A time travel romance
from Switch Press in Spring 2017
(uncorrected advanced reader excerpt)

"Abbi!" An excited voice calls out.

I turn to find a guy with scruffy sandy-colored hair and a brilliant smile coming straight for me, and fast. I look around to see if he is talking to someone else, but no, it's me.

I smile weakly. Should I be glad or scared to discover that someone in 1961 seems excited to see me? Or maybe he's like all the girls in my dorm, and to him I've always been here?

He scoops me into a hug and swings me around, and plants a long, passionate kiss on my mouth.

He-llo!

He grins, revealing an adorable dimple. "Abbi. I never thought it would happen. I mean I hoped so, I prayed for it, and you were right. Here you are, exactly when you said you'd be."

I'm stunned, yet find myself smiling into deep blue eyes. His arms are wrapped comfortably around me as if it's no big deal. He's several inches taller than I am. My hands rest against his chest where I feel his heart racing beneath his shirt. Part of me feels safe and relieved by his attention, but the other part thinks, who the heck is this handsome stranger?

"You look exactly the same." He gazes into my eyes as if I'm the most precious person on the planet.

I don't know how to respond, and I kind of like the feel of him. He's lean and smells good, like the outdoors. After a few awkward seconds, to which he seems totally oblivious, I find my voice. "I'm sorry, but how exactly do we know each other?"

He immediately releases me. "Oh, rats! Abbi, forgive me. For a moment I forgot that you haven't met me yet."

My heart nearly ricochets out of my chest.

"Let's get out of here." Without asking, he takes my hand and leads me out of the Rathskeller. He obviously knows more about what's going on than I do, so I follow with renewed hope in my heart.

He leads me outside and down the lake front path, now a narrow dirt path. He has an easy gait, as if he's used to escorting girls who don't know him. He finds a bench overlooking the water and brushes off bits of twigs and leaves. We sit, his body angled toward me. A soft breeze off the lake blows his hair off his forehead.

"My apologies. I'm handling this all wrong." He holds up his trembling hand. "Look. I'm giddy as a race horse."

For the first time I notice his nervous smile. "It's okay," I reassure him, taking his hand and giving him a reassuring squeeze. His smile relaxes, but his eyes stay glued to mine.

"Please, tell me how we know each other. *When* exactly did we meet?" I hold my breath, waiting for his answer.

He hesitates as if thinking back to old memories. "A long time ago. At least for me it was, but for you — well — it's your future."

So he too is confirming that I continue to travel back in time. I release my breath. "You know about that?"

"I know *all* about it," he says with a serious tone.

"Did I tell you?" I ask tentatively.

"Yes. You told me many things about the future." He holds my gaze as if willing me to remember things that haven't yet happened for me, but I have nothing to offer him, so he continues. "I'm not sure how I would have managed so well without you."

And then it hits me. This guy is the other time traveler that Professor Smith mentioned. He can help me. "How long have you been time traveling? Where have you been? When did we first meet?" I ask eagerly, desperate for answers. He smiles, his lips have a nice curve to them, and there's that adorable dimple.

He is completely comfortable with me, suggesting we have a history. But exactly what kind of history? I see how my future self would enjoy spending time with him. "You know my name is Abbi."

"I do." He runs his hand through the tall grass picking a long, slender blade and slips it into his mouth.

"So you know me from your past, and we're good friends?"

"Very good." A devilish smile lights his eyes, and I wonder exactly how good.

"You know everything about me, and yet I don't even know your name?" I hate this feeling. It's like I've woken up with amnesia.

His eyes dim as if he's wounded that I still don't remember him, but then he says in the sweetest low voice. "My name is Will."

"Hello, Will." I let the sound of his name settle in. I have a friend in the past named Will. A weight eases from my shoulders and I breathe a little easier.